STOLEN LIVES

A NICK WOLF AND LOLA CALDWELL
MYSTERY
BOOK 1

G. WAYNE TILMAN

ROUGH
EDGES
PRESS

BOOKS BY G. WAYNE TILMAN:

Ghost Posse

Zack Bodeway, Texas Ranger

The Legend of Bill Tilghman

Arizona Gunman

Six-Gun From Texas

The Blonde Murders

The Harani Trail (as AG Christian)

The MacLachlan Thrillers:

Honor Above All

Unsanctioned

Highlands Blood

Blood Sky

The Jack Landers Western Mystery Series:

Only the Blondes

Only the Vengeance

Only the Badge

Jack Landers, Sheriff

Heartland Deputy

Cinco Peso

Gun For Wells Fargo Series:

Gun for Wells Fargo

Wyoming Shootout

Stolen Lives
Paperback Edition
Copyright © 2023 G. Wayne Tilman

Rough Edges Press
An Imprint of Wolfpack Publishing
9850 S. Maryland Parkway, Suite A-5 #323
Las Vegas, Nevada 89183

roughedgespress.com

Paperback ISBN 978-1-68549-337-0
eBook ISBN 978-1-68549-336-3
LCCN 2023943515

STOLEN LIVES

1

Nicholas Aaron Wolf was cramped from sitting at the long, narrow Formica counter he had put along one side of his surveillance van. The van was a half-ton Dodge which was ten years old. It had been a county truck, so it had good maintenance and ran well despite its somewhat high mileage. Like a large percentage of the vehicles in Florida, it was white. It had a ladder rack on top, complete with work ladders he had purchased used. Visible only under close scrutiny, the ladders were locked with the smallest high-security locks available and with steel core plastic coated cable. The swiveling camera under the ladders was also difficult to see. It was hidden in a small dome, usually seen affixed to a ceiling in a security area. It was virtually unnoticeable under the ladders. There was a permanent screen on the counter for the camera. The sides of the van were windowless, to give authenticity to the van as a work vehicle. There were small windows in the twin rear doors, but they were dark one-way glass.

A private investigator, Nick Wolf, had installed other things in this ubiquitous van.

He had put the Formica counter on the driver's side of the van. It had a hot spot, his laptop computer, and room for whatever tools he planned to use...especially his all-important Thermos of strong black coffee.

He had a locking box with gear under the long, narrow counter. It had general PI equipment such as nitrile gloves, evidence bags, Steiner binoculars and a video camera with a telephoto lens. He took most photos with his smartphone, given the advancements of in-phone cameras.

Another lockbox had weapons. One was a 12-gauge Mossberg Shockwave shotgun loaded with one two and three quarter inch reduced recoil buckshot loads and eight shorty buckshot loads more closely emulating 20-gauge shells in power. He had a Glock 23 as a backup for the custom one he carried every day, with its Bar-Sto barrel, Apex trigger, and steel night sights. A cleaning kit and plenty of ammunition filled the rest of the space in the box.

Nick had a Yeti cooler with bottled water, energy bars for lunch or dinner, as the case may be. He also had a small marine potty. Having to leave the vehicle or use a Big Gulp cup to relieve oneself was an anathema to surveillance.

He had found a cul-de-sac which overlooked the rear of the subject's residence. He was watching the garage door where his subject kept his car.

The subject was a wheelchair-bound individual who was suing the corporation in whose warehouse he had allegedly had an industrial accident while working. Too many aspects of the case sent red flags up the corporate ladder and their insurance company called Nick.

X-rays showed some back injury indications. His physician of choice was one well-known to be the expert witness on such cases and who was, himself, considered highly suspect by both insurance companies and injury law firms...at least the firms which did not use him.

Nick's client was the local office of the company's insurance carrier. He did very little advertising. His bread-and-butter business consisted of about ten insurance companies and law firms in total. He made a good living just on this retainer business. Any other cases were pure gravy.

He ran an ad online and in several local area phone books and newspapers.

"Aaron Risk Mitigation and Investigations" and his phone number. Nothing more. He used his middle name for the firm because its first two letters all but guaranteed being listed first in the phone book. *Aardvark Risk Mitigation and Investigations would have been nonsensical*, he thought.

Nick watched for several hours to no avail, pouring several mugs of strong black coffee from his Thermos. Then, the rear door of the house opened. His subject's live-in girlfriend wheeled him out in his wheelchair. She was a showgirl at a local casino.

She left him sitting as she opened the garage door.

Nick slipped out of the offside driver's door of the van, having grabbed the video camera first.

He crouched behind the corner of the van as the woman backed a Honda Accord out of the garage. She got out and jiggled across to the subject. The target subject stood and stretched, then walked around to the passenger side and got into the car. She folded the light-weight wheelchair and opened the trunk lid with the remote on the key.

She lifted out a bag of golf clubs and propped them against the fender. The woman, a dancer at one of Tampa's most infamous nude clubs, placed the wheelchair in the trunk, put the golf bag on top and closed it.

Nick was already moving around to the driver's door of the van as she started. As she was backing up and positioning the car to leave the tight rear drive, he was moving the van toward the intersection she would probably take.

The Honda passed the white work van. If they noticed the driver, which he doubted, all they could see was a guy in a ball cap, sunglasses, and a tee shirt.

He pulled in behind them and casually followed about three cars back. In his old department, they would have used several vehicles to tail a subject. One with the "eye" following, another behind to change positions if the first "eye" was made, and a third one on a parallel street.

But the Aaron agency just had its namesake. He would be the eye until he could not be. However, he knew he was driving a vehicle nobody would look at twice. Just another workman going somewhere.

He followed the Honda Accord for at least ten miles. He saw its right turn signal from four cars back and drove past the place the Honda had turned. Nick saw a sign denoting a public golf course. Nick turned around and turned left into the golf course entry.

I'm guessing he drove past a couple of public courses to get out of his part of town. He wants to avoid being recog-

nized. Let's see what we can do to disrupt that plan! Nick thought to himself.

Nick watched the subject, and his girlfriend remove his golf bag from the trunk and walk into the pro shop. He videoed this with his date and time stamp appearing on the video.

He obtained subsequent footage of subject Kauffman playing the first three holes, then ceased filming. Kauffman would hop off the golf cart and walk easily to set up his shot and fire it off with full swing and stability.

Half an hour later, he grinned to himself. This was easier and less time-consuming than he thought it would be.

"Mr. Sullivan? Hi, it's Nick Wolf. I have video of Bob Kauffman and his girlfriend at their garage door. He got up out of the wheelchair and walked around while she put the chair into the trunk of his car. I followed them about twelve miles to a public golf course and filmed him walking with his golf bag into the pro shop. They rented a golf cart and proceeded onto the course. I have video of him playing the first several holes. All of the video is time and date stamped.

"Will this suffice for your defense? Good! I will get it to your St. Pete office before close of work today. Yes? I will be pleased to testify seeing and recording Mr. Kauffman's actions at his trial. See you later," and Nick hung up.

His left leg was stiff from the time he was immobile in the surveillance van, and he limped more visibly when he walked back out to the parking lot and then to his van.

The limp is a lot better than it had been three years ago.

Hell, I could have been long since dead. I can live with this, he thought.

Nick drove to St. Petersburg and dropped a copy of the video at the insurance office.

He only had one parking space at his office and apartment, so he parked the van in a secure garage he rented and limped back to his office. His leg loosened up a bit during the short walk. But it still hurt. It seemed like it was destined to be his future.

He climbed the two landings of stairs to his office with its brass plate on the door and went in, disabling the burglar alarm once inside.

It was four thirty by then. He had framing and drywall up to give him an office and a restroom clients could use. The kitchen and bedroom were separated from his business area by a door. To clients, it appeared just to be a business office. If he ever gave up the Central Avenue St. Pete office, he would simply remove the temporary wall and door and paint it on the way out.

Nick changed into shorts and a golf shirt and boat shoes, reset the alarm and walked down to the rear parking lot. He got into the two-door Jeep Rubicon, albeit stiffly. Two years ago, he could not have owned such a vehicle. Now, he could swing his right leg in and with one butt cheek on the driver's seat, use his hand to assist raising the left leg in.

He drove to a Cuban restaurant and had *ropa vieja* (old clothes, referring to the shreds of beef), beans and rice, and an extra-large *café con leche*. He ordered another extra-large large cup of *café con leche* to go.

Not a bad way to celebrate a case virtually closed. He suspected the insurance company would win without spending another penny after showing

Kauffman and his lawyer the video. He doubted he would be called to testify. If the insurance company turned the evidence over to the Florida Bureau of Insurance Fraud, he would surely be called to testify in the criminal proceeding which would be guaranteed to follow.

Nick went back to his office and home, kicked back in his bedroom recliner and turned the flat-screen on. He sipped the Cuban coffee, ultimately falling asleep watching a mystery with the Irish Garda on either BritBox or the Acorn Channel. He was not sure which as he turned the TV off and brushed his teeth. He set the security alarm and went to sleep immediately.

It was Friday night, and the Central Avenue joints were far from ready to close. Nick slept through the music, none of which he would have chosen, and street noise. He was, however, awakened by a loud argument on the sidewalk below his apartment.

It looked like four guys arguing with one guy and one girl. From his years of experience wearing a star, he knew this one was going to get violent real fast.

"Okay, Finn. You're in charge. I'll be back shortly," he said to his green-eyed cat. He always wondered about the cat's heritage. He had a short tail and taller legs in back. Except for his yellow color, Finn looked suspiciously like a bobcat. However, he was one of the quietest, sweetest creatures Nick had ever been around.

Nick walked down the steps wearing the shorts and a navy-blue tail-out golf shirt from earlier in the evening. His cargo shorts were as he had removed them to sleep. His wallet, money, and retirement badge and creds were in his pockets. He added his backup gun, a Sig 365 micro 9mm to the right front, which disappeared in a pocket holster. Nick stiffly walked down the two landings of steps.

As he stepped out of the shared front door to the café, which was on the first floor, and with the key card door up to his apartment and one other apartment on the second floor, two of the guys rushed the one with the date. While they pummeled him, the other two grabbed the girl. One ripped her crop top off, baring her naked torso.

Nick walked up to him and stepped in closely. He snapped three rapid elbow blows to the side of the man's jaw, and he went down. Nick spun as the other guy came in fast for a head butt, hands reaching for Nick's shoulders.

Nick raised his arms, crossed at mid-forearm in an X-shape, temporarily trapping the man's head. He immediately released and palmed both of the man's ears hard at the same instant. The guy's eyes went funny, and Nick kneed him in the groin. His next move would have been a snap kick to the chest to put him down, but Nick knew his left leg was not stable enough to allow him to retain balance for a kick that high. Instead, he drove a straight-arm fist into the guy's chest so hard it moved him backward and he landed dazed on his butt on the sidewalk.

Nick could hear sirens. A group of twenty-some-things had gathered. Some of them were making smart-phone videos instead of helping the couple.

Assholes! he thought.

It was time to address the two beating the girl's date to a pulp. He hit one from the side with his shoulder and one hundred eighty pounds of bulk. The man bumped into his friend and both of them went down. Nick moved in and risked a short kick to the man's jaw as the man began to rise in an offensive posture. It worked well, and Nick was able to retain his balance.

The other man got up and caught Nick's round-house on the hinge of his jaw. He went down as the first SPPD car pulled to the curb.

Nick turned to a pair who had been videoing with their phones. He flipped his badge wallet open to them.

"You, two. The police will need your testimony and your video for evidence. Do NOT move. You have a civic duty to do."

The first officer, alone, was surveying the situation.

Nick said to him, "Nick Wolf, retired sheriff's detective sergeant." He held up his retirement badge, virtually the same as his original one.

"You are not near forty yet. How the hell can you be retired?"

"Disability. Two rounds in the left leg. Three years ago in Hillsborough on a raid," Nick said as the first backup unit arrived. He lifted the hem of his cargo shorts on the left and one bullet hole scar in the center of his thigh was obvious.

He tossed his shirt to the female victim, who had picked up her torn crop top and was unsuccessfully trying to cover her bare breasts. He walked over to a guy filming her and said, "Delete it. Now!"

The guy gave him an insolent look and he walked up, fists balled, and stared at him from inches away. He took the phone out of the guy's hands, deleted the video and went to the Recently Deleted folder, and permanently deleted it there also. He shoved the phone back to the guy and limped to the officers. One was calling dispatch for an ambulance.

Speaking softly to the officer so the crowd could not hear, he said, "I live here. Which is how I heard the attack on the couple and was able to get down here quickly. I thought I could quash it, so I didn't call 9-1-1. Guess it escalated quicker than I thought. Mind if I go up for a second and get a shirt? The young lady needed mine pretty badly."

The officer said, "You're not going to run off, are you?" Nick handed him his badge wallet and said, "No, here's some collateral to hold until I get back." He turned and limped up the stairs, his leg hurting more than it had for a year.

He returned minutes later with a clean shirt, retrieved his badge wallet and sat in a cruiser completing an incident report for the first arriving officer. He watched out of the open door as the EMTs checked his four combatants. The one he had clocked with a kick to the jaw had a suspected broken jaw. The EMTs thought the second one attacking the female probably had at least one ruptured ear drum from the clap on the ears. The boyfriend was pretty badly beaten, and they sent him to the hospital in a separate Sunstar ambulance from the two attackers. The other two got a ride in a caged rear seat to the lockup.

The officer had the two phone videographers email him their videos. He compared the videos to what Nick had put on the report and the two videos validated his written words about what happened.

"Depending on how these pukes plead, you may or may not have to testify," he told Nick. "I have to go to the hospital and interview the victim. Give me a card, and I will give it to the young lady so she can return your shirt," the officer offered.

Nick handed him a business card and thanked him. He had been so busy he had not taken time to look at her. She was blonde and well-built was about the best description he could conjure up.

"Do me a favor and email me the two videos. It's a litigious world and one or more might sue me for injuring their delicate little bodies. It would help to have the proof of what happened on video if it comes to a court case," Nick said to the officer.

He emailed them to Nick's contact information on the report. Nick immediately viewed the email on his smartphone and verified he had all he needed. He was on retainer to one of the best law firms in Florida and knew exactly who he would call for defense, if needed.

"We will hit the two on the girl with sexual battery for handling her and ripping off her shirt like they did. The other two will get aggravated battery for beating up the boyfriend."

"Good. I suspect they were four bullies embolden by their number and just drunk enough to not have clear reasoning. I hope they get jail time, though I suspect they will be back on the street before morning," Nick said.

The officer just nodded his head with resignation and got back into his car, and drove to the hospital, the female victim sitting in the front, squeezing in by a mobile computer unit.

———

Nick went back up to his office apartment, took a couple aspirins for his leg, and went back to bed. He slept a little and tossed and turned a lot. Finn kept watch over him.

The next day was Saturday. He had a couple follow-up interviews for another insurance client on a hit-and-run car accident where the insurance client was left at the scene seriously injured. In this one, the Florida Highway Patrol was investigating, but his insurance client wanted to find the runner quickly and get their process going.

Nick feared it was a serial drunk driver with no license and in a friend's car. He only had the description as an ugly yellowish-brown Volvo. He interviewed the woman vic in the hospital. She likened the color to something you would find in a dirty diaper.

Delightful...but probably helpful. He remembered those vile-colored Volvos. The color had not been around for years. Unfortunately, he did not have any database to check to see its period of use.

He got in the Jeep and drove to Clearwater. He had worked up a list of paint shops and body shops on his office computer and printed it.

Nick began to check at the shops on his list. After twenty, he still had no joy. On the outskirts of Tarpon Springs, he hit pay dirt.

Somebody had come in to find a match for the horrible color paint. The right front fender, headlight frame, and grill had been dented badly. The customer wanted the dents banged out and the headlight replaced on the cheap.

Nick got the date, the license plate of the car, and the customer information from the body shop. The date was a day after the accident. It and the odd color suggested this was his man.

Back in the Jeep, he did the multi-step entry into a website available to insurance companies and PIs. A more expansive version was available only to police agencies. His version should be good enough.

The tags came back to an old Volvo owned by a woman in Tarpon Springs, north of Clearwater.

He cruised the Jeep past her house. Orange with black spoked wheels and thirty-three-inch Falken Wild-Peak off-road tires, it was not exactly an unnoticeable vehicle. But it was so obvious nobody would think it was a police or PI vehicle either.

A middle-aged woman was mowing her lawn with a lawnmower which smoked like a diesel tractor.

Nick texted a photo of the Volvo to his client's mobile number since it was Saturday. Afterward, he called him on the chance he might be working today.

"Hey, it's Nick Wolf. I think I have located the hit-and-run Volvo you had me looking for. I have not made contact with the owner, though I observed her at home mowing the weeds in her yard. I wanted you to know that I completed my assignment and am ready to call the Florida Highway Patrol trooper who investigated the case and let him know where to find his missing H&R vehicle."

"Nick, go ahead and call the FHP guy and let him make contact and verify it's our car and who the offending driver is. Once an arrest is made, I will cut you a check," his client said.

"Sounds good to me. I'll call the trooper now," Nick said and hung up.

Knowing the FHP was understaffed, he expected to reach the trooper on the road. He was right. He was a she when the phone was answered on the fourth cell phone ring.

"Trooper Caldwell. My name is Nick Wolf. I work with the insurance company representing the injured party on a hit-and-run you are working from last week.

A crappy color old Volvo hit a new Beemer in Clearwater."

"Right! A new three hundred series. Woman is still in the hospital. Do you have something for me?"

"Yes. I'm pretty sure I have the Volvo just over the line in Tarpon Springs. A woman, I believe to be the owner, is mowing the lawn there right now. The damaged Volvo is in the driveway."

"Damn! You want to give me the address and maybe meet me in the neighborhood? I can be there in twenty minutes, providing I don't get any emergency calls on the way."

"I'll be sitting in a bright orange Jeep Rubicon in a parking lot at South Pinellas Avenue and Meres Boulevard. Just come up South Pinellas. I'll be hard to miss," Nick told her.

About fifteen minutes later, he saw a slick top yellow over black FHP Dodge Charger slowing down and turning on her right signal.

He got out, wearing his tan cargo shorts and a LA Police Gear button-up short-sleeve forest green shirt.

Trooper Lola Caldwell was a thirty-ish woman, about five-eight or nine. *Untie the ponytail, put some lipstick on, and she'd be a knockout*, he thought. *Hell, she's a knockout as is.*

"Hi, Nick Wolf," he said as he proffered his hand.

"You don't look like an insurance guy," she responded, shaking his hand.

"I'm a retired detective sergeant working as a PI for the insurance company. Here's my card."

"How can you retire when you and I are about the same age?"

"Wrong place, wrong bullet, disability," he said.

"I'm sorry. That must suck."

"Nah. What would have sucked would have been if the bad guy had been a better shot."

"What happened to him?" she asked.

"He died."

"Oh? When?"

"About a second after he double tapped me," Nick said.

"Who capped him?"

"Two of us did. I hit him first on the way down to the deck."

"Where'd you get him, if you don't mind me asking?"

"No, not at all. Upper forehead. I figured I might lose consciousness and had to end the threat quickly. He was holding two teen girls he had just bought from a trafficker. Besides, the other bullet clipped my femoral artery."

"Not good," the trooper said.

"Nope. My partner ended the date with a twelve gauge to the face. A tourniquet and QuikClot kept me alive until the SWAT medic got there shortly after."

"How soon did the medic get to you?" she asked.

"No clue. Soon enough apparently."

"Been a PI since?" she asked.

"I have. I work for insurance companies, law firms, a few select cases in both investigation and executive protection. It's a living."

"Hmm. How did you find our runner?"

He told her.

"Exactly how I would have done it, given the time to leave patrolling long enough. We are just stretched so thin," she said.

"I know. It's pretty much the way it is in law enforcement. At least you are in Florida. Imagine if you were in a 'defund the police' city or even state," he proffered.

"I cannot imagine."

"Want me to take you to the house and stand by? I need to inform my company when an arrest is made," Nick said.

"Please."

He led her several miles to the house. She pulled into the drive. The Volvo was still there. Nick pulled up to his normal position, which was just below her property line on the driveway side at an angle where people in the house would have a difficult time seeing him, but he could see the house. Especially the exit routes.

Trooper Caldwell walked up to the front door and knocked with authority.

I bet Lola can be one tough customer, Nick thought. *Lord, she's looking more gorgeous by the minute.*

The door opened and the woman who had been mowing the yard appeared. The trooper went in, and the door closed.

Nick watched and saw what he was waiting for.

A man bailed out of the side door and jumped into the old Volvo. He started it and pulled around the police car.

Nick pulled into the driveway and pulled up, nose to nose, with the Volvo. The man in the Swedish car was clearly shocked. And probably under the influence.

He bumped the Volvo with the Jeep's aftermarket steel bumper. Nick eased forward, pushing the car. At about three miles an hour, he slipped the Jeep in neutral and pulled the drive lever down to 4L, multiplying his power and traction. He put the automatic back in drive and started pushing the car across the side yard and up against a rusty old pickup on blocks. The

Volvo was wedged in. Nick got out and walked around to the driver's side door and pulled it open.

The drunk was furious and confused—more the latter.

Nick assisted him out aggressively and put his arm in a "come along" hold with the man's wrist folded back very uncomfortably.

He walked the man to the front door.

"Ring the bell with your free arm or I will break your other one," Nick said, giving the wrist in the "come along" a painful twist to accentuate the benefit of complying.

The woman and the trooper came to the door.

"I think the hit-and-run driver was trying to escape. He did not do a very good job of it," Nick said.

Trooper Lola Caldwell tried unsuccessfully to stifle a grin.

"This is the wife, Mrs. Thomas. She works at the supermarket down the street and was working when the accident occurred. Her husband, who I assume you are presenting to us, dropped her off," the trooper said.

"I will verify her alibi if you want. I suspect you might be busy driving to the Pinellas Jail," Nick offered.

She nodded and smiled sweetly. "Mr. Thomas, I am going to give you a quick pat down and then handcuff you for your and my safety."

She did both.

"Nick, did he actually drive the car just now?" she asked.

"He did. He tried to get past me by bumping my Jeep. I have an aftermarket steel bumper. In four-wheel low, the 4.10 rear axle's power is enhanced. I pushed him up against an old truck and pinned him in."

The trooper got a breathalyzer from her trunk for

him to blow in. He registered 0.16 or double the legal limit. She held off charging him with leaving the scene of an injury accident but did charge him with driving at over twice the legal limit.

"Will you let me know when you verify Mrs. Thomas's alibi? I will charge him for the hit-and-run then," Lola said.

"Take the bum outta here. I am sick of him drinking our rent away. I have the job and take care of the house and yard. All he does is sit on his ass and pour anything he can get with alcohol in it down his throat. I'm done with getting knocked around then bailing him out. Let him rot!" Thomas's wife said with vehemence.

"Do you mind calling the store manager on duty and asking him to verify your presence at work at this time and date?" Nick said, handing her a slip of paper with the information on it. "I can get it, but a call from you will speed things up."

She made the call and explained what she needed and why.

"Ask for Joe Alden. He will be waiting for you with a copy of my timecard," she said.

"I'll text you then wait in the jail parking lot. No need to gun down and come in," Nick said to the trooper.

"Thanks. I should be ready by the time you get the information and get down to the jail," Trooper Lola Caldwell said.

Nick drove to the supermarket and went in. He asked for the manager. Joe Alden was a man about thirty-five.

"I was expecting someone in uniform," he said.

"I work for the insurance company handling a case where Mrs. Thomas's car was involved in an accident. I set out this morning in my Jeep to drive by some locations to find the car. No need to get dressed in business attire. Here is my Florida Private Investigator license and badge if you need it," he said, showing it to the manager.

"Not necessary. She gave me your description. I was just curious. Here's a photocopy of her timecard for the period in question. She was here the day and time she asked proof for. I circled the times she worked that day with a pencil."

"Thanks, Mr. Alden. I appreciate your help and know Mrs. Thomas does. I hope everything turns out okay for her."

"Me, too. She's a hard worker and well-liked. We all knew about her problems at home and feel bad for her."

He left and turned the Jeep southward and toward the Pinellas County jail complex. He drove to just outside the controlled access for prisoner drop-offs. It was a location he knew well from his past. He saw a slick top trooper car, which meant it did not have a light bar on top, and hoped it was Lola's.

Nick turned the Jeep off and texted her, saying he was there with the last piece she needed for the accident arrest. She came out and gave him a killer smile as she took the photocopy.

"A copy of Thomas's arrest sheet for today, especially stating he left the scene of an accident on the proper date would sure expedite me closing the case..."

"I will have it for you in maybe twenty minutes. Can you wait?" she asked.

"Of course."

Sure to her word, she appeared with the arrest sheet in fifteen minutes. She gave him her card with it.

"You have my official cell. I penciled in my personal

one on the back. I am off by dinner time all the coming week if you'd like to grab a burger or something," she said.

"I'll call Monday. I love burgers and somethings," he replied with a grin.

She went back in, and he fired up the Rubicon and headed toward his office and home on Central Avenue in St. Petersburg, smiling all the way.

2

Almost four years ago

Senior deputy Nick Wolf was summoned to the major's office immediately. Unlike most, he was not at all nervous about the call. He had done nothing wrong and was confident if he had been accused of wrongdoing, he could quickly quash it.

At thirty-one, he had been a deputy for seven years. He joined after a couple years as a military CID investigator. Online work in the military had made his remaining night and online classes for a criminal justice degree at the University of South Florida quick.

"Wolf. You've done well as a detective here. Solved several bank robberies, a kidnapping, a money laundering scheme. Lots of good numbers," his major said.

"The sheriff will swear you in as detective sergeant this afternoon. I want you to head up an I-4 human trafficking task force. It will be all local with sheriff's detectives from Polk, Hillsborough, Pinellas, Pasco, and

Manatee Counties. The latter is due to a high incidence in the county, more than its proximity to I-4.

"You will also have some city detectives, mainly from St. Pete, Tampa, and Lakeland. Other cities may be added if you find it necessary.

"As I suspect you know, the I-4 corridor between Tampa and Orlando is a major human trafficking route in the US."

"Shouldn't we have some members from Orlando, Orange County, and at least Seminole, sir?" Nick asked.

"Nope. There is a similar local task force over there. When they appoint a head, you will liaise with him or her. This thing was put together by the Florida Attorney General. She has gotten funding for both task forces. You will be responsible for the supervision, planning, and record keeping on your western half. While the checking accounts have not been set up yet, I have a purchase order number you can use for initial expenditures," he said, handing Nick a piece of paper with the information.

"The County has rented a storefront location in a strip mall midway between the Tampa city limits and the county line on I-4. It looks like a central location to operate from. I understand the other task force has a similar location around Kissimmee. You'll trade your official sedan for a new Tahoe, and I expect will load the odometer up with highway miles. You live over in St. Pete, right?" the major asked.

"Yes, sir. It worries me I don't have any informants who can help much in trafficking, either geographically or the subject matter."

"We know you don't. Make some and exploit the ones your team members have."

"Will I have full access to SWAT when needed?"

"You bet. Direct access. You call the SWAT sergeant yourself. Spend the rest of the day until three picking up your new wheels and transferring equipment over to it. Work up what you will say to your team in three days when you will meet with them at the task force office at noon. You need to go there first and see what security needs to be added. Give me a list and I will work with you to get it done. Any questions?"

"Yes, sir. How will it work with the deputies or detectives for the other agencies. Will they be transferred to this new entity?"

"No, they will remain full employees where they are currently. This will just be a temporary assignment for them. Their pay and insurance and all will be from their parent agency. The task force—you—will pay overtime and gasoline and specialized needs. For example, you will probably need a few surveillance vans set up and maybe a deep-cover car or two. Wherever possible, we will use vehicles the county has confiscated and legally turned to LE use. I have admin folks standing by to help you set up record keeping for rentals, purchases, gas cards and overtime. You and all your people will be cross sworn as state law enforcement officers."

"Thanks for the faith you have in me. I won't let you down."

"I know you won't, Wolf. Now get outta here and get busy. Here's a copy of the budget for your task force and the general rules and way to draw down funds. Study it and don't be late to the Sheriff's office for your swearing in at three. I'll be there, too."

"Thanks, Boss. See you at three." Nick left with the grant folder under his arm and went to his soon-to-be-vacated cubicle to study it.

He had a lot of money to use and would try to list

columns according to category once he finished the rules of use portion. Nick was glad to find out the detectives from the cities and the sheriff's departments would use their own vehicles. He assumed overtime would be the largest drain on the budget.

He wanted to allocate funds for security, cameras, phone lines, and tables and chairs for the storefront he had not seen yet. He planned on keeping the site covert, so would need a cover identity for it. He would go to one of the sergeants he knew had set up a number of cover and sting operations and get some ideas about how to set it up.

Nick had his notes ready an hour later. He planned a trip over to the storefront after being sworn with the new gold detective badge.

He went out and grabbed a quick lunch of a salad and iced tea. He went to his locker and put his recently dry-cleaned dress uniform on before walking to the Sheriff's office for the ceremony. It was quick, and he returned to the locker room and changed back into a sheriff's office golf shirt, khaki slacks, and his low boots. He pinned the new star on his belt badge holder and put his Glock 23, a mag holder and handcuffs on his belt.

The next trip was to HR to get his new ID to match the gold detective sergeant's star, then to the motor pool to officially turn in his sedan for the SUV. He had the techs install a locking equipment box in the back. He began transferring his investigative gear, patrol rifle, and shotgun to the box.

The vehicle switch took a lot longer than he expected, postponing the trip to the storefront until tomorrow morning.

He put gas in the dark gray Tahoe and headed home. The SUV was the pursuit model. Nick thought all Tahoes were pretty quick and knew this one would handle high-speed driving better than most. He already tested the hidden red and blue lights and the siren package in the motor pool garage. The actuators, including switching the sirens to the steering wheel horn button, were just like on the sedan he turned in. He punched it on a low traffic portion of the Howard Frankland Bridge connecting Tampa and St. Petersburg over North Tampa Bay. The gray SUV jumped into passing gear and climbed fast until he backed off. It would do just fine.

He parked in his apartment complex off Fourth Street North in St. Pete and went in and back to his personal computer.

He searched for the Florida Branch of the National Center for Missing and Exploited Children. He only found a phone and an email address. He called the phone prior to five and got an administrative person.

"Hi, this is Detective Sergeant Nick Wolf. I head up a new Human Trafficking Task Force for the Interstate 4 corridor area. We operate under the auspices of the Florida Attorney General. We are just getting going and I wonder if you could provide a speaker to give my officers a big-picture view of trafficking in Florida, especially from Tampa to Orlando?"

He was transferred to a manager and repeated his request. He scheduled a speaker at the task force office for the following Friday before hanging up. He would meet with the task force in three days to see how many people he had, what their background was and who the sergeants were to choose one to serve as number two or maybe two people and split the task force geographically. Nick knew to keep personnel matters fluid until he saw what and who he had.

He and Finn the cat had a largely one-way conversation as he sautéed a fresh fish fillet and turned a massive amount of spinach into one serving in an adjacent fry pan.

He poured some iced tea, served Finn about two tablespoons of the fish set aside before he seasoned it with pepper and Old Bay, and sat down to eat. Finn watched silently, but approvingly.

———

The next morning, he took the Tahoe and timed his new commute. Apartment to the task force office just off I-4 between Tampa and the eastern county line. The major told him the name of the firm which supplied security lights, cameras and alarms for department sites, especially covert ones. Nick called them and arranged for a rep to come by in the afternoon.

The major also had a county construction supervisor slated to come out late in the morning to talk about the temporary walls and doors.

He grimaced. It was a long commute through some of the worst traffic Tampa Bay could throw at you.

The Tahoe had a good navigation system, and it led him right to the storefront. He used the key and walked in. He did not know where the main light switch was, so he used his four-hundred-lumen tactical flashlight until he located it.

The walls were a dull light gray, the floors linoleum, and the space had a reception area with a built-in desk. The walls and floors were ugly but clean. The interior appeared to have been painted after the last tenant moved out.

Beyond the reception area was a large room that was empty, and beyond that was what Nick thought must have been a storage or supply room about thirty by fifty feet. He envisioned greatly enhancing the lighting and turning this into a breakout room and secure file and weapon storage. It had a steel door on the back. He took notes about where he wanted motion detector lighting inside and out and surveillance cameras outside. The big room would be the bullpen where the detectives worked while in the office.

The front door lock should be a card lock. They needed a system to make and be able to delete access cards. Another option he thought would be a passcode lock.

There was a side door. This needed the same access lock control. He wanted the officers to enter this door and not walk past any persons who might be at the reception for whatever reasons. He wanted a removable floor-to-ceiling wall between the one behind reception and before the side door.

His real job though was to get forty rental folding chairs, twenty folding tables.

He called the major, who gave him an additional billing order number to give to whatever rental firm he could find who could accommodate the delivery in time.

Nick had seen a rental company on the way over. They rented tents, folding tables, and chairs. He called them, and they could get his rush order delivered and set up in time for his upcoming meeting.

The space would allow for three admin offices and a conference room, which could be used by victims, for interviews, and by members when they needed to talk and plan outside the bullpen, which would be behind the wall. He noted all of this on his pad.

His last notes were for cable to be run for electrical power for up to twenty work locations. He thought they could rent folding tables and chairs which would accommodate laptops and smartphone chargers. He knew most of his task force members would have their own computers in their vehicles like he did.

He locked the building and drove to the rental company. They did not have office furniture but referred him to a nearby firm which did. He went there and rented a desk, chair, and credenza for himself and two subordinates, three five-drawer locking file cabinets, and forty two-drawer locking file cabinets for the bullpen. He ordered a conference room table and eight chairs. He ordered twenty cubicle units. He ordered a like number of computers for them and more for his two deputies and himself from the county's IT department to be billed to the task force. He doubted he would ever have more than twenty members on computers at the same time, especially when each also had car computers. The probable use would be to print from. There would be other things immediately necessary like trash cans, supply shelves, and office supplies. But he had to get the minimum items set up for the meeting.

Nick would have to play his subordinate selections by ear. He thought once he met them, he would pick two sergeants, one to handle the westernmost agencies, one the eastern ones.

A county construction supervisor and his assistant arrived about eleven. They agreed it would be simple to put in a temporary wall twenty feet behind the reception area wall, to make a corridor to the bullpen and frame up an office for Nick and two subordinates and a large conference room. They measured the runs need to put electricity at each proposed station. Nick found out from him who the county used for Wi-Fi and wrote it down to call before he ended his day. He would also have to get six color printers and have an IT tech person standing by to make sure everything tied back to the detectives' personal laptops during the first several days.

The construction guy also recommended they put a long counter in the back and Nick buy a couple of commercial refrigerators and several microwaves and a couple of big Keurig-type coffee makers. They left with lots of notes about scheduling and material needed. Nick decided to use the credit card he would get on Thursday to buy the refrigerators and coffee makers at a big box store.

"Major, it's Nick. What's the chance of getting an admin person to do some of the bookkeeping and serve as a nine-to-five receptionist? A sworn junior person would be great as long as they have the accounting skills. They would be in this out-of-the-way place alone a lot, so them being sworn and armed would make me feel better."

"On the surface, that seems like a good idea. Let me check with HR and see if we had anyone who would fill the bill. It might be a long shot and you might end up having to hire a temp to do it., but I'd worry about him or her being in a pretty dead strip mall alone a lot too," the major said. "I'll call you back."

Before leaving, Nick arranged for the Wi-Fi and to have a tech available for a few days to help with printer setup.

Nick was thinking about the task force as he drove

through what was arguably the worst rush-hour traffic in the Tampa Bay area.

I'm wrong. It would be unfair to appoint one subordinate from the east end of the task force area and another from over where I live. Both should be nearer to the office. They will be there fairly frequently and don't need this damn commute! I'll get everybody to self-introduce tomorrow by name, agency, and title. Then, I can ask two likely folks to stay over a bit when the meeting is over and talk with them. Maybe some people with supervisory ability. People who were sergeants on the road before making detective...

The major had promised him a complete list of the task force members by nine in the morning. So, he would have the list four hours before the meeting. There would be the furniture delivery and set up of the chairs and some tables in the morning. The actual wall construction would commence on Monday. Things were coming together. Once the office was set up, they could actually start identifying and taking down the worst type of bad guys. Ones who preyed on children.

Nick had been thinking ahead. As they saw things and made arrests, he was probably going to have some counselors on call. He did not want people to burn out or get PTSD from what they experienced. And it very well could happen. Their adversaries were the scum of the earth. Nick figured there was a special hell just for them. At least he sure hoped so.

———

The next morning, he stopped by the headquarters. The major gave him a list of thirty-seven task force members by name, agency, and rank. He knew a detective sergeant from Polk County. As a young detective, he had worked a number of cases with him, and the guy had been a sort of mentor. He was thrilled to have Lee on the team. There was another he did not know from Lakeland PD. Depending on where Lee from Polk County lived, he could have a short or very long commute.

He also learned someone was going to be there from the Attorney General's Office to deputize each as a state LEO, since all the cities and counties did not have mutual aid agreements allowing arrests in adjacent areas.

The Lakeland detective was Kit Ennis. Male or female? He did not care at all and would find out tomorrow.

By the time he arrived, the county construction supervisor was already in, and his team was working. An hour later, the tables and chairs were delivered, and the chairs were set up theater style. His and his two unknown subordinates' desks and chairs were delivered. He had the preponderance of the file cabinets placed along the wall in the bullpen. The computer workstations, printers for the bullpen, and small supply area would be set up in the center of the work area.

He went out and grabbed a salad at a small Greek restaurant nearby, thought about what he was going to say to the new task force members in an hour and a half and decided to do what he did best. Wing it.

He stopped by a Dunkin' Donuts and bought enough coffee to handle eighty cups. He added five dozen mixed donuts. Law enforcement ran on coffee. The donuts were icing on the cake.

Nick returned and told the construction people they could commence full speed ahead at around two thirty, but needed to vacate between twelve forty-five and two thirty while the meeting was going on. A lady from the Attorney General's Office in Tallahassee arrived with state ID cards for everyone, several assistants, and ready to do a group deputation.

People started arriving by twelve fifteen. A couple had marked units. Every car, plain or marked and carrying a light bar, looked like a cop car. There were five detectives from his agency. He knew and liked all. As was obvious, the three marked unit people were not detectives. They were either deputies or police officers from agencies that were not staffed sufficiently to give up a detective for a year, which was the commitment required. Nick figured he could come up with three unmarked units by getting sheriff cars from the retirement list and having them painted in the shop.

He could work the three into plain clothes ranks as there were a lot of street savvy LEOs on the beat. Hopefully, these were examples.

He stood at the door and welcomed everyone. Some stayed outside to smoke, others went in and found a folding chair to crash on.

Everyone was there on his count by one o'clock. He ushered the remaining smokers in and walked to the front of the chairs. Show time.

"Welcome aboard to everyone. I am Detective Sergeant Nick Wolf from the local SO. I've been named to head up this western I-4 human trafficking task force.

"You all represent sheriff's offices in Pinellas, Pasco, Hillsborough, Manatee and Polk and police departments of St. Pete, Tampa, Lakeland, and Bradenton. We may add police departments and another county if the incidence of trafficking warrants it.

"I will appoint two detective sergeants from this end of the district as my number twos. Why this end? I think, since you already made the horrendous commute here, you already know! I live in downtown St. Petersburg and already hate it.

"Luckily, I don't envision many meetings. Maybe one a month. Maybe less. The first one will be an important one and it will be this coming Wednesday at ten in the morning.

"By the time you get here for the meeting, this building will be turned into a bare-bones task force HQ with adequate computer workstations, break room equipment, Wi-Fi, locking files, murder boards, and a conference room. We will have security cameras and alarms and, hopefully, a sworn person to help monitor the reception area, cameras, and help with the bookkeeping.

"Why hasn't all this preparatory stuff already been done? Because I had no idea three days ago this task force would be created or that I would head it.

"You will remain employed for the year commitment with your parent agencies. The task force will cover overtime at your current rate, needed equipment and workspace, and gas cards. For the several of you who have marked units, I will work on getting you some task force unmarked ones to which you can transfer your shotguns, rifles or other equipment. The reason is this is what I would call a semi-covert site. We will have a false name over the door. I watched as you all came in. Virtually every car you have—and mine—took exactly like the cop vehicles they are. But we cannot do a damn thing about it. You will likely need every bit of equipment in them and the ability to run fast in traffic while staying in radio comms.

"Next Wednesday's meeting will include a presentation from the Center for Missing and Exploited Children with an overview of the subject and how the I-4 corridor plays into it.

"By the way, there will be a duplicate task force for the other end. We will coordinate closely with them. They will have a similar building in Kissimmee for their HQ.

"My suspicion is we will be the supply end of the trafficking chain and they the receipt and distribution end. At least most of the time. But I don't know for sure. Our speaker a week from today may validate it or not. We'll see.

"We are honored to have Florida Associate Deputy Attorney General Washington here with us today. She is going to explain what the deputation as a state law enforcement officer means, answer any questions you might have and then swear all of us in.

"After, several of her associates are set up at a table on the side with alphabet ranges. Please get in line and you will be given your warrants to include in your current badge and cred packs. You have probably already smelled coffee and donuts on the other side. Grab some after you receive your warrants. We have another hour or so to go after the deputation, so please stick around. Ms. Washington?"

The attorney at the fourth tier in the office spoke for about fifteen minutes about the authorities given by the deputation she was about to administer. There were no questions and she had everyone raise his or her hands and administered the oath.

Nick joined them in raising his hand and saying his name aloud. He then joined the N-Z line to receive his warrant to fold up and put in his ID case.

The AG office people got coffee and donuts and he chatted with them. He asked how he could get subsequent additions or replacements deputized. Washington said she would use Zoom or WebEx to deputize them. Once she deputized someone online in his presence, she would forward the deputation warrant to him to deliver.

The AG people were on a tight schedule and left shortly. He gave the group another thirty minutes to chat, then called the meeting back to order.

"Okay. Some preliminary thoughts. They are subject to modification after we get together Wednesday afternoon and talk. My idea is to break the group along geographic lines: St. Pete; Pinellas; and Western Manatee, including Bradenton and Palmetto. The second would be Tampa and the western and southern parts of Hillsborough; and northern and eastern Manatee. The third group would be Polk, Pasco, and eastern Hillsborough. I will sit with one, each of the assistants with another. Our purpose will be to compare trafficking experiences and work on strategy.

"Here is my strategy idea. One, we search our areas for missing teens in the past week. It does not mean we or anyone else will give up on ones missing longer. It's just it takes a week or less for traffickers to grab one, move them, get them on meth or some opioid which will make them pliable and put them in place in prostitution or house cleaning or whatever. Just like with heart attacks, there's a golden hour. With these kids, there's a golden week to repatriate them.

"The second strategic prong is really focusing on three things.

"Profile, velocity, and ticket. Profile is trying to determine if there is actually a local profile. The 'ideal' victim for the traffickers. Things like age, sex, and beauty? Unhappy home life? We know a lot of kids are runaways picked up on the street or at bus stations. But are they victims of convenience for pimps? Or are they trafficking targets?

"Velocity is what I mentioned a minute ago. How long do we have for a reasonable move into a targeting victim's final deployment as a prostitute, cleaner or what? A week? Four days once a kid has been reported missing by parents? Priority-wise, where do we go after interviewing the parents? School? Friends? Time will be of the essence.

"Ticket is a short way of saying departure and arrival like a bus or plane ticket to their final assignment. From where do they generally take off? Where is their directed arrival? Are there areas where most leave from? Are there areas where traffickers 'shop' for them? Where do they arrive? Runaways probably bus stations. How about transported victims? Is there a staging area? The assumption of our two task forces is they come from here and go to Orlando. But is it correct? Is the western end sometimes the destination and not the departure?

"Until we figure some of these things out and work up some empirical data, we may be unintentionally leaving crucial parts of our investigations untouched.

"These things are just a starting point. I'd like each of you to think hard about them and other, possibly obvious things, I have left out. Then Wednesday, after the presentation, the area work groups can discuss them, bring in new ideas and we will formulate an overall, and if need be, area strategies."

"Thanks for being volunteered for this"—which caused some laughter—"and for your expertise and the hard work all of us will be doing to make our kids safer and the traffickers who use them to become miserable in Florida's fine penitentiaries.

"Anybody have any questions or comments?"

A hand rose. Nick could see it was Det. Sgt. Lee Strang from Polk County.

"Lee, my friend. How are you?" he said.

"Nick, I'm probably the oldest one here. I have been with the sheriff's office up in Polk for thirty years. I'm not the sharpest pencil in the drawer, but I've damn well seen it all. This thing you—we will be doing—is one of the most important things in any of our careers. Putting away the scum who abuse and make money off our kids. This was not some pre-retirement thing for me. When I heard a scuttlebutt about it, I went to the boss and asked to be included. I, for one, am glad they let me." He sat down without saying more.

"Folks, for those of you who don't know him, Lee is a legend. No matter the crime, he has solved it. He might be the oldest one here, I'm only going on what he claimed. But he's one of the last people in this room I'd want to take on in a dark alley," Nick said.

"Detective Sergeant Kit Ennis from Lakeland PD, would you identify yourself?" Nick continued.

A medium height, strong looking woman of about midforties stood up.

"Sarge, would you and Lee stay over a few minutes for some questions after we adjourn?" Nick asked.

She and Strang both nodded.

"Anybody else? Please start thinking and strategizing between now and Wednesday morning. Put together the most recent unsolved under-eighteen disappearances in your areas and any report information on them. That's where we'll start! I will see all of y'all a bit before ten on Wednesday for the rest of the day. Be safe."

As people began to leave, Lee and Kit walked up to him.

"Think there might be some coffee and donuts left?" he asked rhetorically. The three walked over to the table. No coffee was left, so they made some strong coffee with Keurig cups, and each selected a donut. Or two.

They sat around one of the folding tables.

"Looks like you've been busy for the last three days," Lee observed.

"Just a little, Lee. How have you been?"

"Had a few heart issues, but all under control. This will probably be my last gig before retiring. Like I said, I believe in the effort."

"Me, too, my friend. Kit, we have not met before. Let me introduce myself and ask you to tell Lee and me about you."

She nodded pleasantly. She was quite attractive when she did not have her resting cop face on.

"I'll begin. Mine's probably the most boring," Nick said. "My senior high school trip was to South Carolina for boot camp. After basic and intermediate, I went to spec ops. The 75th Ranger Regiment. After a number of combat and hot spot deployments, I became a CID investigator for a few years in the military. Toward the end, I got deployed again, but as an investigator. Got about two-thirds of a criminal justice degree there. I did not re-up for a second tour. Afghanistan twice was enough excitement and more than enough scars. I got a deputy job here. I guess because of my military experience investigating, I rose to detective quickly. Finished the degree along the way.

"I recently took the sergeants boards. The major notified me I made sergeant by giving me this assignment."

"What are you? Thirty-two?" she asked.

"I am."

"Gotcha by a decade," she said. "I skipped the military and college and joined Lakeland Police Department. Loved every second and like you, got my criminal justice degree online. In seven years, I made sergeant and was a supervisor in patrol. Four years ago, I switched to the Investigative Services Bureau and found my true home."

"That's a great career, Kit. The reason I have asked you two to stay over is to offer you the two deputy positions. Lee, how far away do you live from here? I suspect the two deputy commanders will spend more time here than task force members, so living near is kinda important," Nick said.

"I am maybe ten miles away and none of it is on interstate involves Tampa traffic. I am good to go," he said.

"I am honored and also am good to go," Kit said.

"Thank you both. You have lots I don't have, particularly in the area of supervision. Mine is all in the Rangers versus law enforcement. What do you think about assignments? Should each have a permanent team? Or switch around?"

"I could argue both ways. I'd like to think about it," Lee said.

"Me, too. Stability sounds good, but so does hearing how the several geographic areas may be different," Kit added.

"Okay. I will think about it. Maybe we can meet an hour early on Wednesday and decide. Or not. It may take a couple of meetings to figure out the best way to supervise. Let's exchange cards for now and have one another's numbers. Don't hesitate to call. If something comes up where we need to put our heads together before Wednesday, we can work out a conference call or Zoom meeting. Not being face-to-face for every meeting may have been the only good thing to come out of the COVID fiasco."

3

By the end of the day Friday, the computer cubicles were fastened down and the office furniture for Nick and his two deputies were in place, though the walls were not up yet for either their offices or the conference room. Using power units already in the floor from when the building was a retail store, all the table locations had power.

He had two refrigerated cabinets with glass doors for lunches and several coffee makers and additional Keurig-type single-cup makers scheduled for delivery on Monday.

A Det. Sgt. Walt Wood from the Orange County SO called him at ten o'clock in the morning on Saturday.

"Nick, this is Walt Wood. I got named commander of the AG's eastern trafficking task force a couple days ago. I understand you are my opposite number for the western one?"

"I am. Only a couple days jump on you, Walt. I've been scrambling trying to put things together."

"I just had the lady from the Florida AG's office here

to give a talk and deputize everybody as state officers yesterday. We did it in a vacant storefront. She said you had some stuff moved into yours. I was thinking, if it was convenient for you, about running over sometime and taking a look at what you have done and what your approach is going to be?" Wood asked.

"I'm glad we are in contact. I wanted to get with you and swap ideas, too. Sure, come over and take a look. I am here at our building now. You are welcome to come now if you want. We can talk about ways to coordinate efforts," Nick offered.

"I think I'm about fifty miles away. Give me forty-five minutes?"

"Sounds good. See you when you get here." Nick told him the exit number and how to get to the strip mall before hanging up.

Walt got there forty minutes later. He was a tall, fit guy in his late thirties or early forties. He had already designed and ordered several task force polo shirts for his team and was wearing one. He brought a sample of the nylon raid jackets he ordered too.

"Man. I like those. If you give me your contact, I will get sizes and order them for our folks, too," Nick said. Walt gave him a card from the company and penciled shirt and jacket prices on the back.

"Try to piggy-back on our contract. Since there's no need to differentiate between the two task forces, they can be exactly the same," Walt said.

Nick agreed. Nick led him on a tour of his site.

"You have about the same bare-bones layout as I do for my forty members. The number includes me and two deputy commanders. How do you plan on assigning and supervising?" Walt said.

Nick explained his thoughts. He liked the

commander and deputy commander titles, especially when they had been approved in Tallahassee.

He shared his profile/velocity/ticket approach. Walt liked it.

"As far as I'm concerned, we are running different ends of the same operation. There is no pride of ownership. You like something I'm doing, it's yours. Same the other way around."

"Roger that," Walt agreed. "I think you are generally right about kids leaving your area and arriving in ours. Some probably come your way, some probably go to Miami or Jacksonville. I'm betting more on Miami then to the Caribbean or jumping off points to places like the Middle East. Places from which we are unlikely to recover them."

"Yeah, it makes perfect sense. I wonder if the AG will have Jax and Miami task forces?" Nick asked.

"I hope so, but it's too new. I suspect we are a test balloon. Besides, if it gets too big and too successful, somebody else will try to take it over."

"I agree with you on both," Nick said.

"Have you given any thought to the semi-covert name for our endeavors?" Nick asked Walt.

"Yep. FLAG Police Training LLC. If you like it, I can be the Osceola County Branch and you can be the Hillsborough County Branch. Get it? FL for Florida and AG for Attorney General. The 'police training' should cover the official-looking cars out front and the guys walking in with polo shirts and pistol belts."

"I like it! I am trying to get a sworn person to be kind of a reception, camera monitor and admin. Are you? If so, each of us could have a task force landline answered, 'Flag LLC, may I help you?'" Nick said.

"I just had a new deputy assigned. Business degree. He jumped at it," Walt said.

"I am still waiting, but I have requested the same. I am planning on picking up a couple of vehicles on the replacement list from my county. Keeping—or installing—emergency equipment and radios in them and painting them if necessary. I have a couple road deputies or city patrolmen who will need different cars since they have marked units," Nick said.

"I'd push for late models and not retirement vehicles. It looks like the AG got us more than enough grant money to cover decent vehicles. I'd get some pickups and compacts in the mix which don't jump out as cop vehicles, too," Walt suggested.

Nick agreed.

They talked further. The more they talked, the better the ideas which emerged. All of Nick's scheduled arrivals for the day were delivered so they went to a local Olive Garden for an early dinner before each made the commute home.

Nick did not go to the HQ on Sunday. He felt all thought out, so he decided to spend some rare time on the water.

———

Nick called ahead to the high and dry storage at a marina on Anna Maria Island. He liked the location because it put him close to the mouth of Tampa Bay and to the Gulf of Mexico. Yet, there were mangroves nearby to provide snook fishing when the striped speedsters were not hitting on the beaches.

He left his Tahoe parked at his apartment and took his Mustang. By the time he arrived, his old but perfect twenty-foot SeaCraft was in the water. The one hundred seventy-five horsepower Suzuki started on the first crank, and he idled out of the marina.

Nick put his off-duty snub nose and his badge in the console. He arrived in running shorts and a tee shirt. He dumped the shirt and put on a Mustang inflatable personal flotation device or PFD. He had a signal mirror in the pocket and a personal EPIRB or Emergency Position-Indicating Radio Beacon hooked on it. He also wore a lanyard with the engine kill switch around his neck. If he somehow got separated from his boat in the Gulf, it was a helluva swim home, so he did not take chances.

He loved the Suzuki. It was bulletproof and still fast. The boat would run forty-five in almost all conditions with its stainless prop.

Nick idled out of the marina entry at no-wake speed. Once he got in the Gulf Intracoastal Waterway, he sped up to about thirty. He was in no big rush. He just wanted to be out there. Unfortunately, on a sunny Sunday, everyone else did, too. He followed the markers out to where they numbered in the high 60s and turned left and took the boat up to thirty-five, aimed just off Bean Point.

He was careful off Bean Point to avoid the shoals and entered the Gulf. He had left most of the snowbirds behind and drove several miles off shore, then another left took him along Anna Maria Island toward Longboat Pass. He passed it and continued south the length of Longboat Key to New Pass.

He had two viable choices. Go into New Pass and return via the inside or turn around and reprise his run back on the outside. He ducked in the pass and saw the traffic and turned around, and after clearing the pass, headed north again.

He checked his depth finder/chart plotter. The water was ten feet deep over a hard sand bottom. Hot and sweaty, he drank some water from his cooler bag and dropped the light Fortress anchor on its seven-foot chain and rope rode. He let out fifty feet of anchor and line and let it catch in the sand. In the unlikely event the anchor broke loose, he threw another fifty-foot line with one end secured to the boat by the boarding ladder and the other tied to a life preserver cushion. He would swim close to the line, between the boat and the floating cushion. If the boat broke loose or he got a cramp, he could make it to the nearby line, use the cushion to support him if needed, or otherwise swim along the line to the boat. It beat swimming a mile to shore or to Texas or Mexico or somewhere over the horizon.

After swimming a quarter of an hour and missing having some comely female companion, he swam beside the line to the boarding ladder and climbed aboard. Another water and he recovered the life preserver cushion and started the engine.

As it idled, Nick pulled and stowed the anchor and returned to the helm. He did a 360-degree scan. Nobody was around. Making sure the telltale was spurting a stream of water, indicating the engine was pumping cooling water, he put it in gear and eased up on plane. He got the trim just right and noted a rare forty-seven miles per hour on the speedometer. Not bad, he thought as he let the engine run hard and blow the cobwebs out all the way to Passage Key Inlet, on to marker 68, then, slower, into the ICW to the marina. He tied the SeaCraft, told the dock hand to fill it up and tipped him. The dockhand would then fill the tank, flush the engine with fresh water, hose the boat inside and out, before putting it in its third-story berth in the building, using a huge forklift.

Nick crossed the Sunshine Skyway Bridge, two-hundred feet above Tampa Bay, and got off onto Fourth Street North to his apartment. He stopped on the way for a Tex-Mex dinner, having put nicer shorts and a button-up fishing shirt on at the marina.

————

Nick was at the task force HQ by six thirty Monday morning, drinking some of the first coffee from the machine. He answered his smartphone at six forty-five. It was the major.

"I got you a reception person. She's a new deputy, just past riding with a field training officer. She has an accounting degree from USF's main campus. She has not been assigned a car yet. Any ideas of what kind?" the major asked.

"Do we have a late model mid-size unmarked, but with a radio and siren?" Nick asked.

"Hold on," Nick knew the boss was calling up a computer page.

"How about a new Malibu detective car with full equipment? No cage of course."

"Perfect. Has she been assigned a rifle and shotgun? No? Go ahead, if you don't mind. She may have to hold down the fort, God forbid."

"I've met with Detective Sergeant Walt Wood, sir. He's commander of the eastern task force. We decided on FLAG Police Training LLC for our semi-covert name. Flag is Florida Attorney General. The police training part is to explain the number of cars with short antennae and small hubcaps and tough looking guys and gals with golf shirts and guns showing," Nick said. "We talked strategy and promised to stay in close touch."

"All good, Nick. Will you be ready for your Wednesday meeting with the exploited children's group?"

"I will be ready. The HQ will be almost ready. I think the new walls will be up. I am not sure about them being painted by then. We will have all the furniture and equipment in by this morning.

"The computer workstations are already hot. I'd like an IT guy who can talk to non-nerds about signing in and any apps they will need to add to their already in use car computers.

"I have everyone pulling up-to-date missing kids lists from their jurisdictions in the last week or so. They were asked to bring the full reports with them."

"Why that recent, Nick?" the major asked.

"Anything older and the actual trafficked kids will be gone unlike the runaways. We can help all of them by determining who, why, what, and how on recent cases."

"Makes sense. Just don't forget the ones already in the illicit system."

"We won't, boss. I promise."

Nick accepted the furniture deliveries and had the deliverymen place items in their approximate resting place.

The new addition arrived at two thirty. She was Deputy Dawn Allison. She was young enough and pretty enough to pass for a Miss Florida contestant, but with a gun. She had her new Malibu and seemed quite pleased with moving from a marked unit to an unmarked one so quickly.

"Until we get the polo shirts with logos, you should wear plain or SO polo shirts with khakis, cargo pants of any color, or jeans. I'd recommend comfortable boots or running shoes. As the first line of defense, I want you to wear your Kevlar vest at all times.

"For your first assignment, I'd like for you to make up a shirt/raid jacket size sheet for the task force members to fill out on Wednesday. You can type in the names from this sheet. Please alphabetize them so we can complete multiple sheets at one time. Put something on the top reminding them the raid jackets should be large enough to accommodate heavier bullet-resistant vests instead of the light ones we wear under polo shirts. Oh, and be sure to include yourself."

He went on to brief her on what the goals of the two task forces would be and how they would work. He went over how to answer the landline with calls to the false name FLAG Police Training LLC. He told her he would have her deputized as a Florida state officer the following day via Zoom.

Finally, he spoke to her about her accounting education and how much help he needed in handling the grant budget. She exuberantly told him doing police work and spreadsheets at the same time was her idea of heaven. Her abilities were his idea too, right now. He just did not say so.

The two worked diligently to organize chairs and tables around the computer kiosks. The construction guys got the walls and doors up. Because of the importance of the Wednesday meeting, he scheduled the painting for Thursday. The landline phone went to the reception desk, his and his two deputy commanders, to allow for optional night and weekend answering. For voice mail, he had Dawn record the message.

"How about lunch?" he asked.

She was amenable. She stated she was a vegan but could eat a veggie-only salad and lemon juice for dressing. Dawn added she carried her own lemon juice for convenience.

"Why don't you drive? I want to get a feel for the Malibu, since we have to provide cars for several people."

He found she was a fast and very competent driver. On the way back from lunch, he had her accelerate onto I-4 and run it up to eighty as quickly as the car could. He was pleased with the acceleration of the larger four-cylinder engine, noting his watch as she powered from the on-ramp to the traffic lane. She hit sixty in around six seconds and kept on climbing strongly.

Tuesday saw the security/surveillance cameras installed and the monitor put at Dawn's station and another at his desk. The card-access door locks were put in. Nick ordered sixty cards and had Dawn prepare an issue sheet with names and numbers. She entered a number on each card with a heavy black Sharpie.

He gave her the number of the task force credit card and had her order lunches similar to what he had done for the recent Friday meeting. Since the refrigerator cases were in, they picked up a variety of sodas and water and stocked them in sufficient time to get cold for the next day's meeting.

Nick placed a variety of office supplies on the shelves in the rear storage room and some basics, along with paper and printer cartridges in a cabinet by the computer kiosks.

Lee and Kit came in Tuesday afternoon and moved

into their offices, even to the point of hanging photos and diplomas on the walls. Nick made a note to look for something at home he could hang up. Whatever it was would likely necessitate a stop somewhere to buy a few frames. He had a college diploma and a couple of awards and unclassified photos from his combat time. Maybe they would cover some wall space.

The four were ready for the meeting Wednesday. The lunches would be delivered.

———

Because of the uncertainty of the traffic, task force members began arriving early. The speaker came early to check electronics. Several IT techs were there to help with the logins after the speaker and they helped get the PowerPoint presentation set up.

Nick welcomed everyone for an informative day.

He introduced the speaker, and the man gave an informative talk full of things they needed to know, like categories of trafficking. The time from pickup to delivery which Nick called "velocity, and a ranking of the types of subjects traffickers sought."

Nick watched as forty people took prolific notes, himself included. Dawn at in the open doorway and was able to listen to everything while still monitoring the front door.

Nick introduced the deputy commanders and brought Dawn in to be introduced. He, the speaker and two deputy commanders formed a roundtable and accepted questions from the team members and threw out more questions.

By eleven thirty, they were ready to adjourn for lunch. Several members helped Dawn bring it in and set it up. It appeared Dawn would have no problem securing volunteers at any time. The speaker stayed for lunch and more questions.

He left with thanks following the lunch break and Nick stood up.

"The first thing this afternoon is for you to sign a size chart for several task force polo shirts and a raid jacket. You should dress as you do when you are conducting an investigation for your own agency. Don't forget to stay in touch with your parent agency, too, and leverage off contacts, human sources, and records.

"We should have key cards to get into this building 24/7 and the alarm code for each of you at the next meeting.

"Okay. Dawn is passing out sheets. We will condense them into an order form. We will have another meeting a week from this coming Friday. By then, I hope to have your shirts and raid jackets ready for pickup here."

After the size sheets, we will break you down to meet in three groups with Kit, Lee, and me to discuss what you learned since our last meeting and what we learned from the speaker today, and how we can leverage off the new knowledge. If anyone has some fresh missing cases, tell me or the two deputy commanders and we can jump on them with a vengeance."

He broke them into groups as he, Lee, and Kit had discussed, and they began some unexpectedly detailed and intense sessions.

They broke after an hour and a half for coffee, sodas, or water and some fruit Dawn ordered. Over coffee, the three leaders discussed what each group had provided as to ideas and cases.

Nick called the meeting back after a half hour and made some announcements.

"Okay, guys. We have some hot items to work on. Tampa, St. Pete, and Bradenton/Manatee County each have a fifteen-year-old female, blonde from a middle-class to upscale family missing since yesterday. The three look enough alike to be sisters. Could his be a boutique shopping for particular people for particular clients? Maybe! As you heard today, this type of thing represents a small percentage of the kids taken. However, catch the bad guys here and we may be able to find out about the higher volume operators, too.

"So, we need to jump on these three young ladies' cases right now and with all possible speed. We are within the velocity period between taken and delivered —probably.

"Dawn has made sets of the three reports for everybody.

"Tampa, St. Pete, or Bradenton members: please mark three areas and when I call on you, hold up a hand signifying which area you are. Everybody else, if you are near any of the three, go to the nearest group to where you work. If you are not, just study the reports and start building human sources for trafficking in your area and pick their brains about traffickers shopping for specific types of kids. Report any findings immediately to Dawn at the central number on the sign on the front door. We will collate your information and pass it to the proper members.

"The group on the far left, what area? St. Pete? Pinellas SO, western Pasco? Any task force members near those areas head over with them.

"Center group? Tampa? Same deal. If you are near Tampa, head on over.

"By process of elimination, you guys are Bradenton

and Manatee County, right? Anyone close meet with them.

"Here's how we will do it. We may fine tune as we go, but we have to start somewhere.

"First off, appoint a leader from your rep from the jurisdiction. Before leaving, make sure Kit, Lee, and I have his or her cell number.

"I'd like to work with the leader on the Tampa teen disappearance only because I have existing area informants. Lee, head to St. Pete, and Kit to Bradenton. The three of us should stay in constant contact. All groups work with any missing persons investigators with your agencies. They should be a lot of help and glad to have senior-level bodies to work with them.

"Second, interview the parents and the schools first. Try to find out the names of the closest friends relevant to your missing teen. Then, talk to them. When you get last seen information, pass it to team members from outside your agencies. They should be able to help you with locating surveillance camera footage, door-to-doors, and locating and possibly interviewing new witnesses, Meanwhile, the local agency will take the lead working snitches, oops, I mean informants. I will make some cash withdrawals today and the three of us will split it three ways and deliver informant money to you tomorrow.

"For people not near the three areas of concentration, again, build sources and perhaps some profiles on kids who have gone missing in each of your jurisdictions. Increase your knowledge now before you have an immediate case to work!

"Third point: tell folks you are heading up the search and have a whole team dedicated to it. However, let's not mention the existence of the task force quite yet," Nick said.

"Let me remind you of something we spoke about in the meeting. Every agency here has FirstNet on your smartphones and handheld radios. We will operate broadly on Band 12. It takes priority over all civilian traffic. If we need to devise smaller FirstNet groups, we will. But now, it's our primary way to communicate task force information through multiple systems without adding radio channels."

"Okay folks, go get 'em. And, as you always hear at your home agency and will here: be safe out there!" Nick finished.

Everyone, including Kit and Lee, scrambled for their cars. It was mid-afternoon and a long day faced them.

"Dawn, you are in charge. As you heard, anything hot will come in to you. Pass it to the three of us. Text is okay. This may go into the night. Set up a group text with the three of us and the three local agency heads on the case. Let us know before you head out for dinner. You and I should work out the time to shut down here based on what's going on, okay? It could be a long day for everyone. Don't forget to set the alarm before heading out. Keep the door locked and your long gun behind your desk out front. Call me if you have any questions."

She nodded, and he left.

Nick started the Tahoe and called Detective John Ross, the Tampa task force officer heading the search for the teen there.

"John, it's Nick. I am leaving the HQ now. Where can I meet you?"

"Nick, I am going to the girl's parents first. She lives in a high-priced area in South Tampa. How about speed this way and I will call you if I learn something you should run immediately on. If you don't hear from me, give me a call in thirty or forty minutes?"

"Roger that! Sounds like a plan. Heading your way," Nick said as he pulled onto I-4 westbound, encountering more traffic than was even normal.

He flipped on the hidden red and blue lights and accelerated into the passing lane. The occasional motorist who ignored him was awakened by his air horn.

He merged from I-4 to I-275 and exited on Dale Mabry. As he began the exit into the southern part of the city, John Ross called him.

"Hey. I spoke with the parents. The girl, Morgan, simply did not walk home from school. She is active in her school's soccer program. I am heading there to talk with the school for friends and to her coach. She got her hair done at an upscale salon in the neighborhood the day before she disappeared. Do you mind talking with them? You know how people open up to their bartenders, hairdressers, and barbers."

"I sure do! Text me the address and I will be there inside of twenty minutes," Nick said.

He had turned the lights off but kept his speed a little above the posted limit.

Nick pulled into the parking lot of the salon behind a Porsche 911 he had followed down Dale Mabry Highway and onto Azeele Street.

A blonde stepped out and walked up to him as he exited the Tahoe in his sheriff's polo shirt and gun belt. His gold badge was obvious on the belt in front of his Glock 23.

"Okay, I know I was going fast, but I have to be on the air tonight. Hair takes a while to be made perfect," she said. He recognized her as a news anchor for a Tampa television station. It was not clear whether she was angry, worried, or both.

Nick gave her a disarming grin.

"You and I are just coming to the same place. I'm too busy on a case to write you a well-deserved ticket."

"Well-deserved! Ha!" she responded defensively.

"Twenty over the posted limit is considered well-deserved, but let's talk walking in. I really have to interview some people," Nick said.

"Oh? Is there a story here for me?" she asked, changing her demeanor.

"No. Just have to interview some witnesses. Nothing for you now. Will you be on at six or eleven?"

"Eleven."

"I'll check out your new 'do at eleven then, if I'm off work and back home. Most of the time, my car is my home," he said, opening the door for her.

"Oh! Hi! The receptionist said," recognizing the anchor who moved to a waiting room and began to pour water into a cup and put a tea bag in it.

Nick had intentionally held back, not wanting the television personality to see the photo of the missing Morgan Parker he was getting ready to show to the receptionist.

When the anchor's back was turned to him, he put his finger to his lips and said in a soft voice to the receptionist, "I understand this person was here the day before yesterday. I need to speak to everyone who interacted with her."

The young woman said, "Oh! It's..." and Nick again put his finger to his lips to keep her from identifying his person of interest.

He saw a very attractive woman watching with

curiosity. She looked like she may work here, but also could have been an upscale client.

The receptionist turned to her.

"Yolee, could you talk with this guy?"

"Of course," she said as she walked over and introduced herself.

"I'm Detective Sergeant Nick Wolf with the sheriff's office. Is there somewhere less public we can speak?" he said, nodding to the back of the television lady.

Yolee nodded and led him to a private room and closed the door.

He opened his portfolio and removed the photo of Morgan Parker.

"This young woman was here the day before yesterday. She is missing and we want to speak with the last people who may have interacted with her," he said.

"I was not here on Monday. But I have known Morgan and her mother, Melissa, since Morgan was a baby and Melissa was in her late teens. Maria touched up her color and added some pink strands to her naturally blonde hair. Then Robert trimmed and styled it. Maria is finishing up with color on a client right now. Can you wait twenty or thirty minutes?"

"I'd rather not, ma'am. In missing kids cases like this, literally every second counts."

"Okay. Let me relieve Maria on her job and send her in here," Yolee said.

Nick smiled at her and nodded in appreciation. She walked out of the door and returned with another attractive woman.

"Hi, I'm Maria. You want to see me about Morgan? It's so awful," she said sadly. "We all have known Morgan for years and adore her."

"So, I gather from Yolee," he said and got her information for his file.

"I understand you put some streaks in her hair. Did she talk about why? Any particular special events she was going to?"

"Yes, she was going to the Mama Jama nightclub in the Hyde Park area on Tuesday. They have an under-twenty-one, non-alcohol night every Tuesday. It's where a lot of the affluent kids from the area go to be seen. They have live music and 'way overpriced non-alcoholic cocktails,'" Maria said.

"Do you know if she had been before? And how she got there. She is too young to drive herself."

"I think this was her first trip. Her aunt, Katy Nelson, was going to drive her. She's another longtime client like her mother, Melissa."

"How old is Katy, Maria?" Nick asked.

"Maybe twenty-eight or nine. Something like that," Maria said.

"Since you know the family, I have to ask a standard question. Don't make too much out of it, okay?" he asked.

She tossed her long hair and nodded.

"Do you know or suspect any family issues?"

"Oh, heavens no. Happy, loving people. Grandparents help in raising Morgan. Father is unknown. Melissa is a trust fund baby. No way there are any family issues behind this."

"Is there a chance she might have run away?" he asked.

"I really don't think so."

"Has she ever mentioned any special places she wanted to visit? Disney World, other resorts?"

"She has probably already fulfilled her travel bucket list!" Maria smiled.

"What's Aunt Katy like?" he asked.

"Are you interested in her? She's a doll."

Nick grinned at her.

"Oh, heavens, no," he said. "My question is purely professional. Just wondering if the young aunt might be a bad influence."

"I would say young Morgan is more...hmm...tending toward the adventurous than her older aunt," Maria said.

"Even at fifteen?" Nick said, surprised.

"I guess you don't have teenage daughters or nieces?"

"Right."

"Well the world has changed since we were fifteen. A lot."

"Not good," he said, actually surprised.

"Did she mention a boyfriend?" he asked.

"She mentioned she wished she had one. That's all."

"Has she ever mentioned anything about stalkers? Of any age?"

"Not really, Detective."

"Call me Nick. How about bullying at school or online?" Maria shook her head.

"Do you know if she has much of a social media presence? We have people researching it, but I thought you might know."

"She is on Facebook. We are friends there. I have never seen her send or receive a worrisome thing on it," Maria said.

"Good to hear, Maria," Nick said.

"Any friends of hers who are also customers here?"

"No. I would be aware if they were."

There was a tap at the door. Yolee stuck her head in, saying, "I finished the color for you. Anything I can add here?"

"Please come in," Nick said.

He repeated the questions he had asked Maria and Yolee corroborated Maria's answers.

"Do either of you know why Morgan might have been taken or who might have done it?" Nick asked.

"The only reason I can think of is she's pretty and her family is rich."

"Good points, Yolee. At this time, there has not been any ransom note. We are treating it as a trafficking case since running away has been disputed and there is no indication of a kidnapping yet. Please keep the trafficking part between us, however. And don't discuss any of this with the TV anchor in the waiting room."

"We won't," Maria said, and Yolee nodded in agreement.

"One more question before I get you to bring Robert in for his interview. Do y'all have male customers?" Nick asked.

"As in 'do we do hair for guys with long crewcuts?'" Maria asked, smiling.

"Just asking."

"We do. I am sure we could accommodate you," Yolee said. "You would have to grow your hair longer before we could style it," she said.

"It's a shame you don't need color," Maria added.

Nick grinned. "I appreciate your candor. For the interview and about me being a customer."

"Anything for Morgan and her family. She is a good kid. I pray you find and return her safe and sound," Maria said.

Yolee went out to see if Robert was available to join them as Maria stayed to chat for a minute.

"Robert will be here in a minute or so. He's finishing up with a major cut and style," Yolee said. She had told Nick about him. She said he was a famous hair designer who had worked with celebrities. Nick had enjoyed speaking with both women. Their concern and sincerity was as obvious as their personal appeal.

There was a tap on the door and Robert walked in. He was a handsome man of Cuban heritage with salt and pepper hair and matching mustache and goatee.

"I hope I can help you find Morgan quickly. I have children and a granddaughter. This sort of thing must be put to an end," he said vehemently.

Nick shook his hand. "I am not sure we can end it, but a group of us is setting out to damage its machinery as much as we legally can.

"Please tell me about everything you heard from Morgan Parker on Monday. I will probably interrupt with questions. If I interrupt, it will be because you struck a chord or just because so many of us are anxious to find her and bring her safely home, sometimes courtesy is out the window," Nick said.

Robert gave a concise rendition of their conversation, mentioning the nightclub as Maria did.

"When you find him. The one who took Morgan. Bring him by here and give me five minutes with him," Robert said with emotion as he slammed the bottom of his fist down on the armrest of the chair.

"It would be tempting. These people are predators. Cold animals with virtually no redeeming qualities. I cannot do it, Robert. But I will sure think about it as I cuff him."

Nick added a couple questions to fill in some blanks

for the notes and shook the man's hand. They walked out.

Yolee was there. She reached out and took Nick's hand in both of hers.

"Find the little girl and bring her home to us all safely," she said with a tear forming in one eye.

"I will do my very best. I promise you," he said.

Maria, now in a smock and working on a client, looked up and locked eyes with Nick. She gave Nick a nod which looked like an almost plea. He nodded back with a sad smile but gave her a supportive wink before he turned and walked out the door to call Detective Ross and share his information.

Good people, he thought.

———

Nick filled the Tampa detective in on what he learned at the salon.

"Yeah, I know of the Mama Jama nightclub. We've had some complaints there. Mainly women being given roofies and waking up in a motel room. It's run by a slick Jamaican guy. I've questioned him. His name is Jorell Esson. He has a light complexion and wears dreads. Speaks with a Rastafarian kind of accent, but something sounds fake about it to me. I did not know they have a non-alcohol night. Lemme do a couple of things. I will check for calls for service there, and then I will contact a state alcohol beverage control agent I know and see if there are any violations.

"I've got the men on my team out looking for camera footage. Maybe if the club has some, we can see her leaving. And maybe with whom! I am going to also see if the club was mentioned on any other disappearance reports in the last few months," Ross said.

"Good work, John! I will text everybody and get them to check the club name on their disappearance reports too. What can I help you with?" Nick asked.

"Probably nothing for a while. When I have answers on some of this stuff, I will call you," Ross said.

Nick called Kit and heard the excitement in her voice.

"There is a good indication our teen is being held in a house in Palmetto. I told them to establish a perimeter and wait for us and Manatee County SWAT. We need to hit the house fast. Our senior deputy here is getting a search warrant expedited and sent over at code speed," Kit said.

"Wow, Kit! You guys are on it big time! Text me the address in Palmetto. I know the area and will come as far and fast as I can on the interstate. But, if you get the warrant or decide for her life safety you have to go in immediately without it, don't wait for me!" Nick said and immediately turned his emergency lights and siren on and headed west on I-275 over the Howard Frankland Bridge. It was past rush hour and traffic was strung out. He was able to push the big SUV up to triple digits on a couple stretches on the bridge. He made it to the Sunshine Skyway quickly, crossed it with lights and his siren on alert mode, and exited onto US 19 South to get to Palmetto.

On surface roads, he ran silent and followed his navigation system to the area before slowing down. The group had gathered a block down the street and around a curve from the house. As far as anyone could tell, the subjects inside were unaware of the police presence.

Kit saw him coming in and trotted over to his Tahoe.

"Go in yet?" he asked.

She shook her head "no."

"The search warrant is five minutes out. You must have been hauling ass, Nick!"

"Kinda," he said. They heard an engine being pushed hard and saw a Manatee Sheriff's Caprice rolling in hot.

"That would be our warrant."

Nick pulled on his heavier flack vest, matching Kit's, and they walked over to a hastily designated command post.

A Palmetto lieutenant and a couple of Manatee deputies were there. Officers from both as well as the task force formed the largely unseen perimeter around the subject house.

"Guys, this is Nick Wolf. He's Commander of the Attorney General's task force. It's basically his case, but all of us standing here are on the same team."

"Are we sure there are people in the house? And confident our missing teen is there?" Nick asked.

Several nodded, including Kit.

"My sense is a loudspeaker warning to come out might cause a barricaded subject situation. It's almost dark. What do you guys think about hitting it now? Have Manatee SWAT do a search warrant call and bust the door. Kit, a couple of our task force officers and anyone, Lieutenant, you want to send from your department will follow them in."

"SWAT? Do you guys want to deploy flash-bangs upon entry?" Nick asked.

"Since we don't know what we have inside, I believe so. Maybe a couple. I want a couple of my guys to hit the rear door and use flash-bangs there. Since we will have people coming in front and back, I would like to have the non-SWAT contingent wait outside. We train together to avoid blue-on-blue accidents."

"I concur, sergeant. Just give a call when you are ready for us. We will stand by on the porch. Away from windows! Lieutenant? Want to designate a couple of your guys?" The lieutenant designated two in heavy vests.

"I want Palmetto PD and Manatee SO to take the credit if we safely recover the girl. The task force is still operating undercover. We seek results, not credit," Nick said.

All agreed. Four Manatee SWAT deputies led the way down the street. Palmetto officers cordoned off the block without red and blues.

Nick and Kit walked with the Palmetto senior officer and the front SWAT team.

He heard a "click" on the SWAT leader's radio. "Our team in the rear is set," the sergeant said.

He and the front team moved to the front door in stick formation. Once there, it was found the door opened outwards. Damn! One of the operators unslung a short barrel breaching shotgun to destroy the lock instead of using a breaching ram.

From behind a bush in the front, Nick and Kit heard the twelve-gauge shotgun take off the lock and a SWAT operator pull the door open as he stepped back.

He yelled, "Sheriff's Office! Search warrant!"

An operator on the other side tossed in a flash-bang. The same thing was happening simultaneously on the rear.

With the debilitating flash and smoke, both teams entered. Their night vision devices on their helmets were able to pick up the fellow officers' reflectors for safety.

As the two teams cleared the house, Kit saw a male subject leap from a side window. She moved past Nick, who had not seen him and tackled the guy.

They both went down. He shot Kit in the middle of her heavy Kevlar vest. As the round went off and she was falling, the man turned into Nick's left hook. His right hook was strong, but he had a Glock .40 caliber in his right hand, trigger finger straightened alongside the frame. The man fell and Nick stepped none too gently on his gun hand. He could hear the bones crack. The man flinched but did not scream out because he was already unconscious.

Nick looked at Kit, who seemed stunned, and her eyes were all funny.

"Officer down! Medic!" Nick yelled loud enough to be heard across the Manatee River and halfway way down to Sarasota.

He kicked the man's gun, a rusty Smith & Wesson revolver, away and quickly rolled him face down and cuffed him. A SWAT medic ran up and began to check Kit.

"She's okay! The bullet did not penetrate the vest. Another officer save for Kevlar," the medic said to Nick.

"I got her. Go ahead. I'm hoping you have a fifteen-year-old blonde in there to check over," Nick said.

Almost immediately, a SWAT operator brought the young woman out, half carrying her.

"We need to get her to Manatee Memorial. She's obviously drugged."

"Anybody else need medical attention?" the medic asked.

"The guy who shot Kit is in handcuffs here. He probably has some broken bones in his right hand. He might also have a dislocated jaw," Nick said.

"We'll leave him here for the EMTs to deal with or take to the hospital," the medic said.

He took the limp teen with some help from the operator.

"We can run code and get her to the ER before EMTs can get here. Let's grab something faster than the SWAT wagon and roll!" the medic said. She was in a Manatee SUV and running full lights and sirens a minute later.

Kit was conscious and asked for help taking off the big vest. Her assailant was still unconscious. Nick helped her. She pulled her uniform shirt up, perhaps farther than she intended, and they looked at the maroon bruise in the middle of her chest, just below her bare breasts. A silky tee shirt under the polo and vest was a lot cooler in Florida heat than a bra. Nick pulled her shirt down and helped her up.

He went over to the recovering shooter and dragged him up to his feet.

"Lieutenant, want one of your guys to charge him? He shot a police officer in Palmetto."

He motioned a detective over who charged the shooter and said: "You are under arrest for the attempted murder of a Florida police officer. You have the right to remain silent. You have the right to have an attorney present during this or any future interview. Should you be unable to afford an attorney, one will be appointed to you at no charge by the court. Do you understand these rights as I have explained them to you?"

The man murmured for the detective to do something physically impossible.

"We'll take that to be a 'yes,'" the Palmetto lieutenant said. "And I'll testify he was delivered his rights and was competent to understand them. I also witnessed him shoot the Lakeland detective. Take my report, the commander's, and the victim's as soon as you get the perp locked in the cage of a patrol vehicle."

"Thanks, Lieutenant and Detective. If you y'all could rush Kit's and my statements, we need to get to the hospital and interview the hostage," Nick said. Kit was on her feet but leaning against him for support.

"We might want to get Kit x-rayed while we are there," Nick added. The detective took their reports in record time."

Nick thanked the SWAT team for their professional and brave entry. All inquired about Kit who was leaning on Nick's Tahoe. He waved his task force team over.

"Great job, guys! We need to get to Manatee Memorial. You guys are the reason this young woman is free. If you want to come to the hospital and do the interview, I support it. But we need to get Kit checked out. The vest saved her big time. The bruise is in a spot where she would not have survived a bullet.

"If some of you need to stay and finish your action reports, do so. Any two riding together who can have one drive her car? Thanks! Keys, Kit?" She handed them to the detective.

Nick said, "Let's ride!" He helped her into his Tahoe and pulled out. He moved traffic out of the way as he delivered her as fast as reasonably possible, using red and blues only.

"I'd like to ride with you like this some other time when my chest doesn't hurt so freaking bad!" Kit said. He grinned at her as he crossed the green bridge over the Manatee River into Bradenton and pulled into the hospital ER.

He left the Tahoe off to the side of the ER entrance, engine off, but red and blues flashing.

"Stay there," Nick said. He went around to the passenger side and lifted the small woman into his arms.

"I can walk, not so good, but I really can," Kit said.

"This will get you triaged faster," he said.

"Move aside! Coming through with an injured police officer!" he yelled in a Stentorian voice. Several orderlies and a nurse rushed to them. She sent the orderlies for a gurney.

"She was shot point-blank in a raid. The bullet did not pierce her Kevlar vest, but I am worried she might have some internal injuries," Nick said to the RN.

"It's not usually the case, but maybe point-blank makes it worse. We will check her and do an x-ray to be sure. Follow us to an examination room, then we will usher you outside before we treat her, okay?"

"Absolutely. Thank you very much. She tackled an escaping felon. She's a hero," Nick said.

The nurse did not see Kit elbow him.

He followed her back on the gurney, telling the RN he needed to take her gun belt and the Kevlar vest. He saw them take off the gun belt while she was sitting on the bed and bring him the belt and vest to hold before stripping her for examination. He walked down the hall to a waiting room while that was occurring.

Nick was called back to the room a half hour later. The RN explained the x-ray had shown no serious damage, she would be very sore from the bullet's shock but would recover within several days. Kit received a Tylenol 3 with codeine for pain and was to be released shortly. By the time Kit motioned him in, she was almost dressed and asked if he had spoken to the recovered teen yet. He had not.

"Will you help me with my gun belt and vest?" she asked, and he did.

Nick found out where the young woman, Mary Anne Lewis, was and they went to see her. Several task force members were chatting with her parents.

"Good evening," Nick greeted the group.

"Mr. and Mrs. Lewis, this is our group's commander, Nick Wolf. The lady moving slowly with him is Deputy Commander Kit Ennis, the task force's case investigator for the Lewis disappearance," a detective said. "Kit was shot during the raid on the house where Mary Anne was being held."

"Detective, are you okay?" the mother asked.

"Just a little sore. Thank God for Kevlar vests," Kit told her.

"Have you guys had a chance to speak with Miss Lewis?" Nick asked.

"A bit. Understandably, she's upset over the whole thing with the trauma of the flash-bangs, and all. Her folks say we can talk with her at length tomorrow."

"That would be fine. We will be back here around eight in the morning if it's okay. A couple of you guys from the task force should join us," Nick said.

"Mr. and Mrs. Lewis, I am glad our group was part of the team who recovered Mary Anne safely," Nick said. He turned to his officers.

"Who has Kit's car?"

"One of the team members handed the keys to Nick. It is parked in open parking outside the ER and to the left," he said.

"If you all will excuse us, my red and blue lights have been on flashing since I bought Kit into the ER a while ago. I guess we better head out and get our vehicles squared away," Nick said.

"Thank you so much for bringing our girl back to us safely," Mrs. Lewis said, lapsing into tears.

"This is what our group was formed to do, ma'am. I am real glad it worked out well and Mary Anne is safe and well. We'll see you in the morning. Good night."

Nick assisted Kit down the hall.

"Have you called everybody you need to?" Nick asked.

"I have. I have to admit, I am dreading the drive from here back to Lakeland tonight."

"How about the task force springs for a motel room nearby for you?" Nick asked.

"I think so. Does Tylenol with codeine make you drowsy?" she asked.

"I am not sure. I think I took it in the field hospital in Afghanistan and maybe again in Ramstein, Germany. A lot of those days were a blur. So, I believe codeine probably does. Can you drive?" Nick asked.

"I hate to be a pain in the ass, but I don't think so, Nick."

He helped her to his Tahoe and almost had to lift her in.

"Give me a second, and I will tell hospital security we have to leave your car here. Do you have a long gun in it I need to remove?"

"I have an M4 carbine and a Mossberg 509 pump shotgun in the trunk," she said.

"I'll get those after I arrange for the car to stay where it is. Take a nap, you are fighting to stay awake," he said.

"I need to speak with hospital security," Nick said firmly at reception.

Several minutes later, a supervisor and a security officer responded to him.

"Hi, guys. I brought in a fellow detective who was shot earlier today. Her vest saved her, but the pills they gave her have knocked her out. She cannot drive at all. I have to leave her unmarked police Chevy sedan here tonight. It's dark-blue and is parked legally in the area near this door. I will remove her rifle and shotgun. Would you guys keep an eye on it until morning?" Nick asked.

"Sure. What happened?" the supervisor asked. Nick read him as ex-police, ex-military, or both.

"We raided a house in Palmetto. They had kidnapped a young girl. I am sure it will be all over the news tomorrow. One perp tried to jump out of a window. My detective tackled him. He shot her point-blank in the chest. Her vest saved her."

"I hope somebody shot him," the supervisor said.

"The quarters were too close. I knocked him unconscious. He's going down for attempted murder of a police officer. He'll get hard time."

"Wouldn't shooting him be justified?"

"For sure. But he was between Kit and me. I couldn't risk it, so I clocked him with my off hand. The strong hand was full, and I could have shot him if the shot became been clear. But he was unconscious, so it was not necessary."

"We'll take care of the car. Don't you worry, Sarge."

"Thanks. Good night. And be safe."

Nick walked back to the car and retrieved the two long guns from the trunk. He put them in the Tahoe in his locked box in the area behind the back seat. He had already put her handgun and belt in the locked box.

Kit was sound asleep in the passenger seat. He

gently fastened her shoulder belt and drove away, looking for a motel.

He found an acceptable one about three miles away. Nick knew he could not leave her, but the only room left had a queen bed. He took it and bought two tooth-brushes and a travel tube of toothpaste at the front desk.

He helped the semi-awake Kit into the room and set her in a chair. She was virtually out.

Nick pulled the bedspread, blanket, and sheet down. He carried her over and settled her on the bed. She was still wearing her polo shirt and cargo pants. He removed the pants belt and loosened the tight top button. He took her short boots off and set them on the floor before covering her up.

There was a spare blanket in the closet. He laid it on the love seat and swung his long legs to hang over one arm of the small sofa. Boots off, gun on the floor behind him, and in his sheriff's polo shirt and briefs, he covered up with the top half of the blanket and tried to go to sleep. He made it by three a.m. but had no idea of the time.

At three ten, Kit got up and went to the bathroom.

She hung her cargo pants over a chair and padded over to Nick, who was deeply asleep. She kissed him on top of the head and whispered, "Thanks. I'm glad there are a few gentlemen left in this world and I happened to be with one," and went back to bed.

The next morning, she walked over to Nick, still wearing her polo shirt which did not quite cover translucent panties.

"I thanked you for being so caring and such a gentleman last night, but I don't think you heard me. So, thanks for both again," Kit said and caressed him lightly on the cheek with her fingertips before turning and walking to the bathroom.

His thoughts as he watched her walk were anything but gentlemanly. He gave himself a hard but imaginary cuff upside his head for thinking those thoughts about an associate who could have died in the line of duty last night. But he found it difficult to avert his gaze.

———

By the time she came out, he was dressed and had retrieved her gun belt with the badge affixed.

"Thanks. What a good boss! And a toothbrush and toothpaste too! How in the hell did you avoid being caught by some woman this long?"

"Probably because I found slightly older ones more appealing," he teased.

"See! And he's smart too, ladies," she retorted as he went to brush his teeth.

They went back to the hospital. The very bedraggled Lewises were still there watching their daughter eat breakfast.

"How about taking the lead? I think a woman's touch is called for," Nick said to Kit before they walked into hearing range of the people in the hall.

"Good morning, Mr. and Mrs. Lewis and Mary Anne," Kit said. "We know no time is convenient for a police interview, but it's important and we will try to be out of your way very quickly."

Nick liked the way she did not give them an opportunity to refuse or postpone the interview.

"How are you this morning, Mary Anne?" he asked.

"I'm okay. Still shaky." Nick turned to Kit who took the cue.

"It's perfectly normal under your circumstances. Mary Anne, how and where did these people grab you? The more we know about the how's and where's, the more we can prevent other girls going through what you did."

"I had just finished junior varsity cheerleader practice. I was waiting by the practice field for Mom to pick me up. A car drove up and this guy asked me what time it was. Before I could answer, another grabbed me and shoved me into the back seat. He laid over me so I could not move.

"Mary Anne and Mr. and Mrs. Lewis, we have to ask this," Kit began. "Did any of these people touch you inappropriately? Other than being rough with you."

"No, but both threatened to."

"Was anyone else at the home while you were there?"

"Yes. Another girl my age. She was Mexican or something. She gave them a lot of trouble and the guy who laid over me in the back seat knocked her out and carried her out to his car. I never saw her again."

"When was this?" Kit asked.

"Yesterday morning."

Nick got as detailed a description as the young woman could give, then excused himself.

He called his chief investigator on this case, Hank.

"Hey, it's Nick. We finally got clearance to talk with Mary Anne Lewis. She said there was another girl there, a Latina. She was giving them trouble, so one of the guys slugged her, put her in his car, and left. It sounds like the guy who shot Kit.

"Find out which of the two cars there is his. Both are new and luxurious enough to have navigation systems. Check both for trips yesterday morning.

"He either sent her up the line into prostitution, or more likely, dumped her body."

"Bastards! I'll get right on it, Nick, and call you as soon as I know something."

Nick returned to the hospital room.

The doctor was there and signed Mary Anne's release papers. Nick walked out with him.

"Our case was not helped by not being able to speak with anyone last night when we brought her in," he said. "Did you conduct the initial exam on her?"

"No. But I have the chart. What do you need to know?" the doctor said.

"Did you determine if she had been sexually assaulted?"

He flipped a page back on the chart and read.

"No, Detective. She absolutely had not been. By anyone. Ever."

"Thank you, Doctor. Mary Anne suffered enough trauma without sexual assault on top of the violence. One of the two abductors shot my partner who is in there now. She would be dead but for her Kevlar vest."

"Guns!" the doctor said in disgust.

"No. People. Guns are like the hypodermic needles you use. They are inanimate objects. They take a human to cause harm," Nick said.

Nick and Kit left and walked to her car. He filled her in about the research he had ordered into the abductor's car navigation system.

"Are you sure you are ready to drive?" he asked her.

"Once you give me my shotgun and patrol rifle back, I will be."

He went to his Tahoe and produced them as she opened her trunk.

"Before you go, you might want to see what Hank

found out on the navigation system about where the guy who shot you took his car and the second girl yesterday morning."

"You are right. By the way, despite the pain, I slept pretty well. Better than you, I suspect, on a love seat several feet too short for you," Kit said.

"Oh, I did okay," Nick said.

"Me, too. Having a bodyguard was comforting." He grinned at her but said, "How about breakfast? On me."

"I thought you'd never ask."

"There's an IHOP down the street. Pancakes okay?"

"You bet."

"Once we get seated, we can check with Lee on the St. Pete case and John Ross to see if there are any developments in Tampa. Maybe you can call Dawn and see if anything is going on at our HQ while I am making the other calls?" he asked.

They drove to the International House of Pancakes and parked.

After ordering, both picked up their smartphones.

"Lee says there's nothing going on with the St. Pete disappearance, John Ross says he has some building video footage which may show the Parker girl or may not. They have to study it. Hank just texted he has a strong hit on your shooter's car GPS for yesterday morning. I think we should haul ass over and see where the GPS leads us."

"I'm game. I want to see the bastard who shot me get as much time as possible, though I'd hate it to be for murder," Kit said.

"Well, if it is for murder, it's already committed. Follow or lead?" Nick asked.

"Think you can keep up with me?" He dropped a ten

on the table for the coffee they already drank and canceled the order on the way out the door.

"Nah. I doubt it. You lead, and I'll get there way behind you," Nick said.

She accelerated off in the faster vehicle running just ahead of traffic. No lights or sirens would be appropriate for this type of response. Nick stayed close enough but sufficiently back to not hit her if she slammed on brakes.

They pulled up to the place they were going to meet Hank.

"I thought you were going to drive fast?" he said innocently. She made a face and gave him the finger, unseen by anyone else. He pretended not to see it.

"Hank, you want to lead the way?" Nick asked. With the other task force members, they had an eight-car cavalcade.

Hank drove his Explorer Interceptor about five miles and pulled over at a field. It was overgrown and had not been farmed for a while.

They could see drag marks and some brush still slightly bent twenty-four hours later.

"Okay, guys. It looks like a crime scene. One we don't want to disturb. Let's maybe two of us walk in a ways, twenty feet over and parallel to this trail we don't want to mess up."

As local task force head, Hank walked in with Kit. They stopped and stood about twenty-five feet in and spoke quietly before turning and walking out along the same route.

"Looks like we are going to add murder to Mr. Brown's charge list," Hank said.

"We have a mid-teen Latin female with a bullet wound to the head. Rigor mortis has set in."

"I think we are in unincorporated county. Let's get Manatee homicide and crime scene techs here as soon as possible. They will need a shelter. It's going to rain like hell in another hour or so," Nick said. He stood looking at his boots and shaking his head.

Enslaved kids. Dead kids. Stolen lives. This has got to stop, he thought to himself.

There was virtually no shoulder, so they put flares out and detectives in vests directed traffic around the scene until a couple of Manatee SO marked units arrived and took over traffic control.

Kit, Hank, and Nick sat in his Tahoe. All were visibly distraught with this on top of the stress last night and Kit being shot.

"I am thinking we try to leverage information from —what's the other guy's name?" Nick asked.

"Albion Smithers," Hank said.

"...Smithers about whether they were involved in something bigger. If not, were they going to independently offer the two girls to someone? Who? And maybe if we turn Smithers into being our informant, we can offer him a deal. I don't want to see Brown get any deal better than life or a lethal injection," Nick said. Both nodded their heads.

The requested Manatee units arrived. CSI managed to take plaster imprints of the footprints by the drag marks. Hopefully, they would be identical to Brown's two-hundred-dollar athletic shoes. They also got a shelter erected over the body before the torrential Florida rains started. The medical examiner estimated the time of death to be around ten the morning before. The time was around when Brown left with the young lady.

Hank and his five task force members worked diligently to identify the victim. She was unreported as a missing person and there were no prints on file for her.

He met with Nick and Kit in his agency office to discuss his team's investigation leading to the recovery of the live victim and following up on Nick's information and GPS tracking on the one who was removed from the house yesterday and was now dead.

"So we know who killed her, but not who she was?" Nick asked Hank to corroborate his understanding.

"About the sum of it until we run her prints. But she may not have prints on file at her age. The detective handling the murder wants to put an artist's likeness out to the media to see if someone comes forward. There are a lot of what appear to be migrant workers here. Many work truck farm vegetables, especially tomatoes. However, these are largely citizens who have been here for years. There is no reason for a parent to not step up and identify her."

"Maybe this is what my opposite number on the Orlando end of I-4 suggested. A reverse transport. Someone from over there. Maybe an illegal migrant after all. She appeared to be a pretty young girl. Maybe these two had orders for a pretty Latina and a pretty Caucasian blonde," Nick proffered.

"Boss, you are welcome to sit in if you want. Right now the homicide detective handling the murder and I plan to interview Brown and Smithers from a two-case perspective," Hank said.

"No, Hank. Unless Kit disagrees, it's your turf and your case. Just keep both of us up to date. I suspect this with a recovery and a murder will bring the task force's existence into the public eye. It had to happen sometime. Looks like it's now."

"I agree with Nick. From my perspective, you solved it, and you should run with it," Kit said.

"I will submit a report to the AG's office of the success here to begin to justify the grant money they have fronted to us," Nick said. They left Hank's cubicle and headed for their cars.

"Kit, I forgot to ask about Dawn. Anything of import from her at the HQ?"

"Nope. I think she is lonesome and ready to get into the field."

"Not yet. We need her there," Nick replied.

"I have to go up to St. Pete and get with Lee and the case manager, Joe Horner, on the case there. Why don't you head home and take a day or two of 'damn, I was shot' leave?" Nick suggested to her.

"Is this a new category for leave in the state personnel manual?" she asked.

"No, but it should be. And you were shot. You should go home and sleep for forty-eight hours."

"It would take more of those codeine pills for me to sleep forty-eight hours, Nick. I don't have any more and don't want any more. I will go home and take a long shower, get some clean clothes and treat myself to a meat lover's pizza. Tomorrow, I will go into the office and keep Dawn company," she said.

"Okay, Detective Carnivore. Enjoy your shower and pizza. Don't say I was not a considerate commander."

She reached into the car and ruffled his short hair.

"After you guarded me last night, I'd never say you were an inconsiderate anything."

He grinned at her and started the engine on the Tahoe. He got on the highway and drove across the Sunshine Skyway Bridge in heavy rain. A large anhydrous ammonia tanker was heading under the bridge toward the Gulf. There were whitecaps in Tampa Bay, but he knew they would not faze the large ship.

Nick looked to the left. It was raining so hard he could not see Egmont Key in the distance. Once over the hump, he called Lee. Lee had already driven halfway home to Polk County. They agreed to meet somewhere in Pinellas County in the morning.

Having attempted to sleep on something which was several feet shorter than his frame, he decided to take the advice he had given Kit. He got off on Fourth Street North and drove to his apartment at the far end of the thoroughfare through St. Petersburg.

4

He got home by three and took a long shower as Kit, who lived much farther away from their departure point would probably do in another hour. He forced himself to not think of her taking a shower. Nick knew he needed to get a life. But this was the only one he had now, and it did not include time to establish and nurture relationships.

After cleaning up and putting civvies on, he field stripped his Glock 23 in .40 caliber and cleaned it. He and the Glock had gotten soaked in the storm in Palmetto. The S&W Model 442 .38 snub nose on his ankle received a good oiling too.

He left the Glock locked in a safe and got into the new Jeep Rubicon and drove down Fourth trying to decide on a place to eat. There were plenty, but none appealed to him this late afternoon. He relented and pulled into an old standby famous for its club sandwiches, potato salad and cold beer.

Nick was led to a table for two and ordered. He did

not need the menu. He already knew what he wanted. The place was loud. He watched several twenty-something men and women at the bar. They were the reason for the noise. If he had to guess, he would say they were lawyers. Drunk lawyers.

Nick did not feel compelled to watch them for further infractions. The four seemed too obnoxious to have to deal with, so he turned away and ate a really good comfort food meal.

He paid from the table and stood to leave. One of the males leaned back laughing and fell off his barstool and hit hard. He sat up on the floor and rubbed his head. His hand came away red.

Serves you right, asshole! Hope it hurts. Let the restaurant take care of you. I have seen enough blood today. A lot more innocent blood than yours. He walked out of the door and threw a long leg into the Jeep and pulled the other in. His jeans did not rise up sufficiently to expose the snub nose revolver on his left ankle.

He drove back to his apartment. He decided he needed a tropical fish. Or something. He had a cold Miller's from the refrigerator and watched some television. *Why are British and European detective shows better than American?* he wondered. He dozed off in his recliner and never figured out the answer.

Nick called Lee at eight the next morning.

"What's your status?" he asked.

"Not as good as yours. The Palmetto recovery and murder are all over the news this morning. I guess our task force is not covert anymore. Only took a week, huh?" Lee asked.

"It seems so. I have not turned the TV on. How did we fare?" he asked the older detective.

"Pretty damn good, I'd say. We got good coverage. You were mentioned twice and shown a couple of times. All the stations had you carrying Kit into the ER looking like somebody off one of my wife's romance novel covers. Then, 'Human Trafficking Task Force recovers teen in Palmetto. Locates body of another victim the next morning.'

"You are eloquently quoted saying 'no comment.' But you looked like a serious, dedicated cop."

"Ha! Maybe I should pump some iron, grow my hair long and have Yolee or Maria at the salon where I interviewed them in Tampa dye it blonde. I could become a romance novel cover model like the Italian guy," Nick said in jest.

"Yep. A whole new career. Until your muscles sag like mine and a new stud boy replaces you. At least for twenty years, you'd be the fantasy of a lot of women. Probably many your grandma's age," Lee said, obviously enjoying himself.

"So where are you?" Nick asked, changing the subject.

"Coming down I-275. I will be getting off at Martin Luther King—the one on the Pinellas side, obviously, in about ten minutes."

Nick, a café con leche aficionado, gave him the name of a café where they could meet and talk.

He pulled in first and parked. Knowing his old friend liked the Cuban coffee, he ordered two large ones. Lee parked his Charger beside the Tahoe minutes later.

"Hey, Lee. How are you?" Nick greeted him.

"Frustrated with our missing teen. We have nothing, Nick. Tell me about Kit first, then about the Bradenton and Tampa ones. Sounds like closure on the first and movement on the second."

"Kit is fine. It was a case of fatal shot placement stopped by her vest. She had on a larger raid vest, thank God. Not one of these lighter, under-the-shirt ones like I have on now.

"The young lady was recovered unharmed. Both perps were captured after one shot Kit. I was there and able to restrain him," Nick said.

"I'd a killed the bastard!" Lee said.

"The three of us were too close to each other to risk a shot. Kit could have been hit, maybe in an area not protected by her vest. Hank and the homicide detective working the murder of the young Latina are probably questioning the first guy right now.

"I recommended they try to offer him a deal to incriminate the shooter. My guess is the shooter, a guy named Brown, knows he's in deep crap and will lawyer up. I asked Hank, the local task force lead for us, and the Manatee homicide detective to both work the other guy, Smithers, hard and turn him. We might give him some incentive to give up his buddy. Maybe not make him an accessory in shooting a police officer," Nick said.

"Yep, just the way I would have handled it, Nick," Lee said.

"What can you tell me about the St. Pete case?" Nick asked.

"Not much. The local task force lead for us is Detective Joe Horner from St. Petersburg PD. The vic is a fifteen-year-old girl named Alice Kincaid. She is from a middle-class family in a nice subdivision. Popular and active in high school. No known boyfriend. No indications of trouble at home.

"She disappeared the day before yesterday from the

mall at Tyrone Square. She went shopping with a couple of girlfriends and they split up. When her nineteen-year-old brother came to pick her up at the appointed time, she wasn't there. He called her cell phone. No joy.

"The kid acted real responsibly. Parked and went in to look for her. Notified his parents, and they called the two girlfriends' parents. The girls were already home. They had not seen Alice for an hour or so. Which put the last seen time at four p.m.

"The brother alerted mall security and they did a sweep of the mall with him helping. The place is not all that big, so it looks like they did a fast and thorough job. No joy.

"Joe got wind of it and headed over. Nothing of interest on the sparse cameras. He questioned the two other girls, and his guys went to every store they could remember visiting. Asked about Alice and any suspicious persons or even kids talking with them."

"I've known Joe for a long time. I was glad when the other guys picked him to head the effort for this case. He's a damn good detective. Smart and tough," Nick said.

"Despite any actionable clues, I have been impressed working with him, Nick."

"I hope this Palmetto guy, Albion Smithers, tells us he had a shopping list and will identify his buyer. All three of these fit the same looks profile. The locations from which they were grabbed vary. Bradenton was a school soccer field, Alice was from a shopping center after she had separated from her friends. Tampa had her hair done to go to teen night at an adult club. But she did not walk home from school. Her last verified position was soccer practice.

"The dead Latina in Palmetto is still a total unknown, Lee."

"I hope it's not a coincidence the first three little ladies all looked alike. It could make solution a lot easier!" Lee noted.

"It's still pretty early. Let's finish eating and give Joe a call and see where we should meet him," Nick suggested as Lee took another sip of café con leche and raised a finger for the server to get another one started for him.

Fifteen minutes later, they called Detective Joe Horner.

"Hey, Nick. Where are you?" Nick responded where he and Lee were.

"Don't they have a private room? If you can get it, I'm at my cube with Harry from the SO and Jack from my shop. The other three are out talking to the girl's friends. Why don't we drive over there. It's not ten minutes away. We can talk privately over good coffee."

"Hold for one," Nick said and verified availability of the side room.

"We've got the room. Y'all head on over," he said and hung up.

"They'll be here in ten minutes or so," he told Lee. They moved their cups into the small meeting room and left the door open. It faced the entry of the restaurant.

Hank Thomas and Manatee homicide detective Alex Smith had brought suspect Albion Smithers out of the holding cell early. They were already several hours into interviewing him. He had chosen to avail himself of an immediately available public defender.

The two detectives listed the serious charges against Smithers immediately and told the suspect and his attorney they had spoken with the state's attorney. He had agreed to use the accessory charge on both shooting a police officer and murder of the Jane Doe as a bargaining chip if Smither's was highly cooperative. Otherwise, he would be facing it along with conspiracy, kidnapping, and assault on a juvenile.

The attorney conferred privately with his client. Hank and Alex came back into the interview room and turned the video and audio recorders back on.

"Detectives, my client is interested in helping as much as he can and would like to avoid being an accessory to both the police shooting and the murder of the young woman."

"We are glad to hear he will cooperate. Remember, the prosecutor's willingness to waive on either or both charges will be dependent on the helpfulness of the information he gives us," Alex said.

The attorney nodded.

"Since we are recording this for the record, please signify your agreement or understanding verbally," Hank told him. He did.

"Okay, Mr. Smithers. Let's get to the matters which will help determine if any of the charges against you will be dropped," Hank began.

"Who was the young Latin female who your associate Mr. Brown is charged with murdering?"

"Her name was Rosa Fernandez. She was from Miami," he said.

"Thank you. How did Miss Fernandez come to be at the house in Palmetto?" Alex asked.

"Willie knew this guy down there. The guy called him and said he had a girl who was a good fit for an order from Orlando. He would bring her up and drop her and we'd have to pay him half the fee when we got paid."

"For the purpose of the recording, when you say 'Willie,' you are referring to your associate William Brown?" Alex asked in verification.

"Yeah."

"What is the name of this individual from Miami?" Hank asked.

"I dunno. He is Willie's friend."

"Give us a description of him and his vehicle. Also the time and day he dropped Miss Fernandez off."

Smithers complied.

"Had you done business with him before?"

"No. Willie had."

"Why do you think your associate William Brown removed the young woman and she ended up dead?"

"Her mouth and whining was driving him crazy. He tried to get some action with her, and she kneed him in the nuts, too."

"Where and to whom were you supposed to deliver her?" Hank asked.

"Orlando. To one of Willie's dudes over there."

"Name?"

"Nate."

"Have you ever met this Nate?" Alex asked.

"No. I seen him once, but I didn't get out of the car."

"Describe him for us."

"White dude. Tall and skinny. Brown hair. Kinda long and a man-bun."

"Where were you when you saw him?" Hank asked.

"Orlando area. The Disney World exit. He was there with a van."

"How did you and William Brown happen to be at the exit?"

Smithers looked at his public defender, who nodded for him to answer.

"We was up there to drop off a girl," Smithers said.

"What was her name?"

"Cindy something. I disremember her last name."

"Describe her for us."

"Same as this last one. Fifteen or so. White girl. Blonde hair. Good body for her age."

"When exactly was this?"

"Two weeks ago. On a Tuesday."

"Did he pay you for delivering her to him?" Hank asked.

"Yeah. Five thousand cash."

"How did you obtain custody of this 'Cindy'?" Alex asked.

"We knew what to look for. We seen her walking home from somewhere and Willie jumped out and put a handkerchief with chlorine on it over her mouth. He put her in the back seat and kept her down." Hank and Alex groaned inwardly at "chlorine" instead of chloroform.

"Why her?"

"Nate told him by phone he was looking for blonde, white girls that was pretty. She was a little looker," Smithers said.

"Alex, you keep talking with Mr. Smithers. I have to go to the bathroom," Hank said and slipped out the door. Once outside, he called Nick, who stepped out of the meeting when he saw who it was.

"Nick, it's Hank. Smithers is talking. A lot. He said

the dead girl is a Rosa Fernandez from Miami. I have a description of the guy who delivered her to him and Brown. No name. Also, there is an open purchase order, around five K, from a guy named Nate in Orlando. Picks them up just off Disney World exit off I-4. Tall, skinny white male with brown hair and a man-bun. Drove a van."

"Great work, Hank! I will call Walt over at the Orlando task force and give him this lead now. I will also ask Kit to pass the information on Rosa to Miami-Dade. She's still sore as hell from the bullet and went to the task force office to work today."

"She was lucky, Nick. Real lucky. I am going to slip over to the Manatee crime scene unit which has raid evidence and see if they can pull 'Nate's' phone number off Brown's phone.

"Smithers is singing and throwing Brown under the bus. I suspect he is part of almost everything he's blaming totally on Brown. He just knows we have a hostage who's a witness to the fact he was with her during the time Brown murdered Rosa, so he thinks he has some sort of credibility," Hank said.

"You guys are working this beautifully. Keep it up and let me know what else you learn," Nick said before hanging up. He called Kit on the landline.

"Dawn, it's Nick. Is Kit in her office there?"

"She is. She got in an hour ago. Nick, she's still walking like she's in pain. Is she okay?"

"Yes. I had her checked out at the ER. They x-rayed her and there is only bruising. She will be uncomfortable for a week or so but will not have any long-term effects of being shot."

"I'll ring you in," Dawn said.

"FLAG Police Training, this is Kit."

"It's Nick. How are you feeling?"

"Like somebody shot me in the chest. No tight bras for me anytime soon! It hurts to even take a deep breath!"

There was a pause.

"Nick? Still there?"

"Yes. Everything I'd like to say is against some rule, so I am searching for words. So, let me jump into a request for you."

She smiled broadly and said, "Go ahead."

He gave her everything he knew about Rosa and the suspect who delivered her to the Bradenton area.

"Please try to track down the right detective in Miami-Dade PD. Give him or her the info on Rosa and the creep who delivered her. Tell them we are trying to track down phone numbers from the phones of two suspects who received her to traffic onward to Orlando. If they need to leverage anybody there, Brown knows the guy and Smithers can ID him," Nick said.

"I'll get right on it. Sorry if I embarrassed you."

"No you aren't." Nick laughed.

"Okay. You got me. I am not embarrassed in the least. And neither were you."

"Thanks for taking care of this. I'll talk with you later," Nick said and rang off.

He called Walt over in Kissimmee.

"I might have something for you, buddy!"

"I could use something. Speak to me," Walt said, recognizing Nick from his caller ID.

"We recovered a teen yesterday in the Bradenton area. Two subjects were apprehended on the raid. One shot one of my two deputy commanders. She had her vest on and missed dying by a few layers of Kevlar."

"Good heavens! Lucky officer."

"Very. One killed a teen transferred to them from Miami. We have offered a deal to the other one to offer up the shooter for everything. He is singing his head off. They fulfill want lists of primarily girls to a guy who picks them up at the Disney World exit. Paid five grand for at least one. Tall, gangly white guy with brown hair and a man-bun. Drives a van. First name Nate is all we have now. Does it ring any bells?" Nick asked.

"Congratulations. Is the recovered girl okay too?"

"Yes, she is fine."

"Man-bun does not strike a chord. I will ask around."

"We think his number is in the phone of at least one of the two we have already apprehended. I will share it once I get it," Nick said.

"Probably a burner, but anything helps," Walt said.

"You'd think so, but both of the jerks here have the current model smartphones," Nick said.

"Then, I'm hoping for the latter," Walt said.

"Right. Lived in a dump. Rusty revolver, but smartphones and luxury cars. Go figure," Nick said. "I'll let you know anything I hear, and you do the same."

"I sure will, Nick."

———

Kit went online and found a non-emergency number of Miami-Dade Police. She called it, identified herself, and asked for the senior detective for human trafficking cases.

She was switched to a Detective Sergeant Eduardo Gonzalez. He saw it was an internal referral and answered on the second ring.

"Sergeant Eddie Gonzalez,"

"Sergeant, this is Detective Sergeant Kit Ennis, deputy commander of an Attorney General's local agency human trafficking task force. We are focusing on the I-4 corridor."

"Well! You have your work cut out for you!" he said with a deep, resonant laugh.

"We do. But after only a week, we are making some headway. Slowly but surely.

"The reason I am calling is we have identified a trafficking victim from Miami who was transported up to Palmetto, near the Sarasota/Bradenton area. Unfortunately, one of the traffickers tried to rape her. She kneed him effectively, but he knocked her unconscious. On a raid on the house, we recovered another recent victim okay, though the rapist shot a detective. He was subdued and he and his partner are in custody. The victim told us one subject, Willie Brown, had put the Miami victim in his car and left. We pulled his auto navigation system and found her. He had murdered her."

"How is the detective?" he asked.

"I'm fine. I think I will invest my full 401k in Kevlar," Kit said.

"Did you get checked out at the hospital? I was shot and the pain in my side lasted weeks. I finally went in and found I had been walking around with two cracked ribs."

"My task force leader took me to the hospital despite my loud protestations. They said I'm okay. I'll just be sore for a week, or two, or three."

"You can invest on several weeks of aching, too," Eddie said.

"Do you know the name?" Eddie Gonzalez asked.

"Yes, her name was Rosa Fernandez. We are

analyzing the two traffickers' phones to get the number from Miami where the guy down there called to arrange dropping Rosa at Palmetto. It appears these people pay five thousand cash for a victim."

"No name on the Miami guy. Any description?" Eddie asked.

"The one singing is still being questioned. So far, he claims he did not know the Miami guy. We are suspicious about whether he's telling the truth about him. He says the man was Jamaican, about six feet, thin build, and has dreads. He has sleeved tattoos on both arms. He drove a Mercedes Sprinter. It was an ugly gold color, supposedly."

"I may know him. I have been trying to connect him to trafficking for six months. The phone records would really help!"

"Hold on a minute. I'm on the computer searching while we are talking. Rosa Fernandez is from a family in Coral Gables. Her father is a businessman. She disappeared four days ago. It's unusual the Miami trafficker passed the victim off to others instead of the end recipient. Particularly since these victims have so much monetary value. Yet the guy who took her delivered her all the way up to your area. Maybe four hours. He could have gotten the full fee with another hour and a half driving, right?" Eddie said.

Kit thought for a minute. "Right. It doesn't make sense unless he does not want this Nate to know it was him who did the snatch for some reason. I will share this with the detective interviewing the two we caught red-handed with the recovered girl and whose car GPS showed the trip to the body and back."

"And who shot you?" he asked.

"Yes, he surely did. Right in the heart. Wearing a big

Rolex and shooting a rusty old revolver. Don't people have any pride anymore?" she asked.

"Odd, too. Perps with big watches and big cars usually carry a flashy gun. Something like a gold-plated Desert Eagle. The rusty one must have been the firearms version of a burner phone. A throwaway. I bet if you run it, you will find a very spotty history," Eddie suggested.

"I will make sure it is checked out. Good suggestion. The CSI people probably did it anyway," she said.

"Don't invest on it while you are reallocating your retirement."

"I'm on my office phone. Let's exchange cell numbers and email business cards."

They exchanged numbers and emails and then copies of their business cards. Kit called Hank and left a phone message saying she needed Brown's and Smither's phone logs as soon as possible for a possible link she was tracking down to the trafficker in Miami.

————

As Hank and Alex wrapped up their interview with Smithers and planned an approach for questioning Willie Brown, Nick and Lee drove to Tyrone Square. The older and younger detective felt walking around, getting a feel for where the disappearance occurred would help them understand the crime. Perhaps it would point them to questions they would not have thought of otherwise.

Joe Horner and the two detectives in his group from the restaurant walked with them.

"My big disappointment is the parents never

thought about activating the tracker on the girl's smart-phone. It could have made this a quick case."

"Yeah. I don't know why parents don't activate those. For times just like this," Lee said.

"I will take you to the stores the three girls went to first," Joe said as they slowly walked and observed. They walked the several large anchor stores, then the fashion boutiques the two friends listed. They sat in the food court and watched people. The flow of pedestrian traffic.

"How about the theaters?" Lee asked. "Could she have slipped into one of them to see a movie and been picked up in the dark there?"

"I spoke with the manager just beyond the ticket booth. He said it was impossible to remember a teenage girl with the traffic they have," a task force detective from St. Pete Beach said.

"Do we know if she had her own credit card? I admit I am on thin ice here. I did not know much about teen girls when I was a teen guy," Nick asked.

"I don't know. It's a good question though. My four-teen-year-old daughter has a loadable credit card we control pretty tightly," Joe said.

"Would we have a record of it anywhere?" Lee asked.

"I doubt it," Joe responded, getting his phone out. "I will call the Kincaids and ask."

"Mrs. Kincaid? Detective Horner. Nothing new. I do have a question though. Did Alice have her own credit card? She did? We need to do two things: first, I need the number and second, you need to call the fraud depart-ment of the issuer and tell them what has happened and for them to contact me at the cell number on my card you have if there is any use. Day or night. It does not matter what the hour is. Make sure they do NOT freeze or close the card, okay?" He wrote the number down and thanked her.

"She had a reloadable Visa." He turned to the detective who had spoken with the manager. "Write this number down and go back to the manager. See if he can use the card number to see if she bought a ticket."

He walked over to the theater and went in. About fifteen minutes later, he came out smiling.

"She bought a ticket for a four thirty showing of the sci-fi movie up on the sign in the window."

"Okay, this is good. We are tracking her whereabouts. This may be the last point we can definitively say she was before being taken. Or not. But it's something. Let's go in and see the manager. Let's look at the theater she was in and search it for anything which might have been hers. It might involve interrupting the movie in progress. I couldn't care less. Let's do it!"

Six tough looking obvious cops with guns and badges but sans uniforms marched into the theater and up to the manager.

"Good afternoon. My name is Nick Wolf. I am the commander of the regional human trafficking task force. You may have heard from the news as well as speaking to the detective beside me about the disappearance of young Alice Kincaid.

"We think she may have been taken from your theater two, showing the sci-fi film. We need to search the theater with the full house lights on right now."

"I'm afraid a movie is in progress. I cannot just interrupt it," the manager said.

"I'm afraid you certainly can. In thirty minutes, I can have a court order here shutting down your whole theater and every damn movie. And keep them shut down until we search each one. I am sure the media will be here and ask what is going on. We may have to tell them we had to shut the theater down to search for a missing child at risk over the lack of cooperation of the management."

"I have every reason to call your superior and report you!" the man said, puffing up in self-importance.

"Oh, boy. Here it comes," Lee said in a low voice heard by the manager and everyone within ten yards.

Nick leaned in, his nose an inch from the manager's.

"My superior is the State Attorney General. Want me to call her right now? I can get her on the phone for you," he said in a hoarse, menacing whisper.

The man paused. A bead of sweat formed on his forehead, and another formed as the first rolled down the side of his face.

"You say we can just interrupt the sci-fi?"

"Yes. For the shortest time possible. Maybe you and some of your employees with flashlights can help us search?" Nick said less menacingly but still not pleasantly.

"Ugh. Yes, we can do it."

Nick turned to his team.

"Flashlights?" he asked.

Five detectives produced tactical lights ranging from one hundred to a dazzling six hundred lumens. Nick pulled out his four-hundred-lumen light with the crenelated "DNA collector" edge. The manager gather several attendants and they all walked in. He hit the full house lights.

"May I have your attention? I am with the police. There is no danger! But we have to quickly search this theater for evidence. I have to ask you to leave for a few minutes. Just wait in the lobby. We'll tell you when management will resume your movie.

"As you get up and leave, look around you. Look for a purse, a wallet, a cell phone, anything on the floor. Don't touch it, just call out to one of us. Thanks for your cooperation," Joe said.

People, mainly teenagers, arose and looked around as they shuffled out.

One yelled out, "Hey! Over here!"

Joe and Nick were beside him in an instant. There was a pink purse on the floor under the seat in front of where the kid had been sitting.

Nick kneeled down on the sticky floor and searched with his light. There was nothing of interest near the purse. He took nitrile gloves out of his hip pocket and put them on, retrieving the purse. He stood up in the cramped quarters. Climbed over the seat and checked the area behind. Nothing.

"What do you think about dusting for prints?" Joe asked.

Nick turned to the manager.

"How many times has this theater been used since that ticket was used?" he asked.

"May I see the ticket again?" The St. Pete Beach detective handed it to him. The manager thought for a minute.

"Five showings since this one," he said.

Joe and Nick looked at each other, then at Lee. All shook their heads. Too many occupants in those seats for getting decent prints.

"We'll get out of your way. This is the type of evidence we were looking for. You might have saved a little girl's life. Thank you," Nick said, and the manager knew he meant it. He stuck his hand out and the two shook hands.

"I'll pray for her," the manager said.

"I'll be right there praying with you, sir."

The six men with badges on their belts in front of their guns walked out.

In the lobby, Nick said, "Thank you everyone!" and the manager guided his patrons back in to where their movie would resume shortly.

They went to a table in the food court. Joe spread napkins on it and Nick set the purse down.

Gloves still on, he carefully opened the purse. There was a wallet inside. He removed it. Alice Kincaid's school ID was in it. The Visa was there. There was $17.53 in the wallet, some makeup in the small purse, and other "pocket clutter." Nothing of use.

"I'm thinking she dropped it when she was grabbed," one of the detectives said.

"Me, too. They must not do a very good job of sweeping," Joe said.

"The floors were the sticky mess I remember as a kid. My tennis shoes would kinda stick as I got up to go get more popcorn," Joe remembered.

Nick felt sticky and dirty all over from crawling around but said nothing.

"It wouldn't have done us much good except for checking calls and texts, but the obvious thing missing is her phone," Lee noted.

"She was wearing jeans and a dressy tee shirt top. I suspect she kept the phone in her hip pocket," Nick said, not from personal knowledge but having observed a number of teenage girls in the past half hour.

"Joe, let's get a bag to put the purse in. You have the rest of the case evidence back at your office, don't you?" Nick asked.

Joe grinned. "Now I will."

"I have an idea," he said. He walked over to the

movie theater and took a smart phone photo of the sci-fi movie marque.

"I have a patrol officer working with my home squad at SPPD. She's a whiz at graphics. How about if I have her create a flyer asking what students may have been at this movie, this time, this theater, the disappearance date? Then ask did you see this person, with Alice's photo, and did you see anyone suspicious? Someone looking around a lot. Someone too old or suspicious standing out?"

"Fantastic! One of you guys could go back to our manager over there and see if they have any free movie ticket coupons we can buy. Maybe spread out a lot of rewards? Print up hundreds and your team distribute them to all the surrounding middle and high schools?" Nick asked.

"Exactly what I was thinking? What have we got to lose? A few dollars on printing at a local fast-print shop?" Joe said.

Nick gave Joe fifty dollars of the informant money and Joe sent one of his guys to the theater for the tickets. Nick went with him and bought fifty for the new idea.

He made note of the dollar expenditures for Dawn's records.

By the time he got back, Joe had the purse in a bag begged from a lingerie department.

"You could have gotten the bag from men's socks," Lee noted to Joe.

"You're right, Lee. I could have."

Nick looked at his watch.

"Guys, we have made some headway. We have a plan. I need to find out what we have learned from the two suspects in Manatee County today and if any of it ties in here. Also, I am curious about what Kit found out from Miami we can use. I'll pull it all together on an encrypted group text or email before tomorrow morning.

"I'm going to head out now. See y'all soon. Good work today, guys!" With an expected session of fist-bumping and shoulder punching, he left and headed out with Lee for their vehicles.

"Joe has some pretty good *esprit d' corps* going in his team, doesn't he?" Nick asked.

"Yep. *Esprit d' cops!*" Lee answered as he got in his Charger and started the hemi engine.

It was too late to deal with the commuter traffic on the interstates to go to the task force HQ unless he pulled an all-nighter. Which he had no particular reason to do tonight.

He looked at his watch. Dinner time. He put a chicken pot pie in the microwave and called Kit.

"Good evening! How's the pain level tonight?"

"It's tolerable. A couple aspirin at bedtime ought to allow me to sleep. How are you?"

"I'm okay. Busy day. Nothing real big yet," Nick said.

"I'm on to something with Gonzalez down in Miami, Nick. I should get the phone history from both Brown's and Smither's phones from Manatee County SO in the morning. I will send them to Eddie Gonzalez. He thinks he knows who the guy from Miami is—the Jamaican who delivered Rosa Fernandez to Palmetto. I am thinking he gave up a big piece of the fee because he didn't want Nate in Orlando to know she came from him. He'd already driven four hours with the girl. Why not drive another hour and a half with her to Nate for the full fee? It had to have cost him several thousand dollars.

"Eddie says if his name is on the phone list, he will

pick this guy up. Eddie's being a bit coy. He does not know us and has been trying to get something on him for a while. So he has not given me the Jamaican's name yet," Kit finished.

"Maybe if the name is on the phone list, we can take a road trip to Miami and sit in on the interview..." Nick said, thinking as he spoke.

"I'm up for a road trip. Especially if it leads to Nate's identity. I hate man-buns anyway."

"Well, darn. There goes my plan to grow one," Nick said.

"Don't even joke about it. You would look ridiculous with one. Especially when I suspect your entire friend base is rangers and cops," Kit said.

Nick left the teasing about hairdos. He would as likely grow one of those as he would a unicorn horn in the middle of his forehead.

"Well, the beep you just heard was my microwave, Sergeant Ennis. My gourmet dinner awaits," he said.

"Pray what did you create?" she asked.

"A frozen pot pie to go with a lite beer. Then, an episode or two of a French detective show and bed. I am in love with the star, Candace. As you might guess, she's a bit older but mega hot. And French!"

"I somehow became you tonight and made a salad. It's already long since digested and I am planning some time on my Peloton. I have to maintain a certain level of fitness to meet the demands of my many admirers."

"You certainly do! We demand the penultimate from you. Night, Kit. Sleep well and don't overdo it. You were shot, remember?" Nick said.

"It will be a long time before I forget that. Perhaps never. Night, Nick. Sweet dreams."

He removed the pot pie and cracked the crust with

his fork. He stirred it around and thought it would be a bit dry. He was right. The cold beer helped. But not much.

French TV with subtitles and bed. It would probably be a long day. But, interesting. Nick Wolf thought every day was interesting.

5

Kit received the phone list from the techs at Manatee County SO early the next morning. The same number with a 305-area code appeared several times in the last week.

Her gut told her it was the Jamaican calling Willie Brown. The first was a day before he delivered the Rosa Fernandez. One call was the same day, probably to verify the exact address and delivery time. Then, there were several calls after her death. The last one was late yesterday.

The Jamaican guy was probably trying to find out where his share of the fee for Rosa was. She wondered, *since he knows where Brown and Smithers live, is he on the way to Palmetto to collect?*

She called Eddie Gonzalez at Miami-Dade PD and ended up with his voice mail. Kit left him a message with her concerns and told him she had just emailed him the phone history log from Brown's phones.

She got a call back in an hour.

"I took a team and hit his place just as soon as I saw

the phone log. The 305 area code calls were from his phone. He's big on flash and uses the best of everything. It's the latest iteration of smartphone. The damn idiot ought to use a series of burner phones, but no. His ego outranks his security.

"I put the squeeze on a neighbor. He said our suspect left about dawn this morning. He was not in his van, which is still parked out front. He took his three-year-old silver Corvette. Again, flash. I am emailing you his latest arrest form with picture. As you will see, his name is James Givens. He goes by James. He claims to be a Rasta dude, but he was born in Miami.

"I agree with you. He's coming up to the house in Palmetto to get his money and leave some bodies. He's at least halfway there if you and I are right. Should be time to lay a little trap for him. Let me know!"

"I will, Eddie. Thanks. Let me get on a surprise party. Later!" She hung up and called Nick. After, she pulled her gear on and let the Chevy scream as she headed to Manatee County at least an hour and a half distant from her home.

"Hank, the Jamaican guy from Miami, may be on the way up to get his money from Brown and Smithers. Likely to kill them, too, would be my guess. He left two and a half hours ago in a Corvette. His name is James Givens. I am emailing you his picture and description from his last arrest.

"We need to set up a surprise for him quickly. I think I will bring my orange Jeep instead of the dark Tahoe."

"Okay, Nick. I will have the house stripped of yellow

police tape, be inside and have snipers hidden very discreetly. I will have Brown's car moved back over there. I think one familiar car is enough. Smithers could be out for groceries mid-morning. Call before you get in the area. Your orange Jeep sure doesn't scream 'cop.'"

"I will. See you in a half hour at the most," Nick said as he gunned up and headed for the Jeep."

He picked up I-275 and risked the chance of losing time due to a traffic stop. There was a limit to how fast he wanted to drive the raised Jeep on its wide, tall tires anyway.

He called Kit.

"What's your location?" he asked.

"I am already crossing the Howard Frankland Bridge into Pinellas County. I should be on scene in less than half an hour," she said, adding, "What the hell is all the background noise?"

He laughed. "I am running topless in the Jeep at eighty."

"I'm envious!"

"I bet. You may catch and pass me if you're running Code-3."

"Yep. I probably will."

Fifteen minutes later, a white unmarked Chevy with lights in the grill and upper windshield appeared very shortly in the Jeep's rearview. He moved out of the left lane. She hit her air horn as she blew past. He grinned and shook his head. *Kit is one interesting proposition*, he thought.

She called Hank and gave her position as she exited south of the Sunshine Skyway.

"Run silent and call me when you are within five minutes. I am in the house with a couple of SWAT guys.

I have two snipers set up. We don't have a cop-looking vehicle in sight and want to keep it that way."

"Okay. I will call Nick. He's right behind me in an orange Jeep. Not at all obvious."

"Less obvious to Givens than his no-frills Tahoe," Hank noted. "Which is why he picked it for today."

"I figured."

"At this point, you two should hold back. Make it look like you pulled the Jeep on a traffic stop several blocks west of our location. Let Nick know the plan," Hank said.

"Will do." She killed the call and hit Nick on her speed dial to tell him.

She saw him and pulled in behind, hitting her red and blues.

"Stay in the Jeep, sir," she said over her loudspeaker as she pulled in behind him, nose of the Chevy facing slightly to the right, lights on.

She got out and walked up to the Jeep. From the side, he was a guy in a polo shirt. His gun faced away. She held her notebook in hand and pretended to be writing as they chatted.

Ten minutes later, Hank called Nick.

"A lookout just said he pulled around the corner and is approaching. I will keep the call open and on speaker in the absence of radios," Hank said.

"Okay. He's pulling in. Acting very suspiciously. Or carefully. This is not a social call. He has a nickel-plated automatic out. He's knocking on the door."

Nick and Kit heard "sheriff's office! Drop your weapon. You are surrounded!" Several "pops," of pistol shots followed.

"Get your rifle or shotgun out, we need to move toward the house!" Nick said to Kit as he lifted his M4 carbine from the passenger footwell of the Jeep and put it in gear.

Kit ran back to her car and popped the trunk. She took her Mossberg twelve gauge out and placed it in the front of her car as she got in and followed Nick.

At the scene, suspect Givens had fired his nickel-plated Beretta 92 into the door and immediately ducked right.

The sniper was presented with a target who may have had officers behind him. The sniper's rifle could easily penetrate the walls of the old cottage, so he prudently held his fire.

Hank and the SWAT operators inside heard radio traffic.

"He's running back to his car!"

Hank and two SWAT operators rolled out the front door at the ready. Two more exited the rear.

Givens had made it to the Corvette and started it and shoved the car in gear. Rear tires churned as he stupidly floored it instead of delivering traction by moderation on the accelerator.

"Stop!" Hank ordered.

Givens did not.

"We want him alive if possible! Flatten his tires!"

Front and rear snipers shot out all four tires. Givens roared out onto the street, bumping with flat tires.

He headed toward an orange Jeep, which slid sideways and blocked him. Nick, keeping low, took position behind a front tire. It kept the engine block between him and any oncoming bullets. Kit stopped and got behind Nick's rear tire, her shotgun ready.

Givens could see the cop behind the Jeep leaning around with a rifle. It was aimed through his windshield at his head. The distance was fifteen feet. There was no way the cop would miss killing him. He tossed the Beretta out of the window and put both empty hands out in surrender.

Nick and Kit raised their weapons as they saw Manatee SWAT approaching Givens from the rear. One grabbed the hands stuck out of the Corvette's window and dragged him unceremoniously through it. Luckily for Givens, he was skinny. He came out but struggled, causing himself to hit the ground hard. He was rolled over and handcuffed before he could regain the breath the impact with the ground had cost him.

Nick stood up and swiveled the rifle around on its sling to a safe position and walked forward. He heard a trunk close as Kit locked her shotgun away.

A third SWAT operator had already checked the Corvette for any additional passengers. There were none.

Hank walked up, holstering his pistol. He looked at Nick.

"Want to charge him?" he asked.

"Nope, your case, your collar." The task force commander grinned.

Two SWAT operators gave Givens a thorough search and only found an automatic knife on him. His Beretta was retrieved and bagged. The empties at the door would be photographed and bagged for evidence.

"Your driver's license indicates you are who we expected, Mr. James Givens. Mr. Givens, for now, you are under arrest for shooting a firearm in a residential area. Other charges will be impending, probably to include attempted murder of a police officer, human trafficking and more.

"You will be advised of your rights here and again

downtown," Hank said, then read him the Miranda rights advisement.

"I ain't going to say anything other than wanting a lawyer. And I want it to be a local one who knows the judges hereabout," Givens said.

"Okay. You can select a local one or request a local public defender at no charge to you," Hank told him.

"I'll take a public defender for free," he responded.

James Givens was placed in the rear of Hank's SUV, handcuffed in the back and driven to the sheriff's office for booking and assignment of a public defender.

He lucked out and got a respected criminal lawyer doing periodic *pro bono* work as a public defender.

Before he left with Hank to be booked, Kit was already on the phone to Eddie Gonzalez.

She advised him Givens was in custody after shooting through the door at sheriff's deputies and his attempt to evade on four flat tires.

"I left Miami running fast. I have already crossed the Alligator Alley and am between Ft. Myers and Venice. Any way you can wait for me to sit in on the questioning? Kidnapping the girl on my turf is my case. We can work them together and probably get more information out of him. Lay a bunch of charges and he'll be ready to deal on his connection with your two in custody and the guy Nate in Orlando," Eddie said.

"I agree. I'll pass this to our commander who is standing right here. We'll work the details out when you arrive. I'm going to pass my phone to a Manatee detective to give you an address for where we'll all be so you can plug it into your navigation system," Kit said, handing the phone over to a local detective.

"Nick, he wants to sit in and begin investigating his

kidnapping of Rosa. He says if we add his charges to ours, we will have a lot more leverage."

"He's right. The way I see it, Hank and Eddie can do the interview. We will sit behind the famous one-way glass and listen on earphones. With any luck, he will give up Nate," Nick said.

They got back in their vehicles and drove to the sheriff's office. Nick had Kit lock his M4 carbine in her trunk, not wanting to leave it in a Jeep. He put a "Sheriff's Office Official Business" placard under his windshield wiper after he parked in a "LE Only" space.

They found Hank and Nick told him the strategy he had in mind, which included waiting for Detective Sergeant Eddie Gonzalez to arrive momentarily.

"Eddie and this guy have a history which would benefit us, I think," Nick explained.

They heard a deep voice behind them at the reception counter.

"I'm here to meet Detective Sergeant Kit Ennis," it boomed.

The speaker was a medium height man with dark hair and a thick mustache. He had on a Guayabera shirt. It was cool in the heat of Florida and did a great job of hiding a weapon under the shirttail which was always worn out.

Eddie had a barrel chest and biceps which strained at the material of his sleeves. Nick's first thought was he was not a person he would want to try to go mano-a-mano with.

Kit walked over and stuck out her hand. Eddie took it, pulled her in for a hug.

"This is how we always greet friends in my area!" he said.

"I hope the practice spreads!" she responded and introduced him to Nick.

"Glad your intuition sent you up this way, Eddie! I have arranged for you and our local task force case officer for the recovered and murdered teens both to do the interview. It would probably be good for you all to sit down over coffee and get to know one another and develop an interview plan. His name is Hank Thomas. He's a respected detective in this sheriff's office," Nick said.

"Great! I could kill for coffee! I jumped in the car as soon as I talked with Kit this morning and left mine untouched on my desk," Eddie said.

"Do you prefer café con leche over regular coffee?" Kit asked.

"Is the Pope Catholic?" He grinned.

"Good. I prefer it too. There's a place nearby which has acceptable café con leche. While you guys get to know each other and wait for Hank to become available, I will slip out and get four café con leche grandes," Nick said. He was gone less than fifteen minutes and saw the three of them upon his return.

"Let's go talk in the interview room. I'll send for Givens from the holding cell when we are ready," Hank said.

Nick said to the group he would like Hank and Eddie to do the interview while he and Kit stood by outside observing. Hank updated them on Givens's luck in landing a highly experienced criminal defense attorney as his public defender. He said the lawyer was meeting with Givens now.

They discussed the cases and questions each wanted to see asked. On approach, Eddie suggested bad cop/bad cop. They realized he was serious and Kit asked about it.

"This guy's whole life is a lie. He pulls the Rasta crap. He was born and raised in Miami, and the records show he has never even been to Jamaica. The accent is fake. He is mean, and his firing into a door without really knowing who was behind it shows it.

"He was a person of interest in several murders in Miami but always either had a convenient alibi or the witnesses against him disappeared before the trial. I don't know if they were bought off or killed off. We have been watching him for several years and unable to get anything to stick. This might be it, but it won't be easy. We have to scare the hell out of him. He knows what happens to pedophiles in prison—an angle we could pursue, true or not, to get his attention," Eddie said.

"How do you think counsel would react to unsubstantiated claims?" Kit asked Eddie.

"It's all in how we present them. Let me do the claim. I think I know how to get to him."

Hank got a call on his cell. "They are ready for him and the lawyer to come over."

The two interrogators stayed in the room, and Nick and Kit went to an adjacent observation area.

The lawyer, in a thousand-dollar suit, walked in behind the custody deputy and James Givens.

"You! You sombitch! What are you doing here?" Givens yelled at Eddie. The counsel patted him on the shoulder and shushed him.

"Do you all want me to handcuff him to the eye bolt?" the custody deputy asked.

Hank looked at the counsel, who said, "Not necessary."

"I hope you are right, counselor," Hank responded.

Hank turned on the audio-video recorder. He announced the names of the defendant, attorney, Eddie and himself along with the date and time the interview was commencing.

"All right. Mr. Givens, you have been read your Miranda rights twice and signed an acknowledgment you wished an attorney present. One has been appointed for you and the two of you have consulted before this interview, right?"

Givens looked at his attorney, who nodded, and he answered affirmatively.

"Mr. Givens, we have concrete proof you delivered one Rosa Fernandez, a minor, from Miami-Dade to Mr. Willie Brown and his associate James Givens," and gave the time of arrival and date.

"Do you acknowledge this?"

"No comment."

"Mr. Givens, how and where did you obtain custody of Miss Fernandez?"

"No comment."

"Mr. Givens, is it true you have been a suspect in several child abductions in Miami-Dade in the past three years and witnesses have disappeared before trial?" this from Eddie.

"No comment."

"Isn't it true you have sexually molested certain of these children? Of which one, recently deceased, we have DNA evidence from?" again, Eddie.

Givens got a sick look on his face.

"I object to these unsupported accusations and demand to see what evidence you have," counsel said.

"Counselor, we will present evidence on kidnapping, child trafficking, child molestation, attempted murder of a police officer, firing a gun in a residential area," Hank said, pausing to look at Eddie.

"Did I miss one?" he asked Eddie.

"Probably, we are so early in this investigation and have so much evidence coming in, I am sure there will be several other felonies which will be added."

"You people are just fishing," the lawyer, Paul Abington, said.

"I hope you base your defense on that assumption, counselor," Eddie said.

"Moving forward, you drove from your home in Miami straight to the Brown and Smithers home. Why did you come there?" Hank asked.

"No comment."

This went on for several hours. They learned nothing they did not already know or suspect.

Public Defender Abington questioned the use of his client's own automotive GPS, claiming it was against a Supreme Court ruling. They responded it was from a confiscated vehicle in their custody and the ruling was about police adding a GPS tracker which they did not do.

When he observed things bogging down after almost three hours, Nick tapped on the door and motioned Hank over. He said, "We have the DNA from Rosa Fernandez," loud enough for the others to hear. Hank leaned over and whispered something they could not hear, and Nick nodded his head and smiled.

Though a total ruse, it seemed to get the lawyer's attention.

Nick sat down and stared at them a full minute before speaking.

"Counsel, we have before us a person who is by our evidence a kidnapper, a trafficker, someone who has shot several shots at police officers today. He is guilty of evading, proof beyond live witnesses to include numerous dash cams.

"Perhaps the thing which will follow him most seriously into prison—and he will absolutely go to prison many, many years—is he molests little girls."

"Detective Sergeant Gonzalez and I have spoken with the Assistant State's Attorney. She has authorized us to cut a deal with Mr. Givens.

"You see, your client, as despicable member of society as he is, represents the bottom of the pond we are fishing. We want his end recipient, Nate, in Orlando. And, hopefully, his boss.

"Give up Nate with enough details to arrest and prosecute him and we will drop the attempted murder of a police officer and evading charges."

"Turn off the recording devices. I need to speak privately with my client," Abington said.

Nick smiled at Kit. "He will accept if they drop the pedophile charges. He won't want to go to prison with those. He might not live out the week inside and he and his lawyer both know it," Nick told her.

"Do we have sufficient evidence on those?" she asked.

"Probably not. We could use the allegation. Just like attorneys in a divorce trial use the old trick 'Mr. Jones, when did you stop beating your wife?' when he knows full well Mr. Jones never beat his wife. But he said it in front of the judge who knows the trick and the jury who doesn't. The harm has been done."

"A lot of whispering is going on. It looks like Givens is not very happy all of a sudden," Kit noted.

"Hank and Eddie are good. Plus, we have enough

evidence on him to put him in prison anyway. Givens and Abington both know it," Nick said.

"All right, Detectives. Tell your prosecutor we will accept the offer to cooperate on the man in Orlando if the shooting and evading charges are dropped. And, the abuse of a minor charges," the public defender said.

"Mr. Abington, in all good faith, I will ask her. But I seriously doubt Givens knows enough to buy the deal you have laid out. Let the record show, recording is stopped at two o'clock p.m. while Detectives Thomas and Gonzalez consult with the Assistant State's Attorney on the new deal proposed by the public defender."

Hank reached up and turned the recorder off. He and Eddie got up and left the room. They grinned at Nick and Kit on the way by but said nothing. They did not have to. They had Givens and knew it.

They returned after what seemed like a long time. Hank nodded and winked.

They went into the interview room. Hank turned the recording devices back on, noting he and Detective Sergeant Gonzalez had returned and the interview was resuming at two-twenty PM.

"We have consulted with the Assistant State's Attorney. She is not happy with this turn of events. Not happy at all.

"She will agree to your proposal, Mr. Abington, only if the evidence Mr. Givens provides is sufficient to arrest and have every reason our prosecution of this Nate person will lead to his guilty finding and help lead us to his boss.

"Otherwise, it's all off the table and we throw the full book at Mr. Givens. I would envision life in prison. However, the life part could be seriously lessened by the child abuser charges," Hank said. "I don't like it either," Eddie mumbled, looking hatefully at Givens.

"What an actor!" Nick said. "Eddie really loves this!"

Kit just grinned at her new male bestie and her even newer one through the one-way glass.

Over the next two hours, Givens gave up every name of subjects he had kidnapped, their homes, and how he obtained them, Nate's full name and address, and the location of a remote warehouse in an industrial complex not far from the exit where he would meet Nate. He named Brown, Givens, and other suppliers he had met from around the Tri-state region.

Givens also stated he had passed Rosa Fernandez over to the two in Palmetto because he and Nate had a falling out over payment on their last deal. Nate had told him he was going to find "a new man in Miami."

Givens emphatically said several times, if Nate had a boss, he was unaware of it.

In the next several days, the team leveraged the new information on Brown and Givens since a lot of it involved their illegal actions. Even Brown broke and gave up more information on Nate and his network and the fact Nate ran the whole operation. It was his setup from the beginning. Nick drove the Jeep home and showered, returning to the restaurant they chose in Tampa with his Tahoe.

Nick took Kit, Lee, Hank, Alex, and Eddie to dinner on the last night Eddie had planned to be in town.

The groundwork was laid, the battle lines drawn. While there was haste required, careful coordination was needed to raid the warehouse where an unknown number of teen girls were being held, drugged and cataloged as to whom they would be sent.

Certain ones would be sent to special requestors in

Asia and the Middle East for very large sums. Others would be hired out as au pairs to people who would keep them in a slave-like manner. The next level would be assigned to "specialty" escort services, next to pimps to work the streets, and the remainder as cleaners and other entry-level jobs.

The raid on Nate's operation had to both free existing teens held and obtain customer information to locate already dispersed ones and have authorities in the relevant locations recover them and prosecute their buyers.

The five at dinner in a private room agreed shutting Nate's operation down would put a major dent in the trafficking along the I-4 corridor. The suspects in custody were streetwise and said they were unaware of other operations like Nate's. There may be some pimps hooking up with runaways on a more or less random basis, but this was the big one and had multistate and international repercussions.

The task force would hit it hard and turn the rest of the information over to the Attorney General's Office for dispersion to the other affected areas, wherever they were.

The first job was to meet with Walt at the other end of the corridor and apprise him of their findings. The raid was on his turf. They would have to find out from him how many detectives he needed from the western task force for the raid and arrests and repatriation of Nate's detainees.

Nick called Walt Wood with all of the members at dinner squeezed into his Tahoe. He made the call on his cell phone through the SUV's speakers so it was a conference call.

"Walt, it's Nick on a speaker with leadership from

my task force plus two key outside detectives. Do you have a few private minutes to spend with us?"

"This sounds big. You're damn right I do. What's going on?" the eastern task force commander asked.

"We have broken several of the traffickers from Miami and our area and found out this Nate fellow is the head of the largest trafficking operation in the I-4 corridor. We have his name, address and location of a warehouse near the Disney exit where he is holding and cataloging a number of young women. We have not heard of any males in his custody. We have information on many of his suppliers.

"We need to get with you and your prosecutor and present evidence for an almost immediate raid on the warehouse. It is going to take your SWAT and some of us to lead it as well as a bunch of detectives to debrief hostages and interview anybody we arrest there. We will need medical and children's services backup. Maybe some organization like the Red Cross or Salvation Army.

"Can you put together a meeting at your HQ mid-morning tomorrow for four or five of us to come over with testimony and what other evidence we can and start planning this?"

"I can. Let me reiterate the people I need to have there as well as members of my own team: SWAT, a prosecutor, children's services, and probably our fire rescue paramedic supervisor? We may want to get a group consensus on the outside support agencies," Walt said.

"Guys?" Nick asked, looking around the Tahoe's interior. Everyone nodded.

"Walt, we think the folks you mentioned are all we need for tomorrow. Maybe a super careful surveillance on the warehouse. Perhaps by small plane, drones, and your very best undercovers watching it from a distance?" Nick added.

"Yeah. Good idea. We don't want to hit the warehouse just after he moved everybody. I'm thinking a simultaneous search warrant hit and search of his private dwelling, too."

"Perfect. We don't know where he keeps his records —at home or work. We don't have knowledge of a third site for an office, but I guess it is a possibility," Nick said.

"Hey guys," Eddie spoke up. "This is Detective Eddie Gonzalez from Miami-Dade. I am kind of an adopted member of Nick's team. The teen who was killed in his region was one of mine. It occurs to me getting someone to search property records in Nate's name early tomorrow might show a separate office. Or it might not. Just a thought."

"Eddie, we can jump on the computer and do most of the search before you all get here."

"Walt, I am thinking eight or ten from here. I have some other supervisory guys on a couple of hot unsolved cases, but they are smart as hell. How about call me around nine a.m. and tell me how many bodies you expect tomorrow? Both yours plus the other agencies. We'll pick up enough coffee and donuts to cover a jam session."

"That's nice, Nick. But we have a couple of industrial-size coffee makers. If you want to get a bunch of donuts or bagels or something, it would be great. Think fifteen here as a rough guess. I doubt it will change by more than a few either way.

"While you are driving, how about calling the AG's office and letting them know what's going down? This is big! They might want to fly a Deputy Assistant AG or somebody down from Tallahassee."

"Good point. I will call tonight. I have Ms. Washington's number. She's the one who deputized us. She may want to be there and deputize a couple of the guys sitting with me who are not officially task force but are integrally related."

"She'd be a good one to start with. If she cannot deputize them, our sheriff sure as hell can and will. They will be Osceola deputies for the duration," Walt said.

"Anything else, anybody?" Nick asked the people sitting with him. Nobody had more.

"Walt?" he asked.

"My mind is spinning, but I think we covered it for tonight. Good work, guys! Hey! Kit, are you there?"

"Yes, Walt."

"I heard about you being shot. Are you recovered from the thump on the vest?"

"I'm getting there. It won't bother me a bit when we hit the warehouse. I'll be glad to carry a flag when we charge."

"Haha. You are almost equidistant to our HQ. Take a look at our setup in case Nick isn't treating you right!"

"He carried me into the ER in his arms like in a Hallmark movie. I'll keep him, but thanks for giving me a backup solution."

"Okay. Good night, all. I'll see you mid-morning tomorrow."

"I guess we need to disperse and get some rest. It's going to be at least an hour and a half for most of us over there. Two for me from home. I'm going to invite Joe from St. Pete and John from Tampa tonight.

"Alex, your interview with Hank of the three may be

crucial. And yours is the only murder we know of yet. Any problem with you coming?" Nick asked.

"No. I will call the boss and let him know after I get east of Lakeland." He grinned.

"Watch out around Lakeland. There will be a Chevy on I-4 running in triple digits," Nick said, looking pointedly at Kit.

"I have a twin-turbo Interceptor. I can walk on by her without working up a sweat!"

"Eddie, you thought you were going home tonight. Any trouble staying? And do you need anything from us?"

"No. I am going to Walmart for some fatigues and socks and all. I planned a one-night stay but brought toothpaste and all. Maybe a shotgun if somebody has an extra?"

"You can have mine. Or my M4. Your choice and I'll take the other," Nick said.

"I'm a shotgun kind of guy," Eddie said seriously.

"Shotgun it is," Nick agreed and handed it and a box of double-ought buckshot to him as they got out of the Tahoe.

"Thanks, guys. A helluva day. Let's make tomorrow a better one and a safe one!"

They split for the night as Siri dialed the Florida AG representative for a briefing then John Ross and Joe Horner. Ms. Washington pledged to try to get a state plane. John and Joe were pleased to be asked and promised to be at the office in Kissimmee before ten in the morning.

The game's afoot! Nick said to himself as he drove home at the exact speed limit. His phone rang as he pulled off the Interstate onto the Fourth Street exit.

"Sergeant, I've got a plane!" came the recognizable voice from the capital in Tallahassee.

"Great! Now, let's think about the best airport for you."

"Nope, it's a highway patrol helicopter. I can land at the site. I have given them the address and they have already determined the coordinates.

"They cannot wait for me if I stay through the raid. If I do, we can find me a flight back out of Tampa or Orlando, as the case may be. I can just hitch a ride with you or one of your folks."

"Couldn't be better! Thank you. We all look forward to seeing you tomorrow. I have two guys to deputize for the raid, if you don't mind," Nick said.

"I still have a couple of forms in my briefcase. Not a problem."

"Fly safely and I will listen for you landing in the front parking lot around ten. If you call me with the pilot's specifications, I can have the right amount of space available and some marked units with their lights on at each corner to get his attention and mark the LZ."

"LZ?" she asked.

"Sorry. It goes back to my days in Afghanistan. Landing zone."

"Logical. I will call you and let you know. Good night, Sergeant."

"Good night, ma'am."

———

Nick was up early and at the eastern HQ by eight a.m. Dawn pulled in afterward.

"How would you like to go to a big meeting today and maybe a really big raid tonight?" he asked her and watched her eyes light up like a kid being offered ice cream.

"Are you kidding? You bet, Boss!"

"Get your big vest and whatever you'd wear different than right now out of your car. Put it and the shotgun you have in your hand in my Tahoe. Here are the keys. You will need a pad and some pens. I also want you to be the scribe for the meeting. This could be a day or two, so let me know if you need to stop somewhere and get more clothes, toiletries, or anything," Nick said.

"Maybe a Walmart? I need to get stuff like a toothbrush and a tee shirt to sleep in and so forth," Dawn said.

"No problem if we leave now and shop fast. Oh! I ordered a couple sizes of the flack-type vests. Did they come in?" he asked.

"Yes, yesterday."

"Would you grab one in each size in case we need them?" She ran to the storeroom and returned laden with four vests. She placed them in the rear of the Tahoe overtop her shotgun.

"Ready to roll?" he asked, and she jumped into the front seat excitedly and nodded.

Nick kept the speed normal and pulled into a nearby Walmart. Dawn ran in and returned with a large bag very quickly. The next stop was a drive-through donut shop. Four dozen donuts, a couple dozen bagels, and four cream cheeses, and they were back on the road.

"Hook in tightly," he said. Once they pulled onto I-4, she saw why. Nick pulled into the left lane and moved the big Tahoe. He only used his emergency warning gear when he encountered heavy traffic or a speed lane hog who did not want to move over. When the siren did not work, the air horn did.

"Have you ever run code other than in training? With your field training officer on a call maybe?" Nick asked the young deputy, who seemed to have a grin permanently affixed on her face.

"We had a couple lights and siren calls, but they were all in traffic and in town. Nothing like over a hundred."

"I really appreciate the skill those FHP troopers have. They have to do this a lot. And alone. You will see today how damn stupid motorists will be. Slamming on brakes when you come up behind them in the left lane, swerving in front of you no matter where you are. Ignoring the lights and siren like the guy in the Chrysler just did. Driving alone in his own reverie. Unaware of the world outside his car."

They saw an unmarked Chevrolet sedan ahead, moving fast in the left lane.

"Know who's in the dark unmarked car ahead?" Dawn did not.

"You will recognize the driver," he said as he smoothly caught and eased past the car, which moved over for him.

"It's Kit!" Dawn exclaimed as the car moved in behind them convoy-style and ran with them.

"We need to investigate what can be done to add a channel on everyone's radio designated just for the task force," Nick said, keeping his primary concentration on driving. Dawn just nodded, enjoying every minute of the run.

"Have you ever been in a high-speed pursuit, Nick?"

"Several times. Twice on this interstate."

"What's it like?" she asked.

"Scary when it's over. While it's going on, you are too busy concentrating on a combination of your driving, the fleeing car, and all the traffic around you. You can't just follow the car you are chasing. You are a trained driver, he isn't. Just because he wants to run a hundred twenty through traffic, or hot foot it down the shoulder, or blow through an intersection doesn't necessarily mean you should follow. You have to be the smart one. Let him get away if it gets too hairy! He can't outrun the radio. If he does, we can get him another day."

The traffic thinned out for a while and the two vehicles settled into a steady, mile devouring pace with little adrenaline production. They began to slow as they approached the Kissimmee exit. Nick's phone rang and he answered it on the Tahoe's system.

"Nick, it's Lorna Washington. We are about fifteen minutes out."

"I'm a little less. Ask the pilot the dimensions he'd like for his LZ."

She came back on in a moment saying a hundred fifty feet square would be fine, marked with flares or cars with their lights on.

"Gotcha! Let me get it done. See you in fifteen mikes!"

He called Walt right away and gave him the dimensions.

"I cordoned off a big part of the parking lot. I'll run out with one of the guys, and we'll put crossed flares at each corner of a hundred fifty-foot square right now."

Nick called the Associate Deputy Attorney General of the State of Florida and advised her.

"Okay, we have to really get there fast now," he said and sped up on the surface road, the HQ in sight. He gave his signal early as Kit behind him had not been there before.

They dismounted and left the tactical gear in the Tahoe.

"Commander Walt Wood, this is our admin deputy, Dawn Allison," Nick said. "And one of my two deputy commanders, Kit Ennis, is getting out of the Chevy with the engine steaming."

"It is not! I could have run like we did all day! Glad to meet you, Walt. Hi, Dawn."

She walked up and not terribly lightly punched Nick on the shoulder.

"Some thanks I get for rushing her to the hospital a couple days ago, carrying her in and saving her life," Nick said to an unbelieving Walt and Lee, who just walked up behind him.

They could hear the "whap-whap" of a helicopter getting louder. With a downflow of air not unlike a Florida hurricane, the state police bird landed in a perfect touch down.

Once the rotors came to a stop, a trooper in a flight suit opened the door and assisted Ms. Washington down.

Both task force commanders walked to her in greeting, followed by staff.

"Everybody here?" she asked.

"East task force and guests are all present and accounted for," Walt said.

Nick looked at Lee, who said the same for the west task force.

"We should have driven faster," Nick said, looking at Kit.

"Not necessarily. The pilot had you on radar," the

Associate Deputy Attorney General noted, saying nothing further.

They all went in, Nick, Dawn, and Lee carrying the break foods. Nick saw the rest of his team plus Homicide Detective Alex and Eddie from Miami.

"Let's all sit down. The speakers have name tents on the head table.

The audience looked like about thirty-five people. The eastern task force officers had the new polo shirts, the western had not received theirs yet and wore their agency's shirts.

Once everyone was seated, Walt introduced the people with him at the head table.

"We have a lot to plan and do. I will only introduce the folks up here by name and title. Then, the final person will give us the reason we're all here with such short notice.

"Okay. First, beside me, we are honored to have Florida Associate Deputy Attorney General Lorna Washington back with us today. Sitting next to her is Assistant State's Attorney for Osceola County Marley Stanton. Chief Richard Rankin of OCFD is here to assure we have adequate emergency medical support for any victims we recover and for ourselves. Next to the chief is Sergeant Leroy Jones, head of our SWAT team.

"Finally is the guy who is going to explain a lot to us this morning. He is Nick Wolf, the commander of the FLAG Task Force West. Nick is my opposite number on the western end of the I-4 corridor. Nick, please take it from here," Walt said.

"Good morning. Both task forces have been working hard, as all of you well know. Walt and I keep coming up with one person involved with missing teens on both ends.

"He is a tall white male, thin build, and wears his brown hair in a so-called man-bun. All we knew is he goes by 'Nate.'

"Three virtually identical-looking teens were abducted the same day in widely spread parts of the Tampa Bay area. It looked like a special order was being filled by someone. If we could recover them, it might lead us to Nate and others missing recently.

"We threw our full task force on it.

"Well, we just had a raid based on information uncovered by one of the guys on my task force, Hank Thomas with Manatee County SO. The task force and Manatee SWAT hit a house. We uncovered a victim unhurt and made two arrests. The victim told us another girl we were not looking for had been there and was knocked unconscious by one of our arrestees and removed.

"We obtained evidence of his trip and located a dead victim from Miami. Things have moved fast. With Hank and MCSO homicide detective Alex Smith interviewing and the help of Miami-Dade detective Eddie Gonzalez, the two suspects were soon joined by a third from Miami. I might add shots were fired in apprehending all three. One task force officer was shot when she tackled our suspect number one. She is task force Deputy Commander Kit Ennis. Thank God for her vest. She is fine, though sore.

"We have identified Nate. His name is Nathaniel Adam Boudin. We have his personal address and the location of a warehouse in this county allegedly used to house a variety of teens until they are disbursed to special request buyers, prostitution or some sort of jobs such as cleaning hotels or the like.

"All of you are heroes. Before we start planning two

raids, I want to introduce the people whose good detective work got us here. Please stand when I call your name.

"Homicide Detective Alex Smith, Manatee. Detective Hank Thomas, also of Manatee, Detective Sergeant Eddie Gonzalez, Miami-Dade. And Detective Sergeant Kit Ennis, Deputy Task Force Commander of Lakeland PD."

All were warmly applauded by their peers and sat down, duly embarrassed. Kit made another unseen face at Nick, which he caught and smiled.

"Thanks, Nick," Walt said. "What we need to do now is some admin and planning, then get everyone back together to execute today. Nick has three for Ms. Washington to swear in as state officers for today's activities. Ma'am, you are welcome to stay for the planning and raid, if you like after your swearing-in. Or, if you need to get back to Tallahassee, we understand how busy you are."

"I'll stay, Walt. All I have to do is let the FHP helicopter pilot know he is relieved, and I will get home on my own. What you are doing is so important. It's why we put these two task forces together. I simply have to see today through to its culmination."

"Everyone. There are coffee and donuts in the back of the room. This is a law enforcement operation after all. Let's all get some, invite the pilots in, and then the head table will start the planning," Walt said.

Nick walked over to the people he had recognized. Luckily, Dawn, who did not know anyone but him, Kit, and Lee, tagged along.

"Dawn, Eddie, and Alex. We want to swear y'all in as state officers for this op. Any objections?"

As expected, none had any.

"Stay close. Let's get the helo airborne, and I will introduce you to Ms. Washington for the quick ceremony."

Nick walked out to the helicopter with Dawn and Lee. Washington had caught Kit to hear about her shooting. Hank, Alex, and Eddie were in the group with the two women.

"Hey, guys," Nick called to the pilots. "I'm Nick from the western task force. Why don't y'all come in for some coffee and donuts for the road? Your passenger is going to stay over, so she will release you for real police work."

"Sold us!" one of the troopers said. "Are you the guy in the dark gray Tahoe? Or the blue Chevy sedan?" he asked Nick.

"Do I need to plead the fifth?" Nick grinned.

"Nah. I was just going to tell say you two drive like us," he said.

"I consider that a real compliment. Thanks! Let me show you to the coffee. On the way past, will you share your words with the blue Chevy? She's talking to your boss right now."

"Sure will!" They walked in with Dawn asking them about flying.

"Ma'am? The pilots are going to have a cup of coffee and hit the road. Or sky rather, once you release them officially," Nick said during a break in the conversation.

"Thank you, gentlemen, for my first helicopter flight. It was exciting! Now, I will sit in on my first planning session of a double raid. Mind you, I will sit as a fascinated observer only. Have some coffee and a great flight back!"

The two troopers in flight suits walked off with a very surprised Kit toward the break area.

"We should tag along just in hearing. This may be the only fun we'll have today," Lee suggested.

Fifteen minutes later, they walked out and watched the helicopter take off. Kit stood close to Nick and elbowed him in the ribs, not trying to be at all covert about it.

"Did you sic them on me about driving fast?" she accused.

"Why would the guy in front ever do such a thing? They asked about you. Something about what a good fast driver the young woman in the blue Chevrolet was. They asked why I was holding you back," Nick lied.

"Young?" she said, focusing on the only word she really heard in the exchange.

"Yes. I am sure they said 'young.' Or was it me who said it? I'm not sure now."

She gave him a sweet smile and walked back for another pre-planning donut. *Nick could not comprehend how someone like me, who seemed to live on junk food, stays so trim and fit. He does not know about the daily Peloton workouts and my sacrifices to look twenty-five in my forties. I doubt I'll ever tell him. Sometimes, he's just a big, sweet kid,* she thought. *One who picked me up in his arms and carried me into the ER.*

The head table attendees, plus the full SWAT team met.

Their first act was to immediately review film from the already-deployed drone surveillance on the warehouse to make sure victims had not been moved before the raid.

The second was to study Google Earth shots of the warehouse, its entry and roadways within the industrial park where it was located. They did the same for Nathaniel Boudin's—Nate's—house.

All parties agreed a simultaneous raid would be preferable. The time was a source of discussion for at least twenty minutes. Some were in favor of hitting the warehouse (especially) as soon as a plan was agreed upon and everyone could be put into position. A few wanted the old Indian attack approach during the early morning hours of deepest sleep. It was argued it worked and additionally would have captives safely asleep and not wandering around wherever they were kept.

The advocates for the former argued it would be necessary to ring officers around the area to stop captives being transferred in or out during daylight or evening if a pre-dawn raid as opted. Then, it was discussed under the option, how would they stop vehicles and have a large presence without attracting wide notice of their presence?

In the end, an ASAP approach was chosen.

The planning moved to the tactical phase: who would do what and where would they be placed? What support assets were needed and where would they be positioned?

With regard to the assets, how many child welfare workers would be needed? Again, where to place them to be close, but as unarmed, unsworn persons, how to assure their safety? How many ambulances and where to station them because they would be very obviously positioned ahead of time in the industrial park?

A plan was agreed upon. Everyone had photos of Nate from a now-pulled rap sheet from past infractions. Several task force officers from the local area went home and picked up a variety of their personal vehicles which did not scream "police." They included pickups with mag wheels, a motorcycle, a tiny Fiat belonging to a wife, and a Mustang convertible. They would go in first to reconnoiter. Once done, they would take position out of sight and radio on handhelds.

Because of a plethora of "no-knock" warrant service decisions, the Assistant State's Attorney required verbal notice, which did not help the element of surprise. Ms. Washington from the AG's Office in Tallahassee concurred. The SWAT commander decided to expedite getting in the doors with shape charges in lieu of rams or breaching shotgun rounds.

The first ones in front and rear would be SWAT. The second tier would be the task force commanders and their deputies and a selection of task force detectives with SWAT experience chosen by each task force commander. The third tier, after a "clear!" call, would be children's social workers.

"There is something real dangerous about this raid," the SWAT commander began. "Usually we go it, pop some flash-bangs, maybe even tear gas. We search and yell 'Clear!' Then detectives, CSIs, and so forth come in. I don't see it going down this way today.

"We have never seen the inside. We don't know whether we will have armed resistance with children present. We don't know how many kids are there, if any. We don't know their condition. Are they drugged? We don't know how many staff and their makeup and arms. Basically, we are blinder than normal.

"So, SWAT will hit from both doors. The second contingent of senior experienced detectives will follow very shortly after.

"But, and it's a big damn 'but,' my guys train together all the time. We know what each other is think-ing. No such luxury with us and the second tier. Be care-ful! No blue-on-blue casualties here, okay? If you have to take a shot, but are worried, don't take it! Move to protect yourself and maybe find a position where you can take it with a clear area behind and near your threat. I'm as serious as a heart attack here. We can do this. I know it. But the circumstances suck. We all have to be the best we've ever been. Kids and our lives depend on it."

The rest of the leadership around the joined church folding tables were nodding. All of the sworn officers had had similar thoughts.

"You heard Leroy," Walt said, referring to the SWAT commander. "You all know he's right. 'Best we have ever been' is our mantra for today. Both locations, but especially the warehouse. Leroy, how are you going to divide your team between the warehouse and residence? What support do you need at the residence?" he asked.

"The residence is pretty modest for a guy who probably has as much money as this one does. I am sending four over there, led by my deputy commander. One SWAT medic. I'd say five solid detectives from the task force. No ambulances on scene. Just keep one floating in the general vicinity. No social workers or CSIs. We can secure and call them in if needed," Sergeant Leroy Jones said.

They broke up to gear up.

Nick had Lee, Kit, Hank, Alex, and Eddie with him.

"While it looks like the excitement is going to be at the warehouse, the probability is the real evidence will be at the residence," he said.

"Lee, would you be the senior guy from task force west there? Take any four of five of the members we have here you want."

"Sure thing, Nick. Ha! Watch the big gunfight be there! Which sure won't be my first rodeo!"

He chose Eddie Gonzalez, Hank, and three detectives he had previously known from the task force. They met for a few minutes and got ready to go to the area.

Nick gathered the remainder of his task force members with him and Kit.

"Game time! Wear your heaviest armor. If you have a helmet, wear them. If you have pocket first aid, take it. Long gun and handgun. It will be your choice to shotgun or patrol rifle. Extra ammo for both guns. Tactical lights. We don't know what the lighting will be like.

"As always, both task forces will operate on FirstNet band 14 as our common link. Any questions? Okay! Let's form up behind my Tahoe. Kit, are you driving or coming with me?"

They lined up in convoy formation. Kit got in Nick's SUV. SWAT was in front, and initially, the east task force with Walt in front was in the left lane, the west led by Nick was in the right lane. Ms. Washington and the prosecutor rode in a rear unit with the EMT supervisor.

Walt had arranged for several Osceola marked units to escort, block intersections and generally facilitate the movement of the convoy.

"Treat us like a faster funeral procession," Walt told them.

The SWAT commander looked at his two teams and their support officers. He nodded then looked at Walt and Nick, and they nodded back.

The first two marked sheriff's units took off, running lights and sirens. SWAT next. Everybody else followed, running silently with no lights. The group to the residence departed without escorts.

A mile from the warehouse, Leroy Jones had the marked units douse their sirens and peel off. The SWAT truck turned down a side road and stopped several blocks from the warehouse. He got out and approached the non-SWAT units.

"When you see me leave as fast as I can go, count to sixty before following. I want you to get there about the time I have announced the warrant on the loudspeaker. My guys will take out both doors a second after. They will deploy flash-bangs inside immediately and move in.

"Pull up and walk in. Running causes mistakes. Know what your surroundings are. Trigger fingers straight along the frame of your gun anytime you have one out. Move it to the trigger only if you have to shoot somebody. I will radio Walt on our tactical channel we are going in only if I see you are not already there, dismounting. Either way, SWAT absolutely has to breach and enter as soon after getting there as possible."

The SWAT truck pulled off fast with no emergency alerts energized.

Walt began the countdown standing next to his vehicle. At sixty, he got in and accelerated off. Two lines, one led by Nick, followed. Silent. Fast.

They pulled up in the front of the warehouse as they heard and saw the shape charge on the door blow.

Walt said, "Search warrant!" on his loudspeaker as the SWAT officers went in front and rear. The rear door support task force officers quickly moved off to the rear to join the rear SWAT group.

Seconds after the two doors were breached, the backup officers saw the flashes and heard the explosions of multiple flash-bang grenades.

Long guns at the ready, Walt, Nick, and Kit were first in behind the SWAT operators.

The inside had a number of young voices screaming

in terror. The air was acrid with the door and flash-bang explosions.

It appeared there were only a couple closed-off rooms with doors. One an office perhaps? The other probably restrooms, maybe with showers. They did not know at this point.

The SWAT operators moved through the open building in precise military precision. A vast caged area on the right is separated into one large and two smaller cells. The cells seemed to have cots and a chair for each cot. Nothing more. There was nothing but girls as near as Nick could tell at first glance. Admittedly, he and Kit were looking for threats more than anything else.

The open area on the left had cooking and food storage facilities and shelving. It had a sofa and some chairs and a television for the guards.

The guards were three women with a male. Each was trying to avoid being apprehended by SWAT and were running amok.

Nick swung his M4 down on its sling and ran at one man. The guy put up a fight but lost to the task force commander within seconds. Nick turned to the sound of a nearby struggle.

Kit had tried to grab and hold two women. They were putting up a scratching, punching fight. Nick grabbed one from behind and swung her around, off her feet. She landed and stumbled. He was there to take a wrist in a "come along" grip and handcuff her. He saw Kit have the same success with her apprehension.

Within five minutes, all threats had been mitigated. A SWAT operator used a bolt cutter to sever the shackles of the padlocks, securing the young girls in their cages.

They were quickly moved to the larger cage for their

protection. It was unknown if they were drugged and might run for the door in panic. Three task force officers blocked the door to the larger caged cell and spoke calmingly to the inhabitants.

The staff were all patted down, and handcuffs removed. They were put in the two smaller wire mesh cells and told to not speak. The doors were secured with handcuffs. Task force officers stood at the doors to insure there was no speaking and agreement of what story would be told.

Leroy, Walt, and Nick met and planned their next action based on four prisoners and thirty-nine captives.

Nick called the EMT commander on FirstNet and had him respond with several ambulances silently to do an initial triage on the condition of the captive teens.

Walt called the children's services manager and told her how many teens they had liberated and asked her to send what she considered to be the appropriate initial number of counselors or social workers.

Nick walked over to Walt.

"There is something missing," he said somberly.

"Nate. Not at his house. If he's not here, where the hell is he? We've had surveillance on both places. Since he didn't come home during surveillance and was not there when we hit the house, he hasn't been here. Where, Nick?"

"I don't know. And it appears wherever he is, two of my three Tampa Bay fifteen-year-old's are with him or have already been delivered."

"We need to put out a multi-state BOLO on his vehicles right now!" Nick finished.

"I wish we could do the sheet right here," Walt said.

"We can. I have Dawn here. She has her laptop. She

can cobble a good one together quickly. Let me get her on it."

Nick looked through the crowd and saw her interviewing a former captive. He walked over to them.

"Dawn, I need you for something urgent. Can you turn this interview over to someone else? Or just postpone it for thirty minutes?"

"Of course, Nick. Millie, this is my boss. He's one of the ones who put this raid together to release you. I'll be back soon. I promise!"

The disheveled teen reach across and hugged her as she got up. Dawn, tears starting to form, said, "Everything is going to be okay, Millie. You are safe now."

Kit saw them and came over to work with Millie.

Nick and Dawn walked toward his vehicle to retrieve her computer.

"Neither Nate nor either of the two remaining Tampa Bay teens are here or at his house. He is probably delivering them. Somewhere. I need to have you put out a BOLO so every cop in the southeastern US will be on the lookout for him, his van and car and the two blonde girls. Time is of the essence. He apparently was not at his house or here yesterday when we began surveillance. He could be almost anywhere in the Southeast by now."

They went back into the office area of the warehouse, and she was able to access their Wi-Fi without a password. They did a sheet showing and describing him, the two teens, and his vehicles. Nick motioned Walt over to review the final copy with him. Both commanders concurred and Dawn sent it live.

It was now time to hurry up and wait.

Nick and Walt walked out to the staging area around the SWAT truck. Ms. Washington and Assistant State's

Attorney Stanton were both there. They had been asked to remain outside for safety purposes and any potential conflicts of interest in subsequent prosecutions.

"Ladies, there's good news and bad news," Walt began.

"How about the bad first?" Washington asked.

"Nathaniel Boudin is not here or at his house. Neither are the two blonde victims out of Tampa Bay. We knew he was not here and just finished looking at all the captives. They are not either. We just got the report on the residential raid and search. Same thing there," Walt said.

Washington and Stanton then turned to Nick.

"Does this make you the bearer of good tidings?" Washington asked.

"Probably by default," Nick said. "We have repatriated thirty-nine young women. A very preliminary indication is, if they are medicated, it is very mild. Nobody seems ill. We don't know about whether any were assaulted physically or sexually, but the counselors are aboard, and we will have a task force detective listening in and passing written questions when necessary. It is not as bad as we were expecting. Moreover, nobody, LE, victims or the four custodial keepers in custody were injured or killed. Everybody gets to go home tonight. Unless they are currently in handcuffs."

"What is being done about Boudin and the two young ladies?" Stanton asked.

"We have put out a 'Be On Look Out' for the whole southern US. It went out five minutes ago. The raid only commenced thirty minutes ago at both locations. Kudos to Leroy and his SWAT team!" Nick exclaimed.

Walt nodded vigorously.

"I will prepare a press release and run it by one or

both of you depending upon who is here when it is done," the woman from Tallahassee said.

"Walt, we both have deputy commanders at the residence. Do you want to keep them there for the search? Crime scene people are already working," Nick asked.

"I think so. They are both twenty to thirty-year detectives. Not their first rodeo. They will add value. We have enough people here to do preliminaries on the kids. Maybe we can get something from the staff people in custody about where Nate and the two from the Bay area might be. Why don't we take them? You, me, and our two present deputy commanders?" Walt said.

"Sounds like a plan. Let's do it," Nick agreed and began to look for Kit. He found her finishing up with young Millie for Dawn and she turned Millie over to a child welfare counselor and another task force detective.

"Walt, you, one of his deputies, and I are going to interview the staff here. I think Walt is going to take the guy. He had a gun but dropped it as soon as the flash-bangs went off."

Lorna Washington maintained a long view of the proceedings out of hearing, but the local prosecutor stepped in on the four employees to insure everything was done by the book.

All were advised of their rights under the Miranda Decision. Interestingly, all waived their rights. The male said, "You give us a deal and we will tell you everything we know. We ain't going to protect that weirdo Nate. We had enough to do to protect these here kids from him."

Nick introduced the Assistant State's Attorney.

She listed five potential charges which she was considering for each based only on what they knew. She said information from the captives about lewd acts, touching and the like might add to those charges.

"They ain't bargaining points. Them kids ain't going to accuse us of stuff we didn't do. Because we didn't! Now, you drop the second one and I bet we all agree to spill whatever beans we got," she said. Nick got a school cafeteria cook and server vibe from her. He remembered one at his elementary school who could have been this one's mother.

"Okay. Pending you all giving workable information and nothing new popping up against you, I agree. But again, everything is subject to the quality of information."

Walt, his deputy commander George Wyatt, Kit, and Nick headed to Walt's sheriff's office where they had four interview rooms equipped with video and audio recording devices. They hated not being able to save time by interviewing them on scene, but Stanton insisted, properly, on following the rule of law.

The four workers from the captive detention warehouse were individually taken in the cages of Osceola County sheriff's cruisers.

Lorna Washington and Marley Stanton would observe the interviews simultaneously on screens and with switchable earphones.

Nick sat across from his suspect. She was a tall thin woman. Her strawberry blonde hair was tied in a ponytail. She wore jeans, tennis shoes, and a gray sweatshirt. She could have lived in a run-down trailer or a mansion. She could have been anybody.

She claimed they all knew this was wrong. She said they also knew if they were not there, horrible things would happen to these little girls and, occasionally, boys. She said the staff all hated Nate. He paid them well, mainly to keep their mouths shut. His interest in the "kid's" welfare was about like a used car lot manager taking care of the cars on his lot to be able to get more money for them. Nick thought her observation was not only perceptive but also very true.

She said they spoke with Nate as little as possible. He had a violent temper and was seldom there, except to drop off one or two more kids, to make sure several were showered, groomed and dressed in clothes he brought and generally made ready for him to leave to take them to a buyer. She said she did the hair, having been a hairdresser before this job.

Nick found out his idea about "velocity" was valid. She told him children seldom stayed more than a week. It was a high-turnover business.

"He took three young girls who looked enough alike to be sisters a week ago from Tampa Bay. Do you remember two of them arriving? We freed the third one," Nick asked.

"I do. They were about the prettiest ones we seen here. He said he had a big buyer for them. Up in horse country. Northwest of here. I did their hair the same way early this morning. He left with them about seven."

"How? We had this building under surveillance," Nick said.

"He went out the back and to a friend of his with an eighteen-wheeler. About two warehouses over. They left in it and went to a rental he had. I know cause I heard him arrange it on the phone while I was doing the first girl's hair," she said.

"You said horse country. Marion County, maybe?" Nick asked.

"I don't know. I told you everything."

"I appreciate it. I'll speak up for you for doing it,"

Nick said and rushed across the warehouse floor to where Walt was speaking with the male.

"Ya got something, Nick?" Walt asked, seeing his opposite number walking toward him fast.

"Yes. My two Tampa Bay blondes left here at seven this morning with Nate. They somehow sneaked over to a warehouse two buildings away and left in an eighteen-wheeler. They were dropped at a rental car. My person heard him set it up as she was doing the girls' hair."

"They got out from under our surveillance? Damn! Did she say where the drop off of the teens was going to be?" Walt asked.

"She said 'horse country. Northwest of here.' I asked if it was Marion County. She said she didn't know."

"Musta been the 'Loch Ness Monster,'" the man Walt was interviewing broke in.

"Who?" Walt asked.

"There's a guy up there with a horse farm. Nate is scared of him. Which is why he calls him the Loch Ness Monster. Apparently, he's not real gentle with the girls he buys and uses then passes them on to somebody else."

"Do you know where this farm is?" Nick asked.

"Just somewhere up there near horse country. But not where they raise them thoroughbreds."

"Walt. Inverness is up that way. In Citrus County, I think. The other Inverness, in Scotland, is near Loch Ness, where Nessie, the monster is supposed to live. Almost too much of a coincidence to dismiss!" Nick said.

"Time to get Ms. Washington in here with her far-reaching contacts," Walt said.

They both walked out, taking the handcuffed man

with them, more for speed and convenience than corroboration.

"Ms. Washington. We need your help," Walt said.

Nick related the words from both employees.

"We think this 'Loch Ness Monster' is someone around Inverness. Two people, including the gentleman with us, said Nate was taking my two Tampa Bay victims to him on a horse farm."

"Do you know the sheriff up there in Citrus?" Walt asked.

"I know him well. And the judges too. Want me to call and see if he can put a name on this monster?"

Both men nodded appreciatively.

She sat in Nick's Tahoe, speaking over the audio system so all could here. All except the prisoner, who having done his bit, had been returned to custody inside the warehouse.

Lorna Washington laid out the suspicions to the sheriff.

"We have a small horse farm in the county. Highland Horse Farm. The name ties right in. I never met the owner, but I know a bit about him. He is generally disliked by his neighbors and has been accused of being rough with his horses. I'd like to catch him doing it!"

He gave them the man's name and address of the farm.

"I am going to call the judge and see if he will issue an immediate search warrant. Can you have your SWAT team on standby?" she said.

"I'll scramble them now and keep the reason just between them and me. We can be at the farm in twenty minutes even going silently. If he's got two little girls there, in my county, I want his ass. Sorry, ma'am!"

"You are forgiven. Listen, I have the two commanders of our east and west trafficking task forces. They led a raid on the deliverer's warehouse today and freed a bunch of young women. I'd like to see them and maybe a couple of their task force members in the door behind your SWAT. All of these folks are deputized state officers. I did it myself."

"No problem. SWAT sets the parameters and goes in first. Then, your folks."

"Thanks, Sheriff. We'll let you know when we get there."

"Sheriff, this is Walt Wood. I head the eastern task force. I am going to try to scramble a chopper from my home agency. You have a good place for us to land?"

"I do. Give me a number, and I'll send it to you to give your pilot. We will use the location as our staging area. It's far enough away to not get his attention and close enough to get there fast by vehicles. I'll have transportation for you all. How many?"

"Sheriff, this is Nick Wolf from the western task force. Plan on about four tops?"

"No problem, Nick. Are you all on FirstNet?"

"We are," Walt said. The sheriff and the two task force commanders exchanged numbers and agreed it would be the most reliable comms source.

Walt was able to arrange a high-speed trip on a helicopter.

. Within a few minutes, they heard the chopper outside. The LZ established for the highway patrol helicopter was still obvious and it landed there.

Nick, Walt, Kit, and Detective Bo Kelstrom, climbed aboard in full raid gear with long guns.

The sheriff's coordinates were for a small corporate airport. They could see some sheriff's deputy cars and SWAT were already staged there.

One of the deputies had picked up the search warrant Lorna Washington had arranged with a local judge.

"Men, and ma'am," the sheriff began. "Sergeant Larson is head of SWAT. I'm going to let him take it from here."

"This horse ranch is a small one. Forty acres with a house, a barn, stables for fifteen horses and a couple outbuildings. None of us know the owner, except by his lousy reputation. His name is Rory McCormick. He's got a slight Celtic accent, but nobody seems to know whether it's Scottish, Welch, Irish, or fake.

"Assuming he just took possession of these two young women today, the Google Earth picture shows the main house and another, we lumped as 'outbuilding' but which looks like a pretty nice cottage. He could have them either place. We see a few vehicles parked near the house. We're thinking a couple of the trucks are related to the farm, there is a big Audi, which is McCormick's, and an unidentified Buick sedan. We cannot get an angle from the satellite map to read the license plate."

"My idea is to have seven of my men hit the main house and two hit the much smaller cottage. We will have deputies watching the back of the house and cottage for runners. I don't think we need to simultaneously hit the rear of the residence given our deputies out back watching. Others will be watching the barn, stable, and other outbuildings. We planned it while you guys were on the way up here.

"Since there are four of you, why don't you split two and two between the residence and the cottage? On the cottage, once my two breach the door, four operators should be enough to go in and clear it."

The sheriff added, "When everything is clear, we will have our crime scene folks come in and do their thing. I will have EMTs respond silently and stand by off-premises just before we go in. We will have a SWAT medic in the group which hits the main house. Everybody good?" The collective group signified their understanding and agreement with the plan.

"Why don't two of you ride with the SWAT truck and two in the SWAT SUV with the two operators assigned the cottage?" SWAT commander Larson said.

Walt shrugged at Nick who nodded him toward the larger truck. Nick figured there was a possibility the cottage might be McCormick's playhouse if all of their assumptions were valid.

He and Kit got in the Ford Expedition which was the number two truck in line.

They drove silently in single file to the farm. As soon as the two SWAT drivers gunned their vehicles toward the house and cottage, the sheriff and following deputies moved off to take up positions at the rear of the two houses and around the barn, stable and other outbuildings.

Both inward-opening doors succumbed to the ram and the operators went in. They held off deploying the flash-bangs as they sized the situation. It was not believed McCormick was a violent offender nor would he have armed security.

They were right on both counts. Almost.

The cottage door blew open with one crash of the manual ram. The operator dropped it, swung up his M4 and entered beside his partner with Nick and Kit behind. The two operators fanned out and spotted stairs leading upward. The cottage did not appear to have a second floor from the outside. They moved up the stairs carefully.

Nick and Kit cleared the very open downstairs quickly. The only closed door was probably the kitchen.

Kit eased it open, and Nick moved in low and fast.

He froze inside the door at a scene he did not want to see.

A medium-height man with a reddish beard was holding two young women as a shield. One was Morgan Parker from Tampa, and the other was Alice Kincaid from St. Petersburg.

The man, ostensibly McCormick, was holding a 1911 .45 Automatic cocked against Morgan's temple. He had his arm across the chest of both. The top of their heads came to his chin.

"Drop the rifle, or both girls die right here!" he ordered Nick.

Nick was the only person he saw in the doorway.

Nick was faced with something police officers experienced too many times in their careers. Having to make a life-or-death decision instantly.

He lowered his right shoulder and the sling slid off it. Watching McCormick, he bent slowly and placed the rifle on the floor. He saw McCormick seem to relax for a second and made his move.

Nick drew his .40 caliber Glock 23 faster than he ever had and pressed the trigger as the front sight reached McCormick's hairline eight inches above the top of the girls' heads.

The Gold Dot hollow point hit exactly where Nick aimed, and the man recoiled backward against the rear kitchen wall. He still held the terrified teens and shook his head. The bullet had angled up his skull and given him a painful but not fatal scalp wound.

He let go of the two girls and fired the .45 twice as they fell to each side.

The first two-hundred-thirty-grain bullet hit Nick in the center of his left leg above the knee.

The pain was excruciating and felt like his leg had been blown off. The second bullet hit him in the inside upper thigh and clipped his femoral artery.

In the tachypsychia which accompanies virtually all gunfights, Nick saw McCormick in tunnel vision.

Everything seemed to be in slow motion. He had a clear shot and tried to raise the Glock. He couldn't. With the dulled auditory ability of tachypsychia, he heard something hit the floor.

His Glock was still in his hand. He was confused. McCormick smiled and slowly, it seemed, raised the big automatic.

Nick heard a dull "pop," and McCormick's head exploded crimson, pink, and gray against the wall behind him.

Nick was going down. He was passing out. He instinctively pulled a QuikClot package and a tourniquet from his cargo pants pocket. He could not hold them, and they hit the floor the same time he did.

Everything turned black.

6

Kit pumped another rifled slug into her short-barreled shotgun. It was instinctive. She knew a headless man was no longer a threat. But he shot her friend. She really, really wanted to shoot him again.

Reason took over the tachypsychia she was also experiencing. She snapped out of it.

"Girls, don't look behind you. You are alright! Get over beside me. Now!"

She heard the two SWAT operators bounding down the stairs and they moved into the room, assessed and lowered their rifles.

"Get the medic while I check the task force guy. Ma'am, go sit against the wall. Lay your shotgun on the floor. Try to take deep breaths."

He looked at Nick. The middle of his thigh was probably broken. Maybe beyond repair.

He saw blood pumping. Spurting. But not at a full arterial rate. He saw the QuikClot and the tourniquet. The SWAT operator was still in tactical mode. He did not have to think to use it. He automatically fastened the strap of the tourniquet at the groin and the hip and tightened it. The blood stopped. He ripped the paper cover off the sponge and placed it over the leg wound. As he pressed down, the unconscious man groaned.

Very few minutes later, the SWAT medic came in and dropped his trauma pouch on the floor. But most of his work had just been done perfectly. Walt stood at the door along with the sheriff and several other SWAT operators grimly watching the scene unfold before them.

One keyed his radio for the paramedic unit to roll in on a deputy down. It was close enough the people huddled in the small kitchen could hear its engine as it accelerated.

Walt and the sheriff took charge of the traumatized teens and moved them away.

As the paramedics took over Nick's care, the SWAT medic went over and looked at the gruesome remains of Rory McCormick. A seventy-two-caliber slug from a twelve-gauge shotgun at twenty feet was a fearsome weapon. He was unable to see the head wound Nick inflicted to save the girls. It would come out in Kit's statement and the autopsy.

While the paramedics worked on Nick, the sheriff, his major, and Walt's deputy commander took Nick's and Kit's body cams. Kit relinquished her shotgun and gave Nick's Glock to the sheriff. The three men quickly questioned her and thought they might have sufficient information between her hurried statement and the video history for the subsequent shooting review board which they would largely compromise along with a state investigator.

Walt called his helicopter, still at the staging area, over to the farm. The two paramedics packaged Nick for the flight. They spoke with the pilots. Tampa General, University of Florida Shand's Hospital, and Orlando Health's Orlando Regional Medical Center all had Level One trauma centers. Interestingly, the three were virtually exactly the same distance from the farm. Seventy miles. Since the helicopter's home was in the Orlando area, they chose the Orlando trauma center. A Citrus County paramedic and Kit flew with them.

Nick's blood pressure was low. The paramedic had brought IVs, appropriate drugs, and an Automatic Electronic Defibrillator, or AED, aboard. He monitored the tourniquet and put a temporary cast on the compound fracture with the .45 slug still in the femur of Nick's left leg. The immediate use of the QuikClot hemostatic wound dressing had done its job of stopping the bleeding in the femur wound. It might have even worked on the femoral arterial bleeding, subsequently found to be a nicked artery instead of a severed one. Nick had dropped the two things most guaranteed to save his life by rote. The SWAT operator had realized this from his training and employed both without hesitation; thereby saving a fellow officer's life.

Now, it would be up to a team of surgeons to put the task force commander back together.

The woman beside Nick held his hand and prayed fervently. She had blocked out the horrific damage her own shot had caused.

Kit was sure Nick's quick draw headshot had saved the life of the two hostages. Though the bullet had not acted as planned upon contact, it was an incredible feat. Her belief it saved lives would be stated in her report. She closed her eyes and continued to hold his hand, letting the paramedic do his job and the pilots theirs. Kit even put aside her abject terror about flying in a helicopter. This would be a day of firsts for Detective Sergeant Kristina Ennis. Firsts she never wanted to think about again.

————

While the helicopter was en route to the hospital, Walt and the sheriff took the two teens aside and a female deputy spoke with them until counselors arrived. Then, they redoubled their efforts to find Nate Boudin.

Walt also called Lee and filled him in on what happened. Lee called Nick's parent agency for next-of-kin notification and told them which hospital to which he was being taken.

Lorna Washington named Lee the temporary commander of task force west. Using Walt's phone, she did an announcement of the raid and its repercussions to both task forces on the common-use broadband network.

Members of Nick's home agency and the task force hurried to the Orlando Regional Medical Center to stand by the deputy down.

The helicopter landed and a waiting crew rushed Nick into the hospital on a gurney. Nobody dared deter the well-armed and blood-stained woman in tactical gear or Citrus County paramedic who ran along beside the gurney.

They did a preliminary scan of his two wounds and questioned the paramedic about how long the tourniquet had been on and if it had been loosened. He looked to Kit for the time it had been put on. She knew to the minute. It was when time had stood still for her as she sat back against the wall, shotgun on the floor and tried to watch the SWAT officer tend to her badly bleeding friend.

Nick was prepped and carried into an operating room where several types of surgeons were present. Their game plan was to address the femoral artery first and the femur second.

By the end of the first hour, Nick's Major and a number of others from his agency, Lee and ten detectives from the task force had gathered. Walt was on his way, bringing Nick's Tahoe, with Dawn driving behind him.

The major, in a heavily starched uniform, approached Kit upon his arrival. The tactical vest and blood stains gave her away.

"You must be Kit Ennis, one of the two deputy commanders," he said as he proffered his hand.

"I am. Though I would as soon be about anyone else in the world today."

"Is Lee on the way? I have known him almost thirty years," the major asked.

"I don't know. I would think he is. There is a lot of work still being done at several sites. The kingpin got away. The buyer of the two we had been looking for didn't," she said.

"What happened to him?" he asked.

"He got shot," she said, continuing. "By Nick. A perfectly executed headshot while he was threatening the lives of the two teens he was using as a shield. Nick saved those two girls, Major. The problem is bullets hit and then do strange things. Instead of digging into the man's skull as planned, this one decided to go up his skull and leave a deep graze before flying off into who knows where. The kitchen wall, I guess," Kit said.

"Then, Kit?"

"I shot the man. He died before he hit the floor."

"Where?"

"Between the eyes with a twelve-gauge slug."

"Ouch. Not pretty."

"No, major. Not pretty at all."

"How about I get the hospital chaplain to come talk with you?"

"Thanks. But all I care about right now is the friend. The hero. The one under the knife somewhere in this damn hospital."

"Me, too," the major said.

"Sir? Does Nick have any next-of-kin to notify?" Kit asked.

"He only has a very old aunt up in West Virginia. She's in a nursing home. I called her. I detected more than a little dementia. I guess the practical answer is just us, Kit."

"Nick would say it's enough. He has mentioned you with great respect during the few quiet times we have had to actually speak about things other than the brutes who deal in young kids."

"I can assure you he has told me glowingly about you. A number of times. I see why. It looks like you took a bad situation and mitigated it with expertise. I know your chief will be proud. He's on the way here to be with you. He should be here shortly. The blue line is thin, Kit, but in times like this, the family gathers and supports."

She looked at him and smiled. Through tears she thought she had already cried dry. Apparently not.

Lee, because his mind ran to organization and humor at the same time, computed the group waiting for word on Nick drank eighty cups of coffee and made, collectively, thirty-eight trips to the restroom before the surgeons came out.

The lead surgeon looked at the tired, eager group. He looked strained and tired himself.

"I feel like I am making a press statement. Mr. Wolf underwent four hours of surgery. The primary emphasis was on his injured femoral artery. The secondary emphasis was to stabilize his damaged femur until a specialist could relook at it and finalize repairs in a subsequent surgery.

"Mr. Wolf is young and extremely fit. Both of which are in his favor. He is looking toward a tough road to recovery and one fraught with lots of physical therapy. His gait will never be the same. I think his condition will prompt a disability retirement from police work. I'm not going to take any questions, because I have said too much for non-family. But I realize you are his family. You and a very old aunt out of state are all he has, so I stretched protocols. It will be tonight before anyone can see him. It should be one at a time.

Kit and Lee walked out together.

"Congratulations, boss," she said.

"Ms. Washington wanted to speak with both of us to make a decision, but you were in the helicopter. I accepted the job on an interim basis. I am too close to retirement to take the permanent posting. If it's okay, I plan on recommending you," he said.

"After this, I don't know if I want it. Let's let it slide for a while, Lee," she asked. "I am going to drive back to Lakeland and get a shower, some clean clothes, and come back."

"You think a lot of Nick. Just like I do. I have known him a couple of years. This isn't the first case we've worked together. He will—I guess would—have made a fine senior officer. Maybe a sheriff one day. Now, we'll just have to wait and see," Lee said seriously.

"I do think a lot of him. I'm a decade older, but his quick analysis makes me feel like the younger one. I consider him one of my closest friends. Now I know he doesn't have anybody else, I will sit with him as long and as much as it takes," Kit said.

"After your shooting incident today, you should get a good night's sleep, Kit. And maybe talk to a professional counselor about it."

"If I lie in the bed, I will stare at the ceiling and think about blowing a man's head off. I would rather come back here and worry about my friend. Our friend."

He patted her on the shoulder. Lee could have been her father and she appreciated him more than anyone else in the world at this moment.

"Okay. Come back. But promise me you will get some counseling about the shooting. No matter how tough you are, you need it. I'm serious, Kit. I've been where you are three times. A bit of outside help makes a difference dealing with what happened today. By the way, how are you getting home?"

"My car, as well as Nick's Tahoe, is at the east task force HQ. I left mine there and Dawn drove his back."

"It's on my way home. Hop in," Lee said.

He dropped her at her car in Kissimmee and she drove the short distance west on I-4 to her home in Lakeland. She showered, dressed, and headed back to the hospital in a short time. She was clad in her usual PD polo shirt, cargo slacks, boots, and gun belt with her detective's badge next to her pistol holster. She aimed her car north and laid on the accelerator.

Nick had realized instinctively he was hit hard at the cottage. He could not stand, nor could he hold his gun. It was as if a giant ocean wave rolled over his brain, and he blacked out and fell. On the floor, he dug into his left cargo pocket and pulled out the tourniquet and Quik-Clot. Something inside him told him they would keep him alive.

But he fainted away, the lifesaving first aid items laying unused.

Nick felt someone was working on him. Kit? God bless Kit.

He was being moved. He could not maintain consciousness and had no idea where he was being taken. He was surrounded by noise and shaking. He could not quite make out what was happening. He knew he was on his back and could visualize brightness above him through his closed eyes.

Someone beside him was busy tending to him. He felt Kit's presence rather than seeing or hearing her. He was glad she was there with him.

He thought he was probably going to die. He knew he was shot badly, but he hurt all over and did not know where or how many times he had been hit.

His infrequency of church attendance flashed through his mind, but then he lost total consciousness.

The rest of the day and all of the night were a kaleidoscope of unidentifiable lights and sounds. He knew they were there but could not focus on any of them. The pain had ceased. His ability to move had also ceased.

Am I dead? he wondered. *Is this what it's like?* He faded out.

Kit sat there all night after returning. It was now nine in the morning. Nurses had checked his vitals frequently but said nothing. She thought it must be a good sign. No rushing off or rushing back with an emergency syringe.

His leg was in a partial cast, the surgery site accessible. Her hand was on his arm. In one of the places not festooned with tubes. She was tired and laid her head on the edge of the bed near his arm.

Sometime later, she felt movement. Her head popped up and she looked at him. His eyelids were flickering.

They opened.

He looked at her, confused, then seemed to clear any haze.

"The girls. Are they safe?" he said in a really hoarse voice.

"Yes, Nick. You saved them. They are each back home with their families. They were scared but unhurt."

"The man. The monster?" he asked.

"Dead. Your bullet freed the girls but ran up his scalp instead of penetrating it. He was staggering but aiming at you. So, I killed him. Bastard! Nobody kills my friend."

"Thanks, dear Kit. I goofed up. Bad tactical decision. I should have put the red dot on my rifle and taken a precise shot between his eyes."

"Water over the dam. The girls are free, and you are alive. Nothing else matters," she said.

"Kit?"

"What, Nick?"

"Thanks."

"You are welcome. On one condition. You will never, ever scare me like you did. Ever again. You almost died."

"I thought I had died. A couple of times. I need to start going to church."

"Yep. Probably so. Me, too."

They were interrupted by the nurse's arrival, immediately followed by the surgeon.

"Well, you are awake. About time. I had to answer interrogation by about forty cops last night," the doctor said.

"What's the word on me, doc?"

"You were shot in the upper thigh. The bullet was a full metal jacket .45 ACP. You are damn lucky it was not a hollow point. It nicked the femoral artery. Somebody immediately put a tourniquet on it. The tourniquet saved your life. Then, they put a kaolin clotting agent on your thigh where the other bullet hit. You need to buy somebody a drink, sergeant.

"We repaired the femoral artery. We removed bone fragments from your leg. The bullet is still embedded in your femur. Collectively, we decided to delay the primary leg repair for another day. You had been through enough physical trauma.

"I am going to defer to a specialist we have contacted for the femur issue. He is local and will be by today to look at the images and maybe visit you."

"How will they repair it?" Nick asked.

"There are a couple of options. I'd rather let him study your case and decide. Right now, I could be approximately right and exactly wrong."

"Will I be able to walk again?"

"You will. Badly at first, better over time. I am afraid sprinting is out for good. You will have a severe limp for a while. It should diminish over time. However, it will never go away. I will sign whatever papers necessary for you to be granted a disability retirement from law enforcement."

Nick tried not to show it and to be stoic. The news, however, was like a blow to the gut.

"Thanks for taking care of me, doc. I have my two heroes right here in the room with me," Nick said, nodding toward Kit.

"I gather from this morning's news you are both heroes. A bunch of young, trafficked captives freed and two later when you were shot."

"I'm not a hero. She is though."

"You had all sorts of combat wounds already. I suspect you came into your current line of work already a hero," the doctor said. Nick just shook his head negatively.

"You seem amazingly perky and alert. I am going to check you off as good and continue visiting this morning's million or so patients. I may see you later in the week, but I am passing your baton to the hospital physicians and the bone specialist."

He patted Nick on the arm, nodded at Kit, and left.

The nurse finished his chart and left also.

"Alone at last," Nick said and grinned. "Want to mess around?"

Kit stared at him for minute with his supported leg, partial cast and arms full of tubes. And then she broke out in uncontrolled laughter.

"Maybe later?" he asked, prompting a continuation of her mirth. "Okay. Maybe I'll try a nap," he said and closed his eyes.

She lightly prodded him. "Open your eyes."

"Why?"

"I have been watching you sleep for hours. It's now your turn to watch me sleep!"

"Okay. Go for it."

She laid her head on the edge of the bed and actually fell asleep almost immediately. He stroked her hair and fell asleep, his hand lightly on her head.

———

Lee was setting up a Zoom call with Walt.

"Walt, anything on the trucker who took Nate and the captives to the rental car?"

"Yes, we quickly spoke with the trucking company. They gave his name and even his GPS location. The Pennsylvania State Police have him in custody! I'm sending a task force officer up to interview him. We may get him as accessory to kidnapping, and he knows it," Walt said.

"Did he mention the make and model of the rental car?"

"He didn't have to. He dumped it in Citrus County. They have it and are working on what kind of vehicle he obtained to replace it. Nothing yet. Lee, how is Nick?"

"Kit went back to the hospital. She just called and said he's awake and alert. Saying he made the wrong tactical decision not to cap McCormick with his carbine. Said his mistake was thinking he could buy time and plan by setting the rifle down and using his pistol at the close range. My call on it was he was probably right. The damn bullet just hit McCormick's head at the wrong angle and did not penetrate. Had it done what he planned, McCormick would have had his central nervous system unplugged and the girls would have been fine. And Nick wouldn't have been shot and Kit not traumatized by taking the perp's head off."

"I agree. Bullets do strange things when they hit something hard like a skull. Had it gone straight in, it would have been game over for McCormick. Maybe we should both talk to him and tell him to stop beating himself up."

"We should as soon as we can. I am going to try to get up tomorrow night. He has another surgery, but I don't know how quickly yet. I'll let you know when I hear," Lee said.

"Thanks, buddy. Keep safe and we'll talk soon."

———

Earlier the day before, Nate Boudin had just dropped the two off at McCormick's. He had twelve thousand in cash in his pocket. The sonofabitch had shorted him on the per-person stipend because he delivered two and not the three ordered.

Nate saw a convoy of police vehicles flying toward the farm when he was less than five minutes away from it. He had a ball cap and sunglasses on and was in a car they could not possibly know about.

He got a sick feeling in his stomach. The cops were on to him and, with their SWAT truck, were on the way to raid the farm. The only way they could have traced his steps to the farm was if they had already hit him in Orlando.

He knew he had just forfeited the cash, bitcoins, and the rest in his safe. The dumb employees at the warehouse did not know his business. Nor did they know about the offshore accounts in Belize and the Isle of Man.

Nate knew they would be on his trail somehow very soon. This new team had done something cops had not been able to do for five years. It was time to disappear. For a long time, if not for good.

He needed to dump the rental car. He saw a motorcycle coming toward him on the deserted rural two-lane. He stopped in the middle of the road and pulled the car's hood release latch. Jumping out, he reached under the center of the slightly open hood and released the safety catch.

As the biker approached, Nate waved both arms up and down to get his attention.

The biker, a guy Nate's own age, stopped.

"What's the problem?"

"I don't know. It just died. I know about computers, but not cars. Nothing about cars. And my cell phone is dead. What a day!"

"Lemme take a quick look," the biker said as he put his helmet on the seat of the medium-sized Yamaha.

Nate carefully looked on both directions. Nobody.

As the biker leaned under the hood, Nate shot him between the shoulder blades. He picked up the two empty cases and pocketed them. Next, he quickly dragged the man over to the rear of his Chrysler 300 rental and popped the trunk with the key fob button. He lifted him into the trunk and removed the guy's wallet and keys. Cards but no money. He felt in the front pocket of the man's jeans and took out a wad. Maybe a hundred bucks, he did not have time to count it. He left the Timex on his wrist.

Nate closed the trunk and got in the car. He drove it behind some trees. Taking his handkerchief, he wiped the door handles, wheel, hood release inside and out, and the trunk. The cops would probably think it was his wheels, but why hand it to them on a silver platter.

He locked the car and pocketed the key fob.

Getting on the bike, he started it, adjusted the helmet in place and motored off.

He headed south on highways but not interstates.

The Texas border was still porous. He would go there and cross into Mexico opposite from the directions the illegals used. He had a total of five hundred with his cash and the biker's. Add twelve thousand from McCormick and he had more than enough until he could buy a laptop in Mexico and move some funds around.

Nate figured there would not be any lookouts for a single passenger on a motorcycle, he was good until they found the rental, found the biker dead in the trunk and figured out a bike was missing and what kind it was. In a few miles, he tossed the key fob in a dumpster behind a convenience store. He went in and bought some bottles of water and snacks. They would fit in the fiberglass saddlebags. Keeping to the posted limits, he began a long ride.

He just hoped he could get into Mexico first. In his heart, he doubted it. But he was going to give it one helluva try.

––––––––

Nate went north on US-19 and merged onto US-98. He began to parallel the Gulf of Mexico, curving around through the Florida Panhandle toward Alabama. He stopped in Ft. Walton Beach, Florida and got a crew cut. No more man-bun. At the Walmart Supercenter, he bought some clothes, toiletries, bungee cords, a sleeping bag and an extra light backpacker's tent. They only had shotgun and .22 cartridges, but it was okay. He regularly carried a Walther .22. He bought two fifty-round boxes of .22 hollow points. His last purchase was two burner phones with prepaid cards. All cash. Everything.

Nate got a submarine sandwich, drink, and chips

combo there and wolfed it down. He stopped at a campground at dark and paid cash. As he lay in the new tent, he did a lot of thinking.

Nate had always thought he could disappear in Mexico. Now it was a reality, he had second thoughts. He was a Cajun from Louisiana. He had a third cousin who lived in the sticks just outside of Baton Rouge. Maybe he should crash there and consider his options. He suspected the cousin had connections for new identification, including a passport. It would be easier to use a false name, open an account and have some serious spending money wired in from Belize there than Mexico. Cheaper too, he thought, with no bribes required.

Before Nick opened his eyes the next morning in the hospital in Orlando, Nate was driving the bike past New Orleans on I-10. He figured he was far enough away from whatever lookout the Florida cops issued to be safe on the interstate now.

He got off at the exit for Baton Rouge and called his cousin on one of the burners. Nate had chosen DC and Los Angeles area codes. Paul did not know either number, so he didn't answer. Nate left a voice mail saying it was him, on the run and he needed a roof for a few days. He emphasized there would be no risk and some cash for Paul in his message.

The burner rang a minute later.

"C'mon," Paul's voice said before hanging up.

Nate grinned to himself. It was the chance of making a buck which did it. Not family ties or anything silly like that.

A half hour later, Nate pulled into the grown-up yard of Paul's bungalow. Bungalow was how his mother called her sister's home, now her nephew's. Nate always thought of it as a snaky shack. He hated snakes. Especially the big damn water moccasins along the bayous of Louisiana, with their dark bodies and white mouths with poisonous fangs.

He could put up with it for a few days.

"Whatcha do, cousin?" his gangly cousin with long black hair asked.

"I was moving some goods. I dropped them off and saw a long line of police vehicles heading toward where I had dropped them. The only way the cops could have known was to have raided my little warehouse, and my people told them. I have to lie low. Maybe you know of somebody around here who does quality ID work. I could use a new driver's license and passport."

"You planning on leaving the country?" Paul asked, his Cajun accent as thick as Nate's used to be.

"I thought about poking around in Mexico. It's probably cheaper than somewhere in the Caribbean. Canada is too cold."

"Why not stay here?" Paul asked.

"I might. I have to cover options though. Which is why I need some new identification. You know somebody?"

"Yep. He'd charge you a couple grand for a driving license and a new passport. Can you cover it?"

"I can. It would leave me low on money though," Nate lied.

"When you want to get with this ole boy?"

"May as well do it soon. Then it would be done, and I wouldn't have to worry about it."

"I'll call him. You sure you got a couple thousand hard cash?" Paul asked again.

Paul called the man who lived near Breaux Bridge.

"He's got some time now. You want to go over and set it up. We can stop and eat and have four or three beers."

Nate could never get used to the transposition of numbers, even as a boy living in the area.

"Okay. Want to take your truck? Or ride double on my bike?"

"My truck. Any double-riding, I'll be driving, and some hot girl will be on back."

"Whatever. Your truck is fine. Let me get the money off my bike."

Nate got the money. He split off two thousand and put it in his new weathered jeans front pocket. He put the corpus of his money in the front of his underwear under the tight jeans. It should be secure there. He pulled the shirttail out on his Western-style Walmart shirt and tucked the Beretta in the small of his back.

"You ready?" Paul asked out of the window of his rusted F-150 as he pulled around the side where the bike was parked.

"I'm ready."

They drove to a small house in Breaux Bridge. Paul introduced the man. He used a camera connected to a computer to take Nate's photo with the new short haircut.

They worked out a cover name and fictitious address the forger had used once before.

"That will be two thousand dollars," he said to Nate, or now Gaston Le Marge of Breaux Bridge, Louisiana.

"How about one thousand now and the other when I pick up and inspect the work?" Nate asked.

"It don't work half and half. It's all or nothing. There's nobody who can do my type of work within two hundred miles from here. Take it or leave it," the forger said.

Nate handed him two thousand in strapped twenties. The man counted every bill.

"I can have them to you by tomorrow night. Say six o'clock?"

"Yeah. Six is okay. I'll see you then," Nate said, and they left.

Paul drove to a Cajun restaurant. Nate forgot how much he loved his native food. The owner's teenage daughter was their server. Nate automatically calculated what she would be worth on the market before mentally cuffing himself upside the head. He was retired now. Trafficking had been good to him. He did not like the fool in the Bradenton area killing the girl, even if she was only his on spec from Miami. It was probably him who caused the downfall of his little kingdom.

The business was getting watched too closely. He had enough money he could access to live well for a long time. Or live okay for the rest of his life. All he needed to use was his account number and PIN. They had no idea what he looked like and couldn't care less. And, with his new identity and look, he could travel or live about anywhere.

If he could survive not getting snake bit for the next two days, he could begin the rest of his life.

They ate and talked. Nate realized his idiot cousin had not gotten a whit smarter in the ten years since he had seen him.

After dinner with five Dixie beers each, they went back to the house and bed.

They picked up the new credentials the following night. Nate was amazed at the quality. He compared the driver's license, or as Paul referred to it, "driving license," with his Florida one. Though the States were different, the quality was equal. He had never had a passport, so he had to assume it was equally good.

They went back to the same restaurant. After a similar dinner and same brand and number of beers, they drove back.

Nate lay in bed staring at the ceiling and planning.

All of a sudden, he heard somebody speaking low. He got up and took the Beretta as he padded silently on bare feet toward the sound of the voice.

He realized it was his cousin speaking as he got closer. He was outside on the porch, which overhung the bayou. Nobody else was there. Paul was talking into his cell phone.

"Yeah. I just don't know what he is wanted for in Florida. I just know it's big. He has a fake ID and all. No! I want five hundred for the information. Okay, let me think for a second. Okay, okay. I will take two hundred cash," he heard Paul say, probably to a cop. So his cousin had turned into a snitch...

Paul got up and threw a cigarette into the bayou. Nate heard an alligator growl. Nearby. Like twenty feet nearby. As Paul walked in the door, Nate thrust a butcher knife from the kitchen into his gut.

He twisted it before pulling the embedded blade in a downward slash to remove it.

His cousin looked down at his eviscerated gut and opened his mouth. No words came out. Nate pushed him over the railing into the bayou. He heard two splashes. One was Paul. The other had to be the alligator.

Nate took a dish towel and wiped the handle of the knife before throwing it far into the swamp.

He didn't have much blood splatter on him, so he washed his hands and put the rest of his clothes and his boots on. He took the dish towel and wiped down every place he thought he might have touched.

Packed, he got on the bike and rode to Breaux Bridge and stopped down the street from the forger's house. He knew the man lived alone from his two visits. The house was at the end of a short street. It was quiet, especially as the hands of the clock moved steadily toward midnight. The forger, and his computer, had information about him and his new identity. Which left Nate no option other than to kill him and remove the hard drive.

It was late and the lights were out in the house. He walked in the total darkness all the way around, looking for an unlocked window or door. He had no luck.

The rear door was not as stout as the front. He tried his folding knife on the lock. No luck there either. He got a new tee shirt from the bike, which he had pulled around back out of sight. He wrapped it around the butt of the Beretta and tapped the rear door pane nearest the lock. It broke quietly but tinkled loudly as the shards hit the floor. He reached in quickly and turned the lock and went in, the Beretta ahead of him.

"Is there somebody there? I've got a gun!" the old forger said, clearly frightened.

Nate went through the kitchen, then the living room where he picked up a throw pillow. He wrapped it around the Beretta and peered in the bedroom door from where the voice had come.

He saw the man move in the bed in the dark and fired the Beretta. He hit the forger and he fell back against the headboard.

Nate tried to fire again. He did not understand a major difference between semiautomatics and revolvers. Push a revolver in a pillow or a belly and press the trigger. It goes bang. Do the same with a semiauto, and you likely push the slide out of the battery and nothing. Or, in the case of wrapping a pillow around it, the hammer falls on the cartridge in the chamber and fires it, but as the slide comes back against the enveloping pillow, it jams. No subsequent shot until the jam is cleared. Which is exactly what Nate had done.

Luckily for him, he had hit the forger in the forehead. The small bullet had penetrated sufficiently to kill him.

Nate turned a low-watt bedside table light on and fiddled with the Beretta until it was no longer jammed.

He looked for the empty casing, just like in the movies, but could not find it. He went to the workroom and turned the light on. Dragging the computer from under the desk, he found where the hard drive was and used his folding knife to unscrew the cover and remove it. Nate put the hard drive in his pocket. He went back to the bedroom and opened the drawer beside the bed. Nothing of interest. He looked on the bed. The man had actually been armed after all.

Nate picked up a Charter Arms Bulldog .44 and put it in his pocket opposite the hard drive. He searched the closet and found a cash box on a shelf in the top. He pried it open and found his two thousand dollars and eight more. He was running out of pockets and underwear space.

He found some rubber gloves in the bathroom and put them on. Nate pulled out drawers and threw stuff around, trying to emulate a bad robbery.

After a while, he gave up and went out the back door his third murder of the week on the books and ten thousand dollars, one bit of hard drive evidence, and a gun which would not jam richer.

It did not appear the muffled shot had aroused any attention among the forger's neighbors. Nate pushed the bike down the edge of the street.

Nobody was on the main road, so he started it and headed toward I-10 West.

He was so pumped from the stress he drove all night.

Pulling into Texas, he found a McDonald's. He had a large black coffee and two Egg McMuffins. A cheap hotel was nearby, and he checked in. The clerk asked for some ID, and he proudly presented his new one. Upon being asked for a credit card, he said, "It's been hacked. Take another ten and give me the key to a room." The clerk was tired after a long night and just wanted to get off his shift in a half hour. He complied.

Nate Boudin, now another name, was asleep almost immediately.

He found three prominent Mexican banks on the Texas side and opened accounts in each with cash deposits under the scrutinized ten-thousand-dollar limit.

He motored across the border with his new identification, claiming a one-week motorcycle ride through Mexico.

His guns ditched beforehand, nobody checked for the money, and he rode, smiling, into oblivion.

7

Early on his second morning at the hospital, Nick was rolled into an operating room once again. The specialist had studied his femur wound x-rays and had a plan in mind.

He had to remove the large bullet. The previous surgery had eliminated the bits of bone fragment. Once the .45 bullet was removed, he would repair and support the femur in such a manner both legs would at least be the same length.

Several hours later, he had an assisting surgeon close. It appeared to be a success to the specialist. Nick Wolf would progress from a walker to crutches, to a cane, to an unassisted limp. It would be something called an antalgic gait. He would never sprint again or climb over tall fences.

After a lot of physical therapy, he would walk. Perhaps even walk quickly. He would always be aware of slight pain, worsening sometimes, but he would lead a close-to-normal non-cop life.

It was the non-cop life part which bothered Nick the

most. He was a cop. He loved being a cop. Now he could not be one.

He did not need counseling. He knew what his problem was. Not being a damn cop.

Kit and Lee visited the afternoon after his second surgery and the discussion with the physician. He told them he would be kicked out of the busy hospital within a day. His transfer would be a rehab center for a week or two, then home with home visits by a physical therapist stretching into the future. He was advised his disability retirement papers were being prepared and what his monthly stipend would be on disability. He was qualified for the HR 128 right to carry a concealed firearm in any state as a retired law enforcement officer, with certain exceptions and it was to be included in his paperwork, he advised his friends.

"What will you do? You cannot live just on the disability income you just quoted," Kit asked.

"I really don't know yet. A lot depends on how quickly and completely my ability to walk returns. My mobility will allow some jobs and keep me out of others," Nick said.

"I am going to become a PI when I retire, which is pretty damn soon," Lee offered.

"Might be hard for you to climb up a ladder to peek in a bedroom window," Kit said.

"I have thought about opening an agency. I have not looked into the details yet, but one thing I know. I will not do any domestic work. I've thought about trying to get retainer work for non-divorce law firms and for insurance companies. I want no part of those 'surveilling the No Tell Motel jobs.'" Lee nodded.

"Nick, you know I was just kidding, right?" Kit asked, now concerned.

"Kit, it does not matter whether you were or not. You have every right as a friend to know what type of work I am or am not interested in."

"Okay. I guess I do."

"All humor aside," Lee began, "why can't you stay as the commander of the task force. You don't have scale tall buildings with a single bound as commander."

"I still have the state deputation for now. What I would not have is the county pay, benefits, or vehicle. I have not heard from the state AG's office yet, but I am not holding my breath for an offer. Let me give you the keys to the Tahoe. My county rifle and shotgun are in it. I'd appreciate it if you would look through it and remove anything which looks like my personal stuff. I'll let my major know to have someone pick it up from you at the task force office."

"Sure. I want you to know, I don't plan on letting this acting commander thing go permanent. I still plan on retiring. I intend to suggest Ms. Ennis over here to replace you."

"Good idea, Lee! Have you spoken to her about it?" Nick asked.

"Hello? Anybody realize the person you are talking about is sitting right here?" she asked.

"Well, then, what do you think of both of us recommending you?" Nick asked.

"I may need to think about whether I want it. I think you should also be thinking about Hank down in Manatee. He's really good," she said.

"Yes. No doubt about it. But why not you, Kit?" Nick asked again.

"I know what we do is crucial. I have a real problem with people who steal and sell children. I am convinced the courts are not stringent enough with them. I cannot take the chance my real ideas might come out. They would surely hurt the task force's good efforts. I just blew a pervert's head off. I should be seeking counseling. Instead, I say to myself, 'the bastard deserved it.' Not exactly the sort of image we want our commanders to portray, is it?"

"Probably not. However, I am not sure you are alone in your line of reasoning. The only reason any of us lament his passing is it removes our best source of information about who and how many other little girls he had at his little love nest," Lee said, "and what happened to them."

"Any plans for a forensic search of his farm? Cadaver dogs? Ground penetrating radar?" Nick asked.

"I need to get back with the sheriff. It's certainly a possibility. At least around the barn, stables and such," Lee said, adding, "I have a meeting back at the HQ. By the way, when you are a bit more mobile, we want to have a little get-together for you during one of our all-hands meetings. Also, your major he says he has some of your stuff to send back with me, and I will have some of your stuff to give to him."

"It's real nice of y'all, but really not necessary."

"Hey, this is your baby. You put it together and almost died for it. Don't deny us the opportunity to say thanks, Nick," Kit said.

"Of course, then. One of you might have to bring me. My crop of family and girlfriends are kind of sparse. You are it," Nick said.

Lee headed out and Kit stayed a moment.

"We already agreed I would pick you up here and drive you to the rehab center tomorrow." He nodded affirmatively.

"Hey, did the shooting team meet in Citrus County?" Nick asked.

"That's what I forgot to tell you! It did. It was a clean shoot for both of us. Lee was probably referring to picking up my shotgun, your rifle, and your Glock 23 tomorrow. I'll get mine from him. He will deliver yours to your major in Tampa along with your badge I gave him from your gun belt."

"Good, Kit. I can rely on my backup snub nose for most of my future needs. When you know how to shoot them, they are amazingly accurate. I have seen a couple of guys make remarkable distance shots on TV with one," Nick said.

"When you are ready, will you give me some pointers? I have a Chief's Special and cannot hit much at all with it. I have your ankle rig and revolver, by the way. I took it off of you during the chopper ride here."

"Sure, I'll be glad to instruct you. And thanks for looking after my revolver."

"Do you have anything to wear to the rehab center in St. Pete? I'd hate to help you into the car with your backless gown on!"

"I have the shirt I wore in and my vest. And the pair of briefs they took off of me. They cut my pants off. I have dirty socks and my boots," he said.

"I'll make a quick stop. What size pants?"

"Thirty-four waist, thirty-two length."

"Got it! When should I come by in the morning?" she asked.

"Perhaps eight? I promise I won't leave without you." He grinned.

She reached over and kissed him sweetly but quickly on the lips.

"We don't work together anymore," she explained.

Though surprised, he looked at her and smiled.

She left and stopped at a shopping center on the way home. It was anchored by a major department store known for its quality. And prices. She bought a pair of chino shorts, some white socks and some medium briefs, though she had seen him in boxers in the motel. Apparently, he was a guy with no particular constant in underwear. She added a sweat suit outfit for wear in the rehab center as well as some tee shirts and gym shorts.

Kit felt happy buying things for a man. It had been a long time. She wished they were closer in age, though it did not seem to bother him.

Kit thought about his poor leg and the weight of his tactical tan boots. She went back in and bought some bedroom slippers. They should work with the thin white socks.

———

She arrived back at the hospital in Orlando at seven thirty, festooned with several bags.

He was propped up in bed with his sheriff's polo shirt on, his dirty underwear and socks beside his boots, belt, and vest.

"Ready?" she asked.

"I have the discharge papers. Just no pants."

"I brought your gun belt in case you didn't have your pants belt. But I see you do. Want me to get a nurse or orderly since you basically only have a shirt on?" she suggested.

"Sure. Anything is fine with me. I am just worried about clearing the cast and protecting the surgery site. Modesty is low on my list as long as you are not concerned."

"I thought about the cast. So, I bought you some shorts. Let me thread your belt onto them."

They muddled through it with a modicum of privacy and Nick was ready for her to go to the nurse's station for the orderly and wheelchair ride to her car.

Once at the unmarked police car, the nurse and orderly helped Nick in. Kit watched and learned.

They had missed the morning rush hour.

"Nick, do you have any personal items at your task force office?" Kit asked.

"Just some photos and plaques on the wall. There's nothing personal in the desk."

Kit called Dawn at reception for the task force.

"I'm coming by in about an hour. Would you take Nick's photos off the wall in his office to give to him? Yes, he is with me, and I'm sure he would like to see you."

Kit exited I-4 and pulled into the task force lot. Dawn saw her both from the surveillance camera and line of sight through the front window. She picked up the box with the photos and walked out.

Nick was sitting there with his window down.

"May I hug you, boss?" she asked.

"I am no longer your boss, so you can do whatever you want."

She leaned in, hugged him and gave him a much longer, wetter kiss than his deputy commander had.

Kit frowned but did not say anything. Sometimes she did not think about how attractive Nick was to anybody but her.

They chatted for a while and Nick noticed Kit getting antsy.

"Dawn, we had better be going. We have a while to drive yet, and Kit still has to drop me and return to Lakeland tonight."

"Quite a kiss there, Nick," Kit said.

"It was! Two today. Two beautiful women. My day for sure. I could really get used to this."

"As soon as you are up enough to date, you really need to look for a girlfriend. Better yet, a wife. Then, you could have Dawn-caliber kisses any old time."

"How about Kit-caliber?" he asked.

"You could have some Kit-caliber kisses in your future as long as you understand Kit does not want a husband or even a permanent boyfriend."

"Sounds like an acceptable arrangement to me," Nick said thoughtfully.

They got back on I-4 West and merged onto I-275 South across the Howard Frankland Bridge over Tampa Bay to St. Petersburg.

———

The rehab center was a long one-story building. There was a covered area with a drop-off at the front door. Kit stopped there, and without thinking, she automatically energized her hidden red and blues. If nothing else, it expedited staff rushing out to greet them. Realizing there was no emergency, only a new patient, they assisted Nick into a wheelchair. Kit parked the car and came in with a bag with his new clothes in it.

Nick was shocked how drained he felt after the trip over from Orlando and stop at the task force HQ. He was taken to a private room, something for which he was most appreciative. He certainly did not want to answer the myriad of questions a cop would be asked by a roommate. Especially a cop who had been shot in a rescue with heavy news coverage.

Nick soon realized the whole fifteen minutes of

fame thing has some truth in it. After one day, the news shifted emphasis to more pedestrian things than the rescues in Orlando and Citrus and the shootings in the latter. He had gone from locally famous to "who?" in a space of a day or two.

He did not mind his obscurity at all. All he cared about was getting on two feet again.

Kit had seen him to the room and helped him unpack. He would go from wheelchair to crutches to walker at the rehab center. Maybe to cane. But for now, he was borderline helpless, unable to even get up and go to the bathroom by himself.

The pain had returned as the hospital drugs wore off. Having worked too many cases of non-addicts becoming dependent on Oxycodone, he was very conscious of the dangers of even prescribed narcotics. When the RN in charge interviewed him as a new patient, he looked her in the face and lied his pain level was a two on the ten scale. It was actually a four or five, he thought. He would just tough it out. It was the ranger way.

Kit sat through the interview. The RN left.

"I guess I better take your gun with me. It's probably not safe to store it here."

As naked as he felt without it, he had to agree.

"You have everything you need?" she asked.

"Yes. I need to pay you for the clothes you bought me," he began.

"My gift to you for all you have done for me. And, for being a special friend."

She bent down and kissed him. He noticed the kisses were getting increasingly better and told her so.

"As they say down on the farm by where I was

raised, 'you ain't seen nothing yet!'" She grinned before leaving him.

Alone again. Like most of my life. Oh, well, at least it's familiar to me. I can handle it. Hell, I have to excel and beat it and the system. And I sure as hell will. Within two months, I'll be walking without support. Nothing, not crutches, walker, or cane. Nothing! Or I'll die trying! he said aloud to no one in particular.

Nick settled in to a month of bland food, boring company, and hard-ass physical therapy. The therapist was a lean, medium-height Black guy.

One day during his first week, the air conditioning went down, always a bad thing to happen in the summer in Florida. The therapy room was hot and muggy.

"You want to put off today's session? The repair people are on the way," William, the therapist, asked.

Nick twisted in his wheelchair and pulled his damp Kit-bought tee shirt off.

"Let's do it!" he said.

William looked closely at him.

"Afghanistan?" he asked.

"Yeah, and several other places where nobody knew we were there."

"I see two bullet holes. AKs, I guess. Some shrapnel scars and one which looks like a knife slash. Am I right?" the therapist asked.

"Dead on. Were you there?"

"Yep. Medic. Iraq and Afghanistan. What branch?"

"Yours, probably. Tan beret."

"Yours alright. You guys are some mean motor scooters."

"And you guys were our heroes, brother. I wouldn't

be here a couple times over if it wasn't for medics and medevacs."

William made a fist, and they bumped fists, standing from the wheelchair. It was an immediate bonding only warriors could understand.

"I'm gonna work a miracle on you. You might think I'm the worst guy since your instructors in ranger school. But it will be worth it. I promise," William said.

"Bring it on. Pain is my friend and walking is my goal."

William told him forty-five minutes later, today's session was tempered by being the first and the heat. Nick pulled the tee shirt back on and grinned at him.

"What time tomorrow, Boss?"

"Oh-nine-hundred. Be here!"

"See you then," Nick said as he used his hands to propel the wheelchair back to his room.

He managed a sponge bath in the chair with a damp washcloth. He figured it made him almost socially acceptable.

William had used the analogy with ranger school. He was not kidding. The next four weeks were rough, and he went to bed tired and sore.

On the last day, he stood up shakily, one hand steadying himself on the walker, and gave William a sincerely grateful hug.

"You did it. Anywhere, anytime you need help, call me. I mean it. I can't sprint yet. Maybe never, but I still have a lot of tricks up my sleeve."

"I've watched you through sweat and pain. I know, man. I will. Your progress in a damn month will always be my professional trophy."

"Steak at Bern's on me. Soon!" Nick said as he

walked with the help of the walker to Kit's car. He'd have to save up for the famous steak house. His disability retirement was one-third what his salary as a detective sergeant had been. But he would do it. He owed William a debt bigger than he could ever repay. Walking.

"Well. Look at you, Mr. Mobility!" Kit greeted him. She had been busy at the task force she was now heading and had not seen him for a couple weeks.

His hiking shorts she had bought him hid the wound in the center of his thigh. The tee shirt she had bought him did not hide the ripple of muscles and hint of a six-pack under the cotton. She stared at him for a minute, ran her tongue over dry lips and opened the car door.

"So. What are we going to find at your apartment? Horribly rotten food in the refrigerator? Musty smell? Do I need to get my PPE out of the trunk?" she said, referring to the sealed bag, paper-like fiber protective suit in her trunk.

"Maybe. I called my resident manager and asked her to go in the first week and throw away all food in the refrigerator. Milk, cheese, vegetables. Even bottled things like salad dressing and mustard. Bread, too. She called back and said I must eat out a lot, because there was not much to throw away. She said she left the AC on seventy-two, so I doubt the apartment will be too musty.

"I have had my bills on autopay for a long time, so nothing should have been turned off. She said she put my mail, mainly gun magazines and junk mail, in a box for me.

"I think I owe her a bottle of wine," he said.

They found the apartment as he predicted. Clean, no smell and no food.

"Well, you were right. There is nothing to eat here.

Even the freezer is bare. How far is the nearest super-market?" Kit asked.

"There's a Publix pretty close," he said of a regional chain founded in her city of Lakeland.

"Feel up to some shopping?" she asked.

"Sure!" He took one crutch and the walker but ended up using the crutch under his left arm.

The shopping took a big chunk out of his greatly diminished monthly income. He would transfer some savings to his checking account to cover bills. He kept his financials to himself. He had saved virtually every-thing, including combat pay in the military and a significant part of his salary from the sheriff's office also.

Money was not a concern yet. Hopefully, he would get his private investigation agency started soon enough and producing so it would never be.

Nick did everything he could do in the way of back-ground work to get his Florida Private Investigation license and agency set up. Better to do the online and telephone things now, while he was still cursed with limited mobility.

There was a big uptick on the mobility front. His home visits with a physical therapist commenced. Her name was Lisa Gillis. She was attractive and funny. She was also even tougher than his former army medic PT. She pushed him as hard as she thought she could. After a week, Lisa began to understand Nick's drive and pushed him harder.

After four months, the insurance lapsed on the visits. He could not afford more at his diminished income. She gave him a written series of exercises, stretches and even recommended a yoga studio that frequently worked with clients with physical challenges.

He tried it for a while then went back to Lisa's list of exercises.

He simply felt out of place at the yoga studio, lots of pretty women notwithstanding.

By the end of a year, he had set up retainer contracts with a number of local law firms and insurance companies. He knew surveillance was going to be involved and it was going to cost money to get set up with the vehicle and equipment he would need.

Nick was not a fan of van trucks, but he knew one would be the best choice for surveillance.

He attended a regional auction that included a number of local government vehicles. There were a number of vans and pickups from local cities and counties. He found a clean one and won the bid. He was able to get a friend to take him back over to the site to pick it up. For now, he parked it at his apartment complex. It was plain white and in good condition with a ladder rack on the roof. The description on the auction booklet said it had been assigned to a property inspector's office, hence the ladder rack yet no construction abuse.

The bigger question was where could he afford an office? He decided to investigate somewhere he could have his office and live. The answer seemed to be a one of the two second-floor apartments over a business on Central Avenue in St. Petersburg.

He visited. Even after a year of physical therapy, the climb up the stairs to the apartment was tough. The other apartment was occupied by an older widow who had been there for some time.

Nick stood there with the building owner, who also operated the business on the first floor. There was a separate, key card-controlled door up to the two apartments. There was only one allotted parking space in a tiny lot behind it, a potential problem to be solved.

"Who's my neighbor?" he asked.

"Her name is Thelma. She is an older lady whose husband died a while back. Just lives there with her kitten. She could not be any nicer. You'll love her!"

Nick had never "loved" anyone he was told he would. This time, he would find it not to be true. She was one of the nicest human beings he would ever know.

There was a large room with a kitchen, bath, and bedroom at the end. As he visualized changes, Nick realized one temporary wall and door could create an office, with a hall going to a restroom and kitchen. Another small wall and door could block off the bedroom. As long as he kept the bath spotless and personal items secured in a cabinet, the bath could serve as a restroom and the fact he lived there would not be obvious to any clients who visited.

The rent was several hundred dollars a month less than his more upscale apartment on the end of Fourth Street North, another bonus. Plus, a significant part would be tax deductible.

The owner agreed on Nick making the wall changes and added an addendum to the lease agreement. It stated upon the end of the lease, Nick would remove the temporary walls and paint the apartment such that the changes would not be visible.

He agreed and wrote a check for the deposit. The building was already zoned for business and residency, so there was one less hurdle.

He had waited until the lease on his current apartment was within a month of running out. The timing was perfect.

There were two remaining things to be done before moving. He had to find nearby secure storage for the van and locate a contractor to do the work for the walls, doors, and painting. A year before, he could have done all the work himself. Now, going to a home improvement store, obtaining drywall and the tracks to put it in, doors, paint and getting it all to the second floor and installing it was beyond his mobility.

The purchase of the van and conversion of the apartment and subsequent moving costs put a large dent in his savings. He thought of it as an investment and did not dwell on it.

The apartment on Fourth Street would not be a problem to move out from. He had rental furniture and big screen television. Pack his clothes, kitchen items, and toothbrush, and he'd be done. He doubted he would need a truck. He could just use the van.

Nick drove back to Fourth Street happy with the steps he had just taken. He had decided to sell his two-year-old Mustang GT outright and just use the van for a while. He would use a large national dealership which dealt in newer used vehicles and tended to pay more for the cars they bought outright than new car dealership.

He drove to it the next day with his loan information. By doubling payments, he had gone a long way toward paying it off in just two years. He listened quietly as the car buyer presented the net purchase deal. It compared favorably to the online value he had determined earlier, and he accepted.

He took an Uber and a large check home to his apartment. He immediately took the van to his bank and deposited it, taking a thousand dollars cash for work on the van and a deposit on the construction. He walked over to the resident manager's office and reported his intent to not renew his lease. The thousand dollar plus deposit return would help his business setup also.

Lee called and told Nick he had submitted his retirement papers and Kit had been named permanent commander of the west task force. Nick was surprised she had not called him and shared her news since his support had virtually guaranteed her being named. He had noticed a decline in calls from her. Most of their conversations were generated by him. Nick chalked it off to her being busy supervising the task force and dealing with complex cases. They lived far enough away that dating on a regular basis would have been beyond inconvenient anyway.

Nick drove the van over to his new office and met the installer from the phone company. He needed a landline phone. Once installed, he wrote the new number down. On the way back to the apartment on Fourth Street, he would stop by an office supply store and order business cards with the name of the firm, address and telephone number.

Having graduated to a cane, he went next door to introduce himself to Thelma. She was older than his long dead mother would have been now but was motherly and kind in a manner he had never known. She offered him coffee, something he almost never refused.

They exchanged life stories while her little yellow kitten pounced on imaginary pieces of dust. He was young enough that he could not climb into Nick's lap, so he gave him a lift up.

The cat, Finn, immediately looked at him with emerald eyes and must have instinctively trusted Nick. He made three circles in Nick's lap and went to sleep.

Nick could not tell whether he was snoring or purring as the big man stoked his tiny head with two fingers.

"Nick, I think you have found a new friend!" Thelma said.

"No, Thelma, I have found two new friends."

They visited for a while and he handed the sleeping kitten back to Thelma who positioned him on her lap, still asleep.

"I'll show myself out so you don't have to disturb the kitten. I will see you in a couple days when I move in permanently," he said to his neighbor before leaving.

The stairs from street level to the second floor would be good exercise for him. He got in the van and stopped to order his business cards before driving to a home improvement store on Twenty-Second Avenue North.

He had measurements with him and had a countertop cut to order, bought supports for it, several aluminum ladders, and a steel storage chest. His last stop was a marine store where he bought binoculars, plastic corners to hold ice chests down on boats and a porta-potty. With very little work with an electric drill, he would have the countertop, steel storage chest, cooler, and porta-potty installed in his surveillance van.

Nick ordered a swiveling surveillance camera, a pod for it to be mounted in and a screen and controller from Amazon. He also found small high-security padlocks online and bought those to lock the locker inside the van and to lock the ladders on the roof rack.

Once he had some revenue flowing, he would order magnetic plastic signboards for the van showing different plausible businesses to explain why the van might be parked on a street. For cover, he would use his landline number for the signboards. Nick hoped revenue would begin shortly to cover the plausible deniability of his parked van.

He spent the first half of the next day installing the Formica counter and the four-corner supports for the chest, cooler, and porta-potty.

He would put the ladders on the top for creditability and chain them down later in the day.

Within two days, he would have his cameras in hand and installed.

The last purchase was a used Mossberg Shockwave short shotgun. He ordered the accessory online to allow him to shoot little one and three-quarter inch buckshot, allowing greater capacity and more than adequate power for short-range use. It would fit in the steel case with his binoculars, camera, and the Mac laptop he already had. Just a bit of protective foam and he would be done. After his first insurance fraud case, he realized a video camera with a telescopic lens and date and time imprint was as necessary as any other bit of equipment he had.

The last item for his inventory was a magnetic tracker to put on subject vehicles. While there were some court cases about whether the police could use them, he decided to risk it. It came with a screen and mobile mount for the dash of a vehicle, which was six by eight inches. He mounted it in the van.

He went to an upscale used furniture store and chose office furniture, a recliner, bed, bedside table, chest of drawers, some lamps from there and a mattress from another store. He set up delivery of all items and ordered a large flat-screen television online.

Nick was out of the apartment several days later and settled into the new place with the office.

Nick received a phone call that night in the office.

All the doors were open, so he heard it from the bedroom.

"Aaron Investigations and Threat Mitigations," he answered.

"Hi. I don't know if you are the right person to call or who I should call," a female said, obviously in distress and searching for words.

"This is Nick Wolf. I'm the owner. Tell me a little about your situation. But give me your name so I'll know who I am talking with."

"My name is Pamela Lambert. I go by Pam. I live in Gulfport. I have an ex-boyfriend who keeps harassing me. Now, he says he's gonna kill me if we don't get back together."

"Gulfport has a small but very good police department. Have you called them?" he asked.

"Yes, they sent someone over. She recommended I get a restraining order against him."

"Did you get one, Pam?"

"No, I have mixed emotions about them. They don't protect you, they just give the police another charge to place if the jerk kills you," she said.

"Well...what you said is partially true. They don't protect you and they do give another charge. But they also give the police a reason to come quickly and to place the person under arrest even if they don't harm you at all. I'd recommend you get one for those reasons at least," Nick said.

"I am so scared I took a week off from work. I am locked in the house and would be afraid to leave to go to the courthouse and get one. Could you take me?" she asked.

"Let me ask you some other questions first. What is this guy's name and where does he live?"

"His name is Peter Olson, and he lives just over the line in St. Pete."

"What does he do for a living?"

"He is an accountant. A CPA in St. Petersburg," she said, then named the firm.

"Do you know if he has a gun?" Nick asked.

"We never talked about it. I don't know."

"Does he have a key to your house?"

"Yes. But I keep the chains hooked when I'm home."

"Which also means he could get in and be waiting for you."

"I guess."

"Pam, you need to do some immediate things to harden yourself as a target. First, you need to have a locksmith change the locks with deadbolts as soon as possible. You should keep outside lights on front and back and if you don't have them, have floodlights installed front and back. They can be on motion detectors so they don't shine all the time.

"How are your finances? Is this something you afford to do right away?"

"They are okay. I'm a gynecologist. I live pretty modestly, so money is not a problem."

"Excellent."

"Do you do bodyguard work?" she asked.

"Yes, it falls within the scope of Threat Mitigation."

"Can you come over tonight? Now I know I should have deadbolts, or at least locks he does not have a key to, and I need more lights. I am terrified!"

Nick looked at his watch. Ten o'clock. He was beat from his move prep work today.

"Let me explain my fees." He did, and she accepted them without question, including a retainer check upon arrival.

"My home and office are really close to you. I can be there in less than fifteen minutes. I will bring my white surveillance van and call you on this number when I arrive. Is after-hours street parking allowed in your neighborhood? It is? Good. I will not park directly in front of your house, but more in front of a neighbor's. I'll see you shortly."

He heard a sigh of relief, and she hung up. Nick had absolutely decided to not accept domestic investigations. This was close but closer to an executive protection and security consulting case. He put on khaki slacks and a button-up dark-blue short-sleeve shirt. He wore the snub nose S&W 442 revolver just behind his right hip. The shirt covered it fine.

Taking his cane, he walked down to the van in the rear parking space allotted to him and drove to Gulfport. It was a small city pushed up against St. Petersburg and Boca Ciega Bay, which went out into Tampa Bay, which in turn, emptied into the Gulf of Mexico.

He found her house. It was a charming craftsman-type cottage on a quiet street. Not ostentatious at all, he still thought its value would shock most folks not familiar with the area. It had a one-car garage facing the alley he had driven down first. Her garage entry and rear yard were as dark as a moonless and starless night at sea. As he pulled up to the curb just down from her property line, he saw one weak porch light at her front door.

He dialed Gulfport Police on their non-emergency line.

"Hi, this is Nick Wolf. I am a retired local detective sergeant who is now a PI. My client lives in Gulfport. You have counseled her on dealing with a threatening ex-boyfriend. He's been acting up and I am going to be in or in front of her house until she gets some lock changes and a restraining order. She is Dr. Pam Lambert."

"Yes, I dispatched the call to send someone over to talk with her the other night. What kind of vehicle will be parked there?" the dispatcher said.

"It's a white Dodge surveillance van. Looks like a work truck with ladders on top. It's registered to my firm if you want to run the plates."

"I'm sure we will. Will you be in the van or inside?"

"Both. I just arrived and need to go in and assess the immediacy of the threat. You have my number. Please watch for it, okay?" Nick said.

"Will do. Have a good night, sir."

Nick called Dr. Lambert and told her what he was wearing and that he was approaching her front door. She had a peephole and opened it as he raised his hand to knock.

"Thank you so very much for coming at such short notice, Mr. Wolf," she said, looking down at his cane.

"I'm still recovering from the two gunshots which got me retired. Don't worry. I am capable of handling anything which might be thrown at us tonight or on the way to the courthouse tomorrow."

"Come in, I'm pretty wired, so I am drinking some ginger lemon tea. No caffeine. Would you like some?" she asked, and he nodded he would.

"Let me close the curtains and not give Peter anything to see. Also, we'll see if the locksmith can install one of those doorbells with a camera and screen for you to see who is there. Or it can go to your smartphone. That prevents people from putting their eye up to a peephole and getting shot," Nick said.

"You don't pull any punches, do you?" she asked.

"You are not paying me to withhold information which might keep you alive."

"No, I guess I'm not."

They spoke at length about Peter Olson over tea. His description, including a photo of which Nick took a smartphone picture. He put it in Notes, adding his written notes there later.

He learned about his client including where and how she had met Olson and when it went wrong.

"Are you able to stay here and protect me tonight?" she asked.

"I can. Show me around the house so I can look for points of vulnerability. These houses were built in an era where nobody bothered locking their doors."

She took him on a tour. Along the way, he flipped on the back door light. It was weaker than the dull yellow one on the front. The door chains were worthless. She had a revolver that had belonged to her father. It was a four-inch Colt Official Police which was at least seventy years old. Actually, he thought it was a great choice for a non-shooter. It had old round-nose lead bullets. Cops used to call them "Widowmakers" when they had to carry them because they made police wives widows. They were not dependable stoppers. He slipped out to the van and got her six 125-grain hollow points like he used in his snub nose. Nick then gave her a really basic training session on when to use and when not to use, how to hold, and where to aim.

"I would hate to have to shoot someone. It's against my oath," she said.

"I don't think so, Pam. Isn't 'do no harm,' about patients? I don't think it means attackers."

She thought about his words for a second, then agreed she was overthinking.

"I'll make up the spare bedroom for you," she offered.

"No, I think just a pillow and blanket for your sofa. It would be easier to get into action from there, if need be."

"Won't you be uncomfortable?" she asked.

"I have been uncomfortable every night since I was shot," he admitted.

"Where were you shot?"

"One to the center of my femur. One which clipped my femoral artery."

"How did you survive the arterial shot?" she asked.

"As I fell, I pulled a QuikClot packet and a tourniquet out of my pocket before I passed out. Which was almost immediately. My partner killed the person who shot me. A SWAT operator was there within seconds and applied the tourniquet. He or my partner put the coagulant on my leg. A SWAT medic was there within minutes. They medevac'd me to the trauma center in Orlando in a sheriff's helo."

"May I see your wounds? I am a physician, though I have not seen a bullet wound since I was an intern."

"Sure," he said, pulling up his khakis. She kneeled and examined the wound in the middle of his thigh.

"Do you have a synthetic or stainless brace inside supporting the femur under the skin?" she asked, and he nodded.

She asked about the bullet wound in his groin. He pointed at the spot.

"Wow. A half an inch over, and I am not sure you would have survived, fast tourniquet or not."

"I guess it was not my time. My regret is we had to kill the suspect. He had just purchased two teenage girls from a human trafficker. We freed them and a warehouse full of others, but we are pretty sure the dead guy had bought other girls. If we could have kept him alive for questioning, we may have gotten information from him on their whereabouts. Cadaver dogs and ground penetrating radar from the University of Florida did not indicate any buried remains. The case is still open, though moving into cold case status," Nick said.

"This is all coming back to me from the news a year or so ago. You are the guy who ran the task force! You got some awards for heroism and meritorious service."

"Yep. And a disability equal to one-third of my former salary."

"Sad. Back to a doctor question again. What's your mobility situation and its prognosis now, a year later?"

"Improving. I'll probably need a cane for another six months. I will have an antalgic gait-type limp for the rest of my life. No sprinting, no squats, no bounding over fences."

"You seem to have come a long way for just a year," she said.

"I've had two spectacular PTs along the way."

"Are you sure you don't want a real bed? I believe it would be far better for your leg."

"You are paying for my full service. I would be shorting you if I did not stay in the place where I could protect you the best, Pam," he said.

"And, if you wake up with your leg really stiff and Peter arrives in the early morning, you may be at a disadvantage," she said seriously, convincing him she was right.

"You are probably right, Doc. Listen, I have been around guns all my life. You may not have been. Hold off on using the Colt. Make sure you know who your target is and what the background is, okay?" he asked.

"Absolutely. Any shooting to be done, I will let you do it, unless the circumstances have gone straight to hell!"

"Thanks. Put my number into your cell phone so you can text me immediately if you hear something. I will have my phone on vibrate only, so it won't alarm an intruder if you text me."

"What's our plan for tomorrow?"

"A couple things. First, I will take you to the clerk of the courts, and you will apply for a protection order. Probably a dating one since you and Peter have not been in a domiciled-type situation. It may be a temporary one with the ultimate time protection being set before the judge in Peter's presence."

"A protection order is a restraining order, right?" Pam asked.

"Right."

"We should then contact a locksmith and get some deadbolts installed and one of those video doorbells. And a handyman to install motion detector floodlights on each corner of your house. One thing I can do is toughen your exterior doors by replacing the screws on the hinge plates with ones which are much longer. It will make them a lot harder to kick in."

"That's pretty cool!"

"Last, like we talked about during your tour, we need for you to have a home security alarm system installed with warning signs outside."

"Okay. Will you be able to stay here with me until all this is done?" she asked.

"I will try. It should not be too long to have it done."

She smiled and tried to stifle a sigh of relief.

"This will be the first good night's sleep I have gotten

for a week or two. You want the bathroom first?" she asked.

"No, you go ahead. Since we will hopefully change the locks tomorrow, do you have an extra key so I can lock you in if I have to go outside quickly?" She did and gave it to him.

"Let me make up the bed in the spare bedroom with clean sheets and a blanket. I keep the AC dialed down to the Arctic setting," she said.

"I'll make up the bed while you are getting ready."

"You don't mind?"

"Lifelong bachelor and former military. I'm used to it," he responded as she led him to the linen closet.

The shower situation for an old house with one bathroom worked well. She was apparently a night shower person while he showered early each morning.

Nick made up the bed. She was right about the Arctic setting on the thermostat. It was freezing inside, especially compared to the humid Florida night outside.

He was sitting in the living room making notes when she came in. She was wearing boring-looking silk pajamas and was barefooted. Her hair was wet.

Nick thought she was one hot doc, but quickly shelved the thought. *Professionalism! This is a job, not the date you have not had for a year and a half, fool!* He thought.

"Sleep well, Pam. Call or text me if you need me or hear something."

She smiled and nodded her head. She turned and walked away with Nick trying to keep professional thoughts uppermost. He failed. Her glide was too graceful.

He took a tee shirt and running shorts out of his bag and his Dopp kit. He took the latter into the bathroom to brush his teeth. Back in the bedroom, he changed into the shirt and shorts. He raised his window slightly both to hear and to keep from freezing and went to bed.

At three in the morning, he heard a car slowly passing the house and it turned around and slowly drove by again. It could be a patrol car based on his call to the Gulfport Police earlier to advise of his parked van and presence.

He got up to check. There was a light-colored foreign sedan parked across the street. It could be a larger-class Audi. The same brand Peter Olson has. He saw someone in it but could not clearly see any sort of description, male or female.

He walked to Pam's room and called her softly. She awoke with the expected degree of alarm.

"Pam, it's Nick. I want you to look at a car that just parked across the street to see if you can identify it. We have to be circumspect. Lights out, careful with the shades and blinds, okay?" he asked. She nodded.

They crept to the front side window and Nick opened it ever so slightly.

Pam held onto him and peered around and out.

"It looks like Peter's, but I cannot be absolutely sure."

"Okay. Here's what I want you to do. Call 9-1-1. They will switch you to the Gulfport Police once you give the situation and your address. Remind them about your stalker and tell them you are terrified because of the car which is parked across the street. Tell them it is occupied and does not belong to any neighbor as far as you know."

She responded perfectly and they waited for something to happen.

Within a few minutes, two Gulfport units pulled up

and blocked the car. They had the driver get out. Pam recognized Peter from the police car's lights.

"It's him! That sonofabitch! I bet he is soiling his pants!" she said almost gleefully.

Nick was not so gleeful. Him showing up to sit in front of her house at three in the morning showed two of the three questions one sought to determine the threat a person represents. History, intent, and capability. Tonight showed intent and capability. He was here. If he came again, history would be covered, and he would be a full-scale threat. As far as Nick was concerned, he earned the dubious distinction with just the latter two tonight. This was not imagination. He was a known threat now.

The officers spoke with Peter Olson for fifteen minutes. They wrote down information and then released him.

"Now he's gone, they will probably check in with you. Grab a robe quickly," he said.

Before the two officers could get to the front door, she had the door unlocked and was opening it.

They identified themselves and verified who the person in the car was. They checked him for wants and warrants and noted he did not have a protection order on his record.

"I have been too afraid to leave the house since his last phone call. Mr. Wolf will take me in the morning."

"Are you the PI?"

"Yes. Nick Wolf. I saw the car cruising and got Dr. Lambert to call 9-1-1 while I observed them. Thanks for arriving so quickly, gentlemen."

"We did not find any weapons when we patted him down. He is an accountant. Kinda big, but he did not look too dangerous. He said he did not own any firearms. Is it true, doctor?"

"We never discussed the subject. I really have no idea," Pam said truthfully.

One of the officers was watching Nick closely.

"You are the task force commander who freed all those kids but got shot, aren't you?"

"Freeing almost fifty kids was a group effort. The getting shot part was real personal. And it sucked," Nick said.

"I bet! Didn't you kill the guy who had the kids?"

"I softened him up so he released the kids. My partner finished him."

"Couldn't have happened to a nicer guy, huh?" the older officer said.

"He sure would not have been on my Christmas card list if he had survived," Nick said.

"Y'all call if this Olson guy comes back. And get the protection order. Then we can lock him up when he comes back."

"Thanks, gentlemen. Be safe!" Nick said.

"Yes, thank you so much," Pam added.

They left, and Nick relocked the door. He looked at Pam. She was now stricken with the weight of what had occurred. Olson had come to stalk her in the early morning. Was he planning to come in? This added reality to her fears. She stood there and began to shake.

Nick looked her in the eye and nodded his head almost imperceptibly. She flew into his arms and buried her head into his tee shirt. As he held her tightly, she soaked it with tears. After a while, he guided her back to her bed, leaning on her as much as she was on him.

He covered her up and said softly, "Don't worry. I'm here. You will be safe. I am your protector."

She smiled, and he brushed her hair back and turned the light off.

He thought she had every right to be scared. Their actions over the next few days should somewhat mitigate her fears. But they would not go away until she was off Peter Olson's mind. Which could take a long time.

Most of the planned installations were completed, amazingly to both, the following day. Nick took her to the courthouse and a temporary restraining order was issued. He drove but they used her Acura in case evasive driving was necessary, which proved to not be the case.

"What a day! The alarm folks promise they will be here the day after tomorrow. Do you want me to stay over until then? It might be prudent," Nick said.

"How about your other business?" she asked.

"I can monitor the phones for new business or existing case questions from anywhere with a cell signal. A lot of what I am doing now is prep work on suspects before I actually go back into the field. If you don't care about me using your Wi-Fi, I can do it from here."

"If you don't mind a couple more days, it would make me feel better, Nick."

"Not a problem, Pam. How about a Cuban dinner? On me," Nick offered.

Pam accepted.

"If you don't mind being seen in a work van, I'd like to drive it for two reasons. Mixing up the vehicles is not a bad idea to confuse Peter if he is watching. And second, it needs to be run after sitting a couple of days."

"It's fine with me, Nick. I drove my father's van on

deliveries of eggs from one of his many agricultural endeavors. I was sixteen, so driving anything was a thrill."

He laughed with her. "I doubt this will be a thrill."

He changed into a fresh fishing shirt with Velcro pockets and caped back with mesh for air underneath. She put on a very non-doctor-like crop top and shorts with sandals. This was a new look, he thought, and one he liked. A lot. He wondered if it was deliberate, or this was just how she dressed for an informal dinner.

Nick did his surveillance detection procedures as they locked the house and used the rear door for egress. It gave him time to look over the area across the street, where there were some trees in the yard before bursting out upon the area like they would have done if they had come out the front door.

It appeared all was clear. He showed her around the van and its features, such as the tilt and pan roof camera, the shotgun locker, and some of the camera equipment he had added recently. They went back to the front and began the twenty-minute drive to the restaurant.

Pam could order French food in dialect, but Nick had to assist with the Cuban. Though his ancestry appearance was Celtic, his long-term foster parents were Cuban. Sometimes, he felt more Cuban than anything else. His Spanish was flawless Castilian.

Nick got the impression Pam felt like the dinner was a date. It felt like one to Nick also, which he regretted. It was business. Maybe more after the contract was fulfilled and the Peter Olson situation had been mitigated, but not now.

He noticed she was a bit less conservative in her choice of sleeping apparel after the dinner as well has how quickly she donned it and how long he was exposed to it. He exercised his greatest degree of restraint since Kit determined to not allow their attraction to blossom further until a time when it would not impact his ability to respond quickly and definitively if an attack occurred.

They went to bed after he did a security walk-through inside and out. He made sure the new dead-bolts were locked and verified the motion detector lights were working during his walk.

The thermostat was still set on sub-Arctic. He pulled on a tee shirt with his boxers and slipped the tactical flash and revolver under his pillow.

The home security alarms were installed the following day. Once they were tested and he was confident, Nick told Pam to keep the alarm fob beside her at night to summon the police via the panic alarm. She could use it pulling into the yard and garage, also, he told her.

"Does this mean I lose my roomie?" Pam asked.

"Not necessarily. I was thinking you should go out tonight in your car. I will tail you for security. On the way back, slow down while I check the neighborhood. I will pull into your garage with the van and close the door. Then, I will call you. Pull up out front and leave the car parked near the garage.

"Peter, if he comes by later, will think, for whatever reason, you just parked out front. He will see the white van is gone. Though there are obvious alarm signs hammered into your yard near the doors signifying the name of the alarm company, he still may try something. So, he'll have a bit of a surprise if he does."

"I like the idea. I don't particularly want him hurt... just stopped. An arrest will impact the career he holds so dear," Pam said. "Besides, I need to go back to work and resume my normal life on Monday. I'd rather he try something stupid while you are here!"

"Me, too."

Nick escorted her grocery shopping and to an outlet mall for a new suitcase. She told him she had planned a cruise out of the Port of Tampa the following month.

Pam fixed a really good dinner for them upon their return home. They waited until well after dark for the driving ruse to begin.

She pulled her car out of the garage and drove slowly down the street toward a pre-determined shopping mall. Nick went out to the van and followed her.

They communicated by cell phone. He indicated to give him five minutes to ride the neighborhood and look for a sign of Peter Olson. The only thing which worried him was a blue mid-size down the street from her house. It had Hertz stickers on the windshield but appeared to be unoccupied.

Nick pulled into the garage and closed the power door from the outside with the garage door opener. He went as surreptitiously as possible into the house and disarmed the alarm. He called her to come down the street and park in front. He watched at the window as she parked, came up the walk with a non-descript bag, unlocked the door, and came in. Nick had already cleared the house.

"I have already checked the house, though I am pretty sure he does not have the skill to bypass the alarm system, Pam," Nick said.

"There was a blue Hertz rental parked a few houses down. It probably is a guest of the homeowner or something. I passed slowly but did not see anyone in it. I doubt it's Peter, but we cannot assume anything," he continued.

"I will keep Daddy's .38 close by. Always," she said.

"Good. Just be sure of your target."

"Okay, I promise not to shoot you."

"Even better." He grinned.

They sat around and chatted for a while. Nick had already convinced her of the benefits of British television, and they watched one show before turning in.

"Is a hug permissible on our last night together?" Pam asked.

"Oh, I think so. After all this is over, there might be more opportunities if you'd like," he said.

"I'd like," she said as she gave him a long and non-brotherly hug.

A noise awakened Nick several hours after midnight, more by his estimation than his watch. He listened and heard it again. It was a tapping noise. He walked barefoot, gun and tactical flashlight in hand, to Pam's room.

He called to her in his softest voice, knowing a low spoken word was less likely to be overheard than a whispered one.

She awakened immediately and with full senses. Probably a holdover from her hospital intern days, he thought.

Pam slipped out of bed nude and pulled on a dressing gown. She retrieved the Colt and her flashlight and followed him. The intermittent taps were at the front window. It was as if someone was throwing pebbles against it, like lovers or kids in a movie, to gain attention from within.

"My assessment is he thinks you are alone. He knows he can't bypass the alarm and thinks he can trick you into doing it. It's a stupid ploy for a bright guy.

Which indicates to me he's in panic mode. Which makes him dangerous."

"Should we call the police?" Pam asked.

"Yes, but only when I tell you," Nick said as she followed him into the guest room, where he put on pants and boat shoes and got his cane and a pair of handcuffs.

"If you disarm the alarm system, I will slip out the back door and circle around. If I capture him or he runs for the rental car, I will yell for you to call 9-1-1."

"Okay," she said, getting her cell phone from the nightstand on the way past.

The noise was from the front, and she usually used the rear door. So the alarm panel was close to it in the back.

She disarmed, and he slipped out of the door. She relocked it as he instructed.

High-lumen tactical light still extinguished, Nick holstered his gun. He knew he could draw in less than half a second if needed. He had proven that at the horse farm outside of Inverness.

Cane in the left hand and light in the right, he crept around the house. From the street right, he did not see anyone, so he went back around in a counterclockwise direction.

Nick saw a man crouching behind a bush at the corner of the house.

He walked silently on the dewy grass in his boat mocs. He aimed the flash in the dark. Ready, he turned it on and blinded the man behind the bush.

The man froze long enough for Nick to get to him and swing the cane hard to his leg at the side of his knee. The man, who he now identified as Peter Olson, collapsed onto his right leg. The next blow was diagonally between the shoulders, and he went down.

Though hurt and surprised, Olson scrambled on all fours to Nick and tripped him. He straddled the ex-detective and cocked his right arm for a long punch.

Nick's short jab to his jaw stopped the roundhouse Olson had planned. His head flew back, and the next punch was in his throat. It was carefully done to hurt and impair but not crush Olson's windpipe and his ability to breathe.

Nick shoved both open hands hard against his adversary's chest, knocking him off. Also on all fours, or perhaps on all threes, Nick got to the stunned Olson and handcuffed him from behind. He had used the cane to leverage himself to his feet.

"Pam, call 9-1-1. I have Olson and have him secured. Tell the Gulfport PD he is in custody and get out your restraint order."

By the time Nick had the stumbling Olson on the front sidewalk, Pam was by his side berating her ex-boyfriend and two patrol cars were pulling to the curb.

Nick had his right hand holding Olson's left in a "come along" hold he could turn very painful in an instant. The other side was leaning against his cane. His left leg had twisted in the fray and hurt like hell.

Though the officers were aware of the retraining or protection order, Pam showed them the paperwork.

An officer took a report on the circumstances, about being lured out and the scuffle. Both signed the report.

The officers charged Olson with violation of a protection order and swapped Nick's handcuffs for one of the officers'. He would be out before daylight, but Olson had an arrest permanently on his record. One which could possibly threaten his employment and professional status. And his ability to own a firearm.

Would any of these things prohibit him from coming back after Pam again, she later asked Nick. He replied they would not. It depended on whether he got over his obsession and wanted to maintain his job status or was just crazy when it came to her.

Both hoped for the former.

———

Several weeks later, Nick's household grew. By one yellow cat. Thelma decided to move in with her daughter, who was allergic to cats. Finn, almost his already, moved in permanently. Nick found him to be the distinguished gentleman of cats.

8

Current day

Nick had dated Pam for a year until she was offered a partnership in a gynecological practice in affluent Naples, Florida. They parted best of friends.

About that time, the grant for the human trafficking task forces ran out. The detectives at both I-4 corridor task forces returned to their respective agencies. The problem did not go away; just the money.

Kit returned as a lieutenant, on the way to her unsaid goal of chief.

In the ensuing three years, Nick's PI practice grew substantially. His computations indicated ninety percent of his revenue came from ten law and insurance firms. The other ten percent came from security consulting and the rare executive protection job.

Unlike television and movies, where a detective or PI had some dramatic, all-encompassing case, he worked multiple cases at once as other real-life detectives and PIs did worldwide.

He had not had to draw his gun, now a Glock 19 backed up with a Sig 365, once. However, Nick remembered how quickly things went to hell. He never went anywhere without one or both pistols close at hand. He was in a dangerous business in a dangerous world, the raw side of which he had looked in the face many times during both his military and law enforcement careers.

Nick had managed to retire his cane shortly after the Dr. Pam Lambert case. A year later, his business had grown sufficiently to finance a personal vehicle once again.

He bought a one-year-old orange Jeep Rubicon two-door with a convertible top and thirty-three-inch tires. He loved it, though he had to struggle to climb in until very recently. It already came with thousands of dollars' worth of off-road upgrades. He added steel bumpers, LED lights all the way around, and kept a fire extinguisher, trauma first aid kit, and web tow rope inside at all times. He also added a lockbox in lieu of the console compartment. There were times he could not take a weapon inside somewhere, such as an airport, post office, or courtroom. The very open Jeep was no place to leave a gun unless one had a vault bolted in.

It had been three days since he had met and worked with tall Trooper Lola Caldwell. Her number on the back of her official Florida Highway Patrol business card and mention of burgers was not even a veiled suggestion.

Nick picked up his cell phone and called her.

"Hey, can't talk. In the middle of a three-car accident investigation on US-19," she answered.

"No problem! Call about that burger when you can. Be safe!" he said, and they disconnected.

Lola called him an hour later.

"What a mess! An old lady, a drunk, and a big mouth. I ended up arresting the drunk and threatening bodily harm on the big mouth. I am afraid I might have to deal with him again soon.

"If you are in a burger and cold beer mood, so am I," she said. "I am three miles from home and need to get out of this sweaty vest and uniform. I can meet you somewhere or you can come by here. I live around Twenty-Second Avenue North and Sixtieth Street North in St. Pete."

"You are not very far from me. I'll pick you up. Say where and when," Nick said, and she gave him the address for an hour and a half hence.

The hour and a half gave him time to shower, change into clean cargo shorts and an Under Armour pullover. He took the remaining time to prepare several invoices for cases closed, one with a law firm, two others with insurance companies.

If I get any new insurance or law retainers, I am going to have to add an investigator and maybe an admin person. Several will put my business into a whole different sphere. I will have the added costs of salaries, benefits, workman's comp, different tax situation, and time away from what I like—investigating. Expanding your business sounds great until you look at the real effects. Maybe if the admin load grows, I should look at a casual employee. A part-timer a couple days a week.

*I'm not getting rich, but I am making more than enough to do and buy everything I really need or want. As my revenue and savings grow, maybe buying a building as a headquarters with living space in it would be a good investment and tax benefit...*he thought. He would give the subject more thought. But he had a lady trooper to think about right now.

He climbed into the Rubicon with increasing ease and headed out Central to Sixtieth Street North and hung a right.

Lola had her own house—a typical Florida stucco ranch on a concrete slab. Hers was painted yellow, probably the most popular color for Sunshine State stuccos. The yard was well-kept but not a landscaper's delight. His would be the same if the tables were turned.

He saw a red VW GTI in the drive next to the black and yellow FHP Charger.

He pulled in and rang the doorbell. Lola answered it with a crop top and Daisy Duke cutoff jeans. Very cutoff. Her hair was wet and she was drying it with a towel.

"I had a fender bender to write up on the way home from the three-car circus," she explained.

"I'm early. Take your time." He sat down.

He heard a hair dryer. Lola came out soon, her raven hair blown out wild. It was a super-hot look, he thought and told her so.

"Why thank you, sir!" She looked at him.

Lord, she has a killer smile, he thought.

"You live alone. Do you have a pet or anything?" she asked.

"I inherited a cat named Finn from a wonderful older lady next door when she moved away to live with her daughter."

"Is Finn still with you?"

"He is. He's one perfect little guy. We talk all the time. He gives good advice, too!"

"On your love life?" she asked.

"No, on relevant subjects, like whether to expand the business. I actually have no love life."

"By choice, Nick?" she asked with a sympathetic,

almost worried look on her face. He had been right. She was so gorgeous in her sparse civvies.

"Hell no. Your and my career choice limits the number of possible mates. Then, I got shot and became somewhat of an invalid. Strike two. I'm walking better now and think I am ready to actually date.

"I don't mind being a test drive..." she said, hesitating.

"Lola, you would be the top prize. Never a test drive." She flashed the smile again, and he knew all was going to be well with them.

They decided on a distant place famous for burgers and really cold beer. It was eighteen miles away. Across the Howard Frankland Bridge, past the Tampa Airport and in a suburban area of the city.

It was not the place so much as the glorious day to drive across Tampa Bay, wind blowing in the open-top Jeep and chatting. Making one another laugh.

They arrived and ordered. Halfway through, Nick's phone rang. He looked at it and saw the number was blocked on his caller ID. Lola saw him get a puzzled look on his face. He knew the irritating auto warranty calls were spoofed. This smelled like government.

"This is odd, Lola. I've got to get it."

"Aaron Investigations and Threat Mitigation, this is Nick Wolf."

"Nick, I don't know if you remember me from your days with the sheriff's department. This is Judge Andrew Mabry of the Thirteenth Circuit."

"Yessir. I remember you. You were or are Chief Judge. I testified in a number of cases before you on people I arrested as a detective," Nick said.

"Exactly. Listen. I need your help and need it right now. How quickly can you get to my office in Tampa?"

"I am already in Tampa, sir. I have my off-duty trooper friend Lola with me."

"She can come. This is not a secret, just urgent. Can you come now?"

Lola heard the conversation due to the stressed, loud voice of the judge and nodded her head up and down.

"We are leaving now. Can I reach you on this number when we arrive and gun down?" Nick asked.

"Yes, but don't bother gunning down. I will clear you and the trooper through."

"See you in ten minutes, Judge. We are dressed very informally."

"Irrelevant. Call when you arrive and ID yourselves to the bailiffs." He hung up.

Nick motioned to the server and laid two twenties on the table, more than covering the burgers and two beers.

They walked as fast as Nick could to the Jeep.

"I am so sorry, Lola. But this sounds really serious. I have no idea what he wants with me. I have really been looking forward to our date. Can I call it a date?" Nick bumbled.

"You better. I am considering it one. This could be really interesting. I'm glad I'm going along!" she said.

"Get ready to flash your badge for Tampa PD. I am going to break the law!" Nick said as he floored the accelerator and the Jeep roared off toward downtown. Its exhaust had a staccato growl.

A Tampa PD cruiser lit them up a block into the trip.

"I've got this," Lola said and slid down from the tall Jeep, her FHP badge held high. She walked over to the cruiser and spoke a couple of words before coming back and climbing in, grinning.

"We have an escort," she said as the Tampa cruiser pulled past, waited for them to catch up, and hit the lights and siren.

"Judge Mabry's name carries a lot of weight, apparently," she said as Nick managed to stay behind the car.

"These guys are good in traffic, but we troopers can move through anything better," she said boastfully. Nick nodded, knowing she was exactly right.

They reached the courthouse in record time and the police car doused his lights and curved away. Nick saluted him as he turned, and he responded by a quick beep on the air horn.

They pulled up to the gate for judges and official vehicles. They were waiting for them and waved the Jeep through.

Nick flashed his retired detective's badge and Lola her trooper shield to the first set of bailiffs and were waved around the walk-through metal detector and directed toward the judge's chambers.

They got in an elevator alone. Nick turned to Lola. She was stunning in the little outfit and without her law enforcement expression.

"I've been planning to say this all day, but I seem to be running out of opportunities. You are breathtaking, Lola. You are simply beautiful."

She seemed stunned someone would think she was beautiful. She thought for a moment and leaned up, though slightly due to her height, and gave Nick a memorable kiss. The door opened and they walked toward the judicial chambers. They tapped on the door for "Andrew Mabry, Thirteenth Circuit, Chief Judge."

A judicial assistant let them in. Nick was not

surprised to see the Chief Deputy Sheriff present. He was a new one. Nick had been gone four years, and a lot had changed.

The judge looked at their attire and smiled.

"I am sorry to interrupt an obvious date. However, you will soon understand the alacrity with which I needed your presence. Do you know the Chief Deputy?" he said. Both shook their heads, and he introduced him.

"Chief, Nick was one of your top detectives. A sergeant, I believe. He was the commander of the I-4 Corridor Missing Teens Task Force. He was retired after taking two rounds rescuing two young ladies he had tracked to Inverness. Nick, please introduce the young lady."

"Gentlemen, this is FHP Trooper Lola Caldwell. We were at a local restaurant when the judge called."

Both men nodded.

"Nick, I want to hire you to bring back my granddaughter. She went to school this morning and did not arrive. The school called my daughter, and she called me.

"The sheriff was out of town, so I called his number two here. As you know, we are well inside the twenty-four-hour missing persons requirement. My granddaughter is fifteen and a half, so she is eligible for the Amber Alert protocols. The chief will work on the Amber Alert.

"If you will accept the contract, I'd like you to start with my daughter, my granddaughter's school, friends and whatever magic you worked freeing around fifty teens four years ago. The sheriff's office will have lead— my daughter lives in the county—and will officially start once the missing person time requirement has been met. I want you on top of it well before that time, Nick. Will you do it?"

"Of course I will, Judge Mabry. I will need your daughter's name and address. We will go straight there and begin gathering information from her. What is your granddaughter's name?"

"She is Madison Elaine Newton," Judge Mabry said, taking a photo out of a frame on his desk and handing it to Nick. He then wrote his daughter's name and address on a slip of paper and handed it across his desk.

Lola leaned over and whispered something in Nick's ear, and he smiled.

"Your honor, Lola has offered to take some overdue vacation time and help us find Madison. Do you mind?" Nick asked.

"Not in the least! The more, the merrier."

"Judge," Lola began. "A call from you would really smooth the no-notice vacation time with my boss."

"Give me his or her name and I will call as soon as you leave for my daughter's house." Lola wrote the information on the back of one of her official business cards.

"I will call you and advise whether I reached this person directly or had to leave a message."

"Thank you, sir."

"Judge, Chief, we better get rolling toward your daughter's home. Let her know to look out for a very unofficial-looking orange Jeep Rubicon," Nick said. The judge nodded, and they left.

"Lola, I really appreciate the help. You are officially a contractor of Aaron Risk Mitigation and Investigation."

"It's certainly a good cause. And I look forward to working on it with you," she said.

The daughter, Shelby Mabry Newton, lived about

thirty minutes outside of Tampa in unincorporated Hillsborough County. They made it in twenty.

———

"Well, Daddy said to look for two people who don't look like cops," was their greeting from Shelby Newton.

"Perhaps we have a different persona when not interrupted on a date. We need to get some information from you very quickly to start working to get Madison back safely," Nick said, his voice not reflecting the irritation he felt.

"I guess I was not very nice..." Shelby said.

Ignoring her half-ass apology, Nick said, "We need to sit down and get a lot of information fast. This is Florida Trooper Lola Caldwell. I am retired Detective Sergeant Nick Wolf."

"You're the guy Daddy said ran the task force which saved fifty girls Madison's age, then got shot," she said.

He nodded and took out his notebook. Lola removed hers from the small Maxpedition sling bag she carried everywhere. Everywhere when she could not hide her Glock on her person, Nick knew. Today's outfit made hiding anything larger than a tiny .25 caliber impossible.

"Your father gave us no details. He said you would. So we will hit you with a barrage of questions. Please answer directly and answer only what we ask. There will be time at the end to elaborate, okay?"

She nodded.

"Trooper Caldwell will jump in any time she has a question. First, when exactly did you determine Madison was missing?"

"This morning when the school called at nine."

"How late was she by the time they called?"

"About forty-five minutes."

"When did she leave home and how? Walking? Bus? Ride?" Lola asked.

"About seven forty-five. She walks to school."

"Please elaborate on the route she walks," Nick said. She did, and they both took notes.

"What was she wearing? As much detail as possible, please."

"A white tee shirt with a unicorn on it, blue shorts, and red tennis shoes."

"What color was the unicorn? The length of the shorts and were the shoes high tops or low?" Nick asked.

"Pink, pretty short, and low-quarter shoes."

"Does she normally walk with a friend? Or meet up with one along the way?" Lola asked.

"Neither."

"At fifteen and a half, does she have a boyfriend? Date at all?"

"She does not have a boyfriend. She does date. He's a harmless, nerdy kid. I have taken them to the club in Hyde Park which has teen nights. I always pick them up."

"I'm familiar with the club from my task force days. We'll need the name and any information you can provide on the young man. Did she have a smartphone with her?"

"Always. She's on it all day."

Nick suspected her mother was too and taking innumerable selfies to post on social media.

"Have you called her?" Lola asked.

"Of course! It goes into voice mail," she said with irritation.

"Instantly, or after ten or so rings?" Nick asked.

"Instantly."

"Okay. Which indicates the phone is turned off or the battery went dead."

"Does it have tracking set up?" Lola asked.

"No. She's a well-behaved girl. Should I?" Shelby answered.

"No matter if a missing person was kidnapped, ran away, is off with someone voluntarily, they are unlikely to give permission at this point to approve being tracked. But even if it's a one-in-a-million chance, we have to try setting it up. Please get your phone out," Nick asked.

She did, and they went through the process of just the Find My Phone tracking installed standard. There were other apps, but they would have their answer from the "Do you approve of being tracked?" question. There was no response, indicating she either did not want to be tracked or, more likely, no longer had control over her phone.

Nick wrote Madison's number in his notebook and called the judge.

"Judge, we are at your daughter's. There was no tracking on Madison's phone, but it would help if you had law enforcement check the number to see what the last location of use was? Okay. I'll look forward to your call. Thanks."

"Has Madison had any potential stalker calls or emails, as far as you know? Keep in mind, perverse adult males often use the picture of a boy her age to start a conversation online."

"No, what kind of daughter do you think I have?" Shelby retorted angrily.

"Ms. Newton, there is no reason to snap at us. We

are asking standard questions used in every missing teen case. Every single one. If you want to help us get your daughter back safely, hold the attitude, please," Lola said before Nick could.

Shelby frowned and nodded.

"The questions will get more invasive, but they are what the detectives will ask you when the twenty-four hours have passed, and they handle this as a missing person case. So, you may as well break in on us. We are providing an investigation starting hours before theirs," Nick said.

This time her nod was more resignation than anger. Was she hiding something? Her body language suggested it and it was also a vibe he felt from Lola.

"How was your relationship with your daughter, Ms. Newton? Did you argue much? Did you have words before she left for school?" Nick asked.

"No!" she virtually screamed.

"Ms. Newton, the standard parental answer is 'of course we argued. She is a teenager. But it was always over trivial things.' You want to rethink your answer?"

"Yeah. I'll go with the standard one you said," she obviously lied.

"Next question. Are you married?"

"Never married."

"And, you are estranged from her father?"

"Yes."

"Is he a participative father? Do they have a good relationship?" Nick asked.

"No. The sonofabitch walked out a month before she was born," Shelby said.

"Has he ever tried to contact you about seeing her? Or contacted her as far as you know?"

"He made an attempt about a year ago. Some BS

about wanting to get to know his daughter. I didn't buy it for a minute. Where was he and child support when I was struggling?"

Yeah, as if you ever struggled for money with a rich judge as a father and living in an upscale house with a Mercedes SUV in the driveway, Nick thought. He could tell Lola, though stone-faced, was thinking the same thing.

"Is he still in town?" Lola asked.

"He's over in Largo," she said, referring to a small city across the Bay in Pinellas County.

"What's his name?" Nick asked, and she told him it was Noah Thompson.

"Do you have his number from past calls?" Lola asked.

"Why would I keep it?"

"Maybe for notifications about situations like this," Lola suggested, getting a smirk in return.

"May we see her room?" Nick asked.

"Why?" Shelby snapped.

"Because we want to get a feel for who Madison is. Going through her room is what every detective does on a missing persons case."

"If you say so." She led them to her daughter's bedroom and noticed Nick's limp for the first time.

"How can you be a detective if you limp? Doesn't it disqualify you?" Shelby asked.

Nick could see Lola balling up her fists unconsciously.

"Yes, Ms. Newton. It does disqualify me. I was shot twice freeing two young ladies Madison's age and left permanently disabled."

"Does being crippled prevent you from doing a sufficient job finding my daughter?"

"I hope not. It has not hampered any other case I have solved in the past four years."

She frowned, not buying it.

The first thing Lola gravitated toward was Madison's Mac laptop.

"Ms. Newton, do you know your daughter's password?"

"Of course not. I don't invade her privacy."

Ignoring the remark, Nick asked, "Does she have a diary?"

"Yes. I bought her one. I don't know if she uses it. It should be on her desk if she does."

"Thank you. This might take a little while. Feel free to have a glass of iced tea or something while we work here," Lola suggested.

"And let you pull through my daughter's stuff without me watching?"

"Yes. Exactly," Nick said, engendering a cold stare before she left the room in a huff.

Lola mouthed, "Bitch!" and Nick grinned and softly said, "Big time! I promise our next date will be a lot more...personal."

This time it was the trooper's turn to grin.

Lola began going through Madison's chest of drawers and then closet while Nick sat at her desk.

"Eureka! Here's the password written on a yellow Post-it stuck to the side of the Mac. My investigative skills are surprising even to me!" he said as his partner rolled her eyes.

He logged in and started reading texts. There was a string from a sixteen-year-old boy. They got increasingly personal, then suggestive. He wanted to meet her. Maybe even on the way to school and walk with her.

"We might have her kidnapper right here. This

should immediately be looked at by experts to identify the sender. I have a suspicion it is a trafficker and not a sixteen-year-old. He does not leave any phone or address. Nor a car description if he's going to meet her along the way to school. Most sixteen-year-olds who have a car of any type would boast about it and describe it, I'd think," Nick said.

He immediately called a friend who was a hacker and knew more about tracking down computers than virtually anyone in law enforcement. Nick had helped him out of a scrape which guaranteed hard time. He wanted to groom the hacker, who went by the street name, Pi, as a source.

"Pi, long time no see. This is Nick Wolf. I am on permanent disability retirement as a detective due to two unfortunate bullet wounds which crippled me a little bit. I need your help and will pay you five hundred dollars for something real easy for you to do. We have the computer of a fifteen-year-old girl. She has probably been kidnapped this morning by a human trafficker. We have her computer but cannot remove it for legal reasons. There is a conversation on it with a purported sixteen-year-old which is very suspicious. My PI partner and I think there is some probability it is the trafficker. I can give you the IP and need to get the IP of one person who has sent several emails. Can you do it for me? Really quickly? Her life is literally at stake here."

"Sure thing, Nick! It's a lot easier than people think, but you can still pay me the five bills. There are several ways I can do it, but the easiest is a search tool I use all the time. Just give me the bad dude's email address," Pi said.

"Gotcha! Okay, now I will put it in a search tool to find the dude's full particulars. The tool will charge my credit card, but your five hundred will take care of it just fine.

"We have a setback. Not a problem. This dude uses a VPN or virtual private network. It's smart. You should have a VPN too. I'll include the best one for you during our little billing process, Nick.

"What the VPN does is bounce the IP location all around the world. I have five or six popping up. Some are standards. Let me study this. It may take longer than I thought. Can I call you early in the a.m.?"

"Sure. Is there any way the police computer forensics people can look at this computer when they take it tomorrow and find out we did this ahead of them?"

"Negatory. No clue at all. I move like a wraith in the night for you, buddy!"

"Okay, Wraith, I will await your call. Call me as soon as you get it. I don't care about the hour."

They terminated the call.

"Five hundred? Is five hundred bucks a bit rich for what he's doing for us?" Lola asked.

"In view of the head start we have, and the retainer check the judge gave us, no. I want us to find her and deliver her safe before my former associates do," Nick said.

"I'm with you one hundred percent," Lola said.

"Think about whether we should pass on her evasive responses about an argument this morning with her daughter to the detectives who catch the case," Nick asked.

"I believe we should. You never know if it might be a root reason for the girl running away if she was not kidnapped by traffickers. I suspect a lot of missing teens run away instead of being kidnapped. They may fall under the influence of a trafficker or pimp later, but maybe not first."

"I think you are right. I was shot before the fifty or so were debriefed by the task force. But Kit, my successor, said some were runaways like you said and some were specifically targeted to meet buyer's orders. The rest? Who knows the exact number because so few relatively have been repatriated. The flaw is repatriation with the very people who may have abused them in some way to cause them to run away to begin with."

"Nick, the whole thing is a sad conundrum," Lola said. They said goodbye to the mother, who responded with an angry look.

They started at the house, walked a block along her route then started knocking on doors for the "house to house." Many people were at work, shopping, or off on some other endeavor. Many did not answer the door, there or not.

Nick fully expected Lola in her crop top and Daisy Duke cutoffs would have more doors answered than he would. He was wrong. Housewives predominated, and he won. He was completely shocked yet did not figure out why until Lola explained it to him.

Their path knocking on doors all the way to the school notwithstanding, they only learned one thing from the interviews. An older lady, often the best type of witness, had seen a strange dark-colored van parked near her house a little before nine this morning. It was either dark-blue or gray or black. She did not know if it had Florida plates or any writing on the sides.

"Should we go in and interview in the school dressed like this?" Lola asked as they approached the school.

"I think time suggests we have to, Lola," Nick said.

The school resource officer was a deputy Nick recognized. He explained why they were there and introduced Lola who showed her badge and credentials. She escorted the two to the principal's office.

"I am Mrs. Adams, the principal. You too do not look like police officers dressed like that! But if my favorite deputy here vouches for you...what can I do for you?"

"Mrs. Adams, I am a private investigator. Your SRO here knows me from my days as a detective sergeant and as head of the teen trafficking task force. Which is why Judge Mabry hired me the second he learned his granddaughter was missing. This is Trooper Lola Caldwell. She is part of the investigating team. We are dressed like this because we were having lunch on a day off when the call came in. Time, as I am sure you know, is of the absolute essence here."

"Time which you gifted us when you called Madison's mother so promptly. We are starting our investigation well before the missing persons twenty-four-hour requirement," Lola added.

"I am glad. I know every child in this middle school. It's a small one and every student comes from the upscale development which surrounds us.

"I like Madison. She is popular and a good student. When I called her mother, she seemed to blame the school because her daughter was missing. I have to be careful. As you know, her grandfather is very influential in this county. In fact, the entire region."

"We received a bit of unfortunate attitude from the mother also. I can assure you everything you say to us will be held in the strictest of confidence," Nick said.

"What are your feelings about home life in the single-parent residence there?" Lola asked.

"I don't know the father. Neither does Madison.

Knowing Madison and her mother, however, I attribute Madison's delightful personality to his DNA," the principal said.

"Changing tack to a more comfortable area, how about Madison's friends? Especially boys?" Nick asked.

"She is liked by everyone. Not a student leader, just a nice person everyone likes. I am not aware of a boyfriend. A number of the students go to the teen night at a club in Tampa," the principal said.

"Have any of them gone missing?" Nick asked, knowing of one. He saved her.

"I think one from South Tampa. None from this school. The one from South Tampa was freed after a gunfight out of town," she said.

"I know quite well about Morgan Parker from South Tampa. I was there when she was released."

"Hence your disability retirement?" the perceptive principal asked.

"Yes, ma'am."

"Are there any girls Madison was particularly close to? Girls she might confide in if she had, for example, an Internet relationship with some boy?" Lola asked.

"Yes. A couple I can think of."

"Could you call them in to speak with us one at a time? You are encouraged to be present in lieu of a parent," Nick said.

"Let me call the two mothers. I'd like either for them to be present or approve me sitting in their place," Principal Adams said.

She went onto her computer and pulled a student file and called the contact number, usually a cell phone.

"Hi, this is Principal Adams from the middle school. Your daughter is fine. But I have a request to make." She paused a moment, then continued. "One of our students, Madison Newton, has gone missing. I have some investigators here working on the case. They would like to speak with Maisy about her friend. You can come and sit in or delegate me to. Either way, just be aware time is very important in finding Madison."

She paused again while the mother spoke, then said, "I understand completely. These are very conscientious investigators. I will sit in for you, but I have every confidence in their professionalism. I will call you after. Thanks so much," and she terminated the call.

"One down, one to go," she said as she punched in the new number. She got an answer and said virtually the same thing, again winning the right to sit in during the interview of the second student.

They were called to the principal's office one at a time.

Nick suggested Lola take the lead with him, suggesting any questions she had not asked. He thought the female, who looked like their fun aunt, would have more rapport with the two. He was correct. One even asked Lola where she got her top.

They learned both girls knew about the mystery boyfriend, though neither suspected he could be an adult. They giggled over him being older and having a car. Both were shocked when they learned what prompted them being questioned.

Their statements only corroborated what Nick and Lola found on the computer but did not answer whether the emails were a legitimate kid or an older predator. The answer would hopefully come with the identification of Madison's so-called boyfriend's computer IP address.

It was approaching dusk.

"I have an idea to extend our date," Nick began, and Lola perked up with interest.

"Let's go back to Pinellas and change into club clothes—whatever they are—and go to the club in Hyde Park for a look around. It keeps cropping up on teen trafficking cases, but four years ago, we were not able to prove anything," he said.

"You just want to see how I clean up, don't you?"

"Okay. You got me. Of course I do. But we've done about all we can do tonight on the case otherwise."

"Let's take my car. My POV," she said. "Easier on my party hair."

"Your red VW GTI personally owned vehicle sounds good to me. Let's go. Want me to drop you at your house to get ready? I'll run back to my place and clean up. I will come back to pick you up in less than an hour," Nick said.

"Sounds like a plan."

They drove back to Largo from Hillsborough County, and he dropped Lola off. He went home and played with Finn a while before showering and putting on dress slacks, loafers, and a short-sleeve silk shirt. The Sig 365 with the Wilson Combat lower module disappeared under the shirt in an inside the beltline holster. He had an ankle holster for it as a backup gun but considered the ankle rig too slow when using it for a primary weapon.

He hit a spray of Chanel Bleu for Men onto his chest and left for Largo. Lola was ready.

Her black hair was as glossy as it would be wet. It beautifully set off her blue eyes. She had on an eye-catching black cocktail dress and high heels making her equal to his six feet.

He just stood there and drank her in when she opened the door.

"I'm going to take this as approval," she said.

"On a scale of one to ten, I'd say a fifteen."

She gave him a long kiss.

"I saved the lipstick to put on later in case you said something like that."

"Thank the good Lord you did. I'd have hated to miss that kiss."

They got in the fast VW, and she drove to Hyde Park as he gave directions to the club, which he surveilled four years ago.

"I don't think they have a metal detector or check for weapons. If they do, we will show badges. If they don't allow even for cops, we will tell them to go do something physiologically impossible and leave," Nick said.

They did not have a metal detector. They did have a purse check policy and their badges did not override it.

The guy at the door was big and a smartass. He made a couple of desultory comments about cops and shoved Nick toward the door.

Big mistake. Nick turned, and the man put up his fists in a classic boxing position. Nick came inside and head butted him in the nose, breaking it. He then kidney punched the bouncer with his bad leg extended. The man fell over Nick's leg and down both steps to the converted old home.

Lola met him at the bottom, her badge and gun both prominent as another bouncer saw what was happening from inside the door.

"Touch the trooper, and you die!" Nick snarled.

The second bouncer came out the door onto the porch.

"Stay out of this. Police!" Nick said. The man spun

around toward Nick and threw his shirt tail back, reaching for a gun. He stopped in mid-reach as Nick's Sig appeared, pointing between his eyes, his trigger finger moving off from its position along the slide and onto the trigger, ready for a press.

"That will be enough, Izsak!" a voice from the doorway commanded.

Nick stepped back and saw the speaker was a light-tan complexioned male with dreadlocks. The owner.

"What's going on here?" he asked to nobody in particular.

"He did not like our badges and guns and made some rude remarks, then tried to shove me down the steps. I was far more gentle with him than I should have been. Your second man tried to draw a gun. I think I am going to place a call to Tampa Police to resolve this matter. Both men need some time in a lockup to consider how intemperate they were," Nick said.

"Sir, I do not think the police need to be involved. Come right in as my guests. I will deal with my staff and counsel them on respecting the police."

Nick looked at Lola, her black dress riding high as she squatted over the man, her Glock 45 and badge both in hand. She shook her head.

"Thank you for your courtesy. I'm afraid my date feels the night has been ruined. We will leave. I have the name and contact information of several of your guests if either man decides to file a false report," Nick lied convincingly.

"Oh, I am quite sure they won't when I have finished with them," the apparent Jamaican said politely.

Nick, Sig re-holstered, went down the steps and held out a hand so Lola could arise without further display of long beautiful legs.

They walked to her car, Nick limping sideways to make sure no one behind them was going to draw a gun.

She touched the door handle, and Nick opened her door as soon as he heard it click.

She got in and he went around to the other side, his left leg feeling like it was afire.

"I guess we weren't as covert as we hoped to be," he said.

"No, but we are one helluva team. I noticed your limp was more pronounced as we walked back, Nick. Are you okay?"

"It twisted a little when I held it out to trip the first guy. It will be fine. You are one great partner. One for whom I am going to buy the fanciest dinner we can find."

Tampa was known for fine restaurants. She picked seafood and Nick knew exactly where to take her.

Lola retouched her makeup when they arrived and fixed her hair with a toss of her head.

Nick Wolf walked into the restaurant with her on his arm, prouder than he could ever remember.

They were seated quickly as it was not a Friday or weekend in snowbird season, when returning northerners, Midwesterners, and Canadians were in Florida to escape cold weather at home.

Each had one glass of wine and ordered. She chose salmon, and he ordered Chilean sea bass en Papillote. Both entrees were accompanied by steamed broccoli and new potatoes and preceded by a small salad.

They finally had a relaxed time to have the talks most people have on first dates. Both had finished college while working. Nick started online as a military investigator and finished both at night and online as a deputy sheriff. Lola did both online and night classes as a trooper.

Nick spoke in detail about his combat experience and the wounds which preceded his two four years ago.

"At least I have interesting scars," he finished.

"Maybe one day..." Lola said, leaving the obvious unsaid.

"Surely one day..." Nick answered.

"Nick, are you one of the many vets who has PTSD?"

"No. I was checked out prior to CID school. Nothing showed. My outlook is pretty straightforward. I'm the good guy. They are the bad guys. Everything in between comes under 'shit happens in this world,' so I deal with it."

"I feel the same way, Nick. We are in a business where we run toward the gunfire, not away from it. We do it by choice. You chose a tan beret. And the badge. I chose a tan uniform and the badge. I admit it's a little lonely and scary sometimes being a trooper all alone on the road, not knowing what's next and if there is any backup within miles."

"That's a tough one, Lola. I respect you all a lot. I almost wish you were a deputy. You'd make more money and have backup more readily available. And, if alone, at least a second car is responding with you and close."

"It's tempting. Today has stirred my investigative interests. I have tried to muffle them. Accident investigations are not like the ones you did as a detective or like what we are doing now. These are the ones that get my juices flowing."

"I certainly understand. Your questions today and mine were so seamless. It's like we have been doing this together for years," he said.

"So you noticed it, too?" she asked.

He smiled and nodded. "You said it best. We are a good team."

"We are. Speaking of good, this dinner is deliciously memorable!" she said, changing the subject, which was going one way really fast. She liked the direction, but the speed scared her.

"It is. Or was. How about dessert?"

"Did you like the way I looked with the bare midriff and short shorts today?"

"You know I did!"

"Well, you will understand why I will skip dessert then!" she said.

"Understood and approved."

They talked another hour over coffee before he paid, and they left.

He walked her up to the door.

"I want you to come in. To stay. I really do. But we are moving so fast it scares me," she said.

"Will you admit we are heading in the right direction, Lola?"

"Oh, yes."

"Your answer and a kiss will be good enough for me, then."

The kiss was the best yet, and he climbed painfully into the tall Jeep Rubicon, smiling.

"I'll call you early so we can get back on our investigation. Without any recent informants to press, there does not seem to be anything else we can do today. How early can I call you?" he asked.

"I will be up drinking coffee at five."

"How about I come over and have a second cup with you an hour later?"

"Sounds perfect to me!"

"I'll bring my white surveillance van in case we need it."

"See you at six!"

He spun the orange Jeep around and headed back to his place and an impatient cat.

*Lord, I hope she likes cats. It would be awful if she was allergic to them...*he worried on the way. Finn was like family. His only family.

He was up, showered, shaved, and dressed in tan chinos and a short-sleeve shirt with the tail worn out. He had the larger Glock under the shirt and had to be more careful to make sure its blocky shape it did not print if he moved wrong. It only held two rounds more than the little Sig, but also offered the use of +P+ more powerful police rounds with its greater weight and longer barrel. The barrel on the smaller gun would not provide sufficient time for all of the powder in the hotter round to burn. And the recoil would be painful.

The older Dodge van started dependably as usual. It had a 318 V8 putting out two hundred twenty-five horse-power. The engine was adequate for a van that weighed only forty-two hundred pounds.

He pulled up at Lola's at five to six. She met him at the door in a bathrobe and led him to a screened porch overlooking a privacy fenced yard. An urn keeping coffee warm was on a table with two cups. One had a little coffee left in it. She poured a full cup into both.

"Slàinte for a good day of investigating!" he said.

"May the wind blow beneath your kilt and keep you cool as you fight oppressors!" she responded.

They drank, smiling at each other, and planned the day. He already had a list made out of former task force members in Tampa to reach out to, especially Detective John Ross.

Lola got up with her loose robe and turned to go into the house to get dressed. He stared after her long after she had disappeared.

She appeared a few minutes later, hair in a ponytail and wearing a slacks and vest outfit over a contrasting top. Nick knew the reason for her vest. The same reason he kept his shirttail out.

He gave her the quick tour of the van and an extra key to the locker where the short-barreled Mossberg Shockwave shotgun was stored.

"Is it carried cruiser style?" she asked.

"Yep. Loaded with an empty chamber and the safety off. Pump it once, and you have one full-size lower recoil double-ought buckshot load followed by eight one and three-quarter inch buckshot."

"I am not familiar with the short ones. What's their power like?" Lola asked.

"Kinda like twenty-gauge buckshot which many use for deer hunting. Sufficient for government work. Especially after the big one comes out first."

Nick's phone rang, and it was Pi.

"I am ninety-nine percent certain I have your man planted on the island of Belize," the hacker said.

"Hmm, which makes a trip across town to check him out tough," Nick said with the phone on speaker. "But it proves he is our guy. If he was just a run-of-the-mill pedophile, he could not pick a target he could not reach. He also probably has a Confederate in the Tampa area to do the snatch. I guess I know where I'll be heading today. You have the same address for the check?"

"I do. Same post office box. I will text you the suggested VPN to use. You might share it with your partner, too."

"I will, buddy. Thanks for your help so fast. I will let you know how it comes out if it does not make the Tampa paper or news," Nick said and hung up.

"Do you have a passport?" he asked Lola.

"No, never thought I needed one," she said.

"Then I'll slip down to Belize solo. I have a passport. I suspect it will only be a day. We may be on to a major source and will let the other detective's human sources slide until we let this play out. Can be a real vacation day for you!"

"If there's nothing we can come up with me to investigate, I may spend the day in the backyard working on my tan," she said.

"I believe there are direct flights to Belize City from Tampa. I looked into it for a snook fishing trip a year or so ago and never went. I worry about using my real identity but worry more about traveling on a forged passport."

"Well, it's not like you are going to break the law... are you?"

"Probably not. It depends on how reluctant this person is to share the information we need to recover Madison safely.

"I guess you don't have to be as strict about questioning. Or do you?" she asked.

"I don't know. I cannot do Madison much good if I'm locked up in a rat-infested jail."

"Let's be sure that's not a possibility. We may have something special brewing here and I'm liable to miss you something fierce," Lola said, leaning over to give him another kiss.

"Lola, this kissing habit? Let's keep it up, okay?" he said.

"Deal!" she smiled.

"I can lock my armaments in the locker with the shotgun. We can stop by a mall or something and get everything I need to add to the outfit I am wearing. Toothbrush, razor, deodorant, shorts, and tee shirt. I have a ball cap and sunglasses here in the van.

"If I give you the key and the alarm passcode, would you mind staying at my place without me tonight? I need to make sure Finn has food and water and good company. He deserves it."

"Finn?" she asked.

"Finn. The world's greatest cat."

"Great! I love cats!" she said and alleviated his greatest relationship worry.

In the mall parking lot after shopping, Nick transferred his new purchases into the flat dark earth colored bag he used as his emergency get-out-of-town bag. He put its prior contents into the locker with his two handguns.

The strip center had a travel agent. They stopped in and came out a half hour later with a roundtrip ticket to Belize City and the name of with a fishing lodge in the small-town Pi's VPN search hit on. It was a village named Sarteneja in northern Belize and the travel agent showed several vacancies.

Nick spoke fluent Castilian Spanish and had often used it and a false name as a cover. His light-brown hair and blue eyes were not unusual for a Cuban of recent Spanish heritage. He took the last name of his long-term foster family, Jorge. He used Roberto as his first name and would use the cover at the fishing lodge unless they asked for a passport. The bus, instead of a rental car, would further serve to hide his arrival in Sarteneja.

They realized Lola had never even seen where he lived and had his office, much less been inside.

He gave her directions, the address, his key and the alarm code and location just inside the door. He also gave her Finn's feeding amount and schedule of twice per day.

The flight was on American Airlines from Tampa to Miami to Belize City. They pulled up at American Airlines departures two hours before the flight. They switched places, kissed, and she drove off, with him watching her depart in the surveillance van.

The travel agent had already printed out Nick's boarding pass. He went straight to the gate after clearing security.

A stop at a newsstand yielded a couple of bottles of trustworthy water, which he did not believe plane water was, and a Jack Carr novel and a Fred Burton book on chasing real life terrorists. Two favorite authors. He was ready. The small Mac laptop from the van was in his bag. He had already memorized the case notes he needed. Nick saw an ATM on the way to the gate and replenished his cash by four hundred dollars.

He was ready. Almost. A very large cup of coffee to take aboard completed his preparation. He did some quick research on Belize and found out he had to declare every dollar he was bringing. He did a quick count. Five hundred two dollars and twenty-seven cents. He noted the amount on his flight ticket jacket.

Just before boarding, he got a phone call from Lola.

"Hi! You ready to board? Good! Finn and I are getting along famously. He is in my lap, purring as we speak. I found the cat food and a scoop in the bag. I'll give him a scoop in the morning and one at night, right? Okay. Your office and living quarters are so neat! It must be your military background, though a tiny bit of woman's touch is begged for," she said.

"I am amenable to your woman's touch. Oh, and of course in the apartment too," he said and could feel her smile through the phone. "They just called for us to board. Thanks for staying over and looking after Finn. I will probably see you the day after tomorrow. I will let you know by text or email, okay? I love you. Be safe," he said, uttering words he had perhaps never said in his life.

"I love you too! And you also be safe. Get our man!" she said and hung up.

He rose and took his carry-on to the boarding line.

9

Lola played with Finn, then went out for a run. She decided to drive over to the nearby town of St. Pete Beach and run along the beach. She picked up a takeout fish taco dinner on the way back to Nick's.

She had worked virtually all of her life and not traveled very much, something she regretted and planned to remedy.

Staying somewhere other than whatever was her home at the time was almost alien to her. Staying at Nick's, however, seemed strangely comfortable. Finn was affectionate but not intrusive. She thought he was the perfect gentleman of cat world.

Everything in the apartment and, she suspected the office, was neat and logical. If she needed something, a condiment for example, she just looked in her first choice, reasonable place, and there it was. Even his closet was logical.

Lola put his primary and backup guns and their holsters and extra mags in the top of his closet. She added his fast-opening pocketknife to the guns.

During their conversation at dinner, Nick had spoken of enjoying the foreign mysteries on BritBox and Acorn so she scanned both and picked a French show about a female detective named Candice to watch.

The recliner with the purring cat was so relaxing she found herself waking up at two in the morning. Finn stirred and moved over as she got up. Lola stripped to panties and looked in Nick's closet. He even had tee shirts on hangers. She chose one and slipped it on. It smelled fresh like fabric softener.

Lola found herself wishing it smelled fresh like Nick, in which she would not need the shirt. She could just have him to snuggle up against. She wondered if he was having the same thoughts about her, sleeping in Belize. She was pretty sure he was.

She decided to take the surveillance van to Tampa tomorrow morning and see what happens at the Mama Jama nightclub in its off-hours. She had a bad feeling about the place she just could not kick.

Lola went to sleep with the faint sound of purring coming from the foot of the bed.

Only one thing missing, she thought as she drifted off.

———

Lola awakened and fed Finn. His water and litter box did not appear to need action on her part.

She fixed a bowl of raisin bran and a cup of coffee from the Keurig. After a shower, she left in the van and decided to try to interview Madison's father. She hoped she could catch him before he left for wherever work was.

Madison's father, Noah Thompson, lived in Largo.

His house was barely a mile from hers. She saw a car in the drive and knocked on the door.

A medium height and build man answered it, surprised to see a pretty woman at his doorstep at six thirty in the morning.

"Hi, Mr. Thompson. I am FHP Trooper Lola Caldwell. I am part of a group investigating a missing teen." She showed him her badge and credentials.

"Good morning," he said pleasantly. "But why have you come here? I don't know anything about a missing teen," he said.

"Then, the judge's daughter, your ex-wife, has not contacted you?"

"She's the mother of our daughter but not an ex-wife. I have tried to contact her about getting to know my daughter. She has rebuffed me at every turn. And it's impossible to do it by court order when her grandfather is the most powerful judge in the region!"

"So, you are unaware your daughter is missing and presumed kidnapped?"

She could tell from the expression on his face he was shocked.

"When? From the home?" he blurted out.

"We think she was taken on the way to school yesterday morning," Lola said.

"The horrible woman I dated and who got pregnant, and her father cut me off from any future contact, has not called me."

Having met the woman, Lola did not doubt for a moment he was telling the truth.

"Have you met or at least spoken with your daughter?"

"I have seen her from a distance. I have tried to call but without any luck."

"So, she has not come here? Or called you?"

"I wish, Trooper. I wish. But no, she has not done either," Thompson said.

"Is there anything I can do to help?" he asked.

"Only advise us if she contacts you in any way. We will keep you in the loop as our information develops," Lola said as she gave him her card and left.

She drove across the Howard Frankland Bridge to Tampa and headed to the Mama Jama Nightclub. Lola was curious to see what kind of movement they had during the day, when the club was not open.

Lola parked the van under a tree. It was still cool enough in the morning to be able to sit and watch diagonally across the street comfortably.

She sat for an hour, wishing for a cup of coffee, but knowing if she had one, she would have to pee. A major dilemma of surveillance duty, though she would have brought Nick's Thermos full of Canadian Tim Horton dark roast coffees, had she remembered the porta-potty in the rear of the van.

Damn! He thinks of everything. I should have remembered. I could be having my second cup by now.

She sat immobile for several hours. This was like sitting on a knoll by the interstate with her radar on. The difference is she did not anticipate the adrenaline rush of accelerating in up to triple-digit speeds to apprehend a speeder.

At ten-thirty, she saw a beige Mercedes come from around the house. The garage—possibly even originally built for carriages at this old of a dwelling—must be in the rear.

She saw the owner, Esson, with his dreads, driving. She could not tell if there was anyone else in the dark windowed car.

Lola started the Dodge van and followed. Esson led her onto I-4. She kept several cars between his luxury sedan and her ubiquitous truck. They cleared Tampa city limits and headed toward, and then past, Lakeland.

She kept several cars between her and the Mercedes. The traffic had thinned out appreciably since Lakeland.

She focused on the car ahead, but had noticed a large pickup truck behind her.

On a long straight stretch with no traffic now they had cleared the commuters, the truck pulled up beside her.

A dark passenger window dropped, and a Black man looked intently at her.

They recognized each other at the same time.

It was the bouncer from the club! The one whose nose was still covered by a bandage from Nick having broken it.

The truck was a large one, probably an F-350 to her eye, which was trained for such things.

It dropped back, then swerved toward the van's rear quarter.

He was doing a basic PIT maneuver. She was stunned at his disappearance from view and helpless to react.

He jerked his wheel and seven thousand pounds of truck slammed into the smaller van's left rear panel at the tire.

The van careened across the road so violently its highly trained driver could not control it. It hit the shoulder and flipped, rolling several revolutions.

The older generation airbag exploded into Lola's face as everything spun and she, though constrained by her shoulder belt, was hurled from side to side violently during the rolls.

The van rolled into the grass, coming to a rest on its roof seventy-five feet from the shoulder of the interstate. Lola was dazed and disoriented, hanging upside down by her lap and shoulder belt.

She vaguely smelled gasoline, then the hot smell of fire as she struggled with the seat and shoulder belt.

The big pickup, which had virtually no damage, pulled over to the shoulder and sat briefly a hundred yards ahead. The driver watched in his large wing mirror as flames appeared. Still no cars coming up from behind. Several on the westbound lane across the median had seen the "accident" and were coming to a halt.

He watched the van as flames grew. As he pulled away, window still down, he heard the dull "pomp!" of a contained explosion and the van became engulfed in flames.

His boss's follower was dead. The door bouncer called Esson on his cell phone and advised him as he drove off at a normal highway speed attracting no attention whatsoever. He was pretty sure the people on the other side had not seen him hit the van. They only saw it rolling and catching on fire.

Several motorists crossed the grassy median and pulled in a hundred yards behind the emolliated van. As they exited their vehicles, one called 9-1-1, which alerted fire rescue and the FHP. Because this was likely a vehicular death, or homicide, additional deputies were sent for traffic control while the troopers investigated the accident.

Nick made a quick change of planes in Miami and took off for Belize City's Phillip S. W. Goldson International Airport. He arrived and took almost an hour to clear immigration.

His research had suggested a bus to Sarteneja. He boarded a Valdemar Perez bus and settled in for an interesting several-hour ride.

He had not shaved for several days and decided to let his shadow grow. It would fit in with a guy coming to a remote fishing village to fish and make it more difficult to be identified.

The bus dropped him in the heart of the village. He heard English and Spanish, and a combination spoken as soon as he got off the bus. He chose a Spanish speaker and asked directions to the fishing lodge in Spanish. The man pointed southwest and said it was on the Caribbean about a mile down the main road. He said there was a sign pointing him toward the left after he had walked most of the mile.

Nick set off, still limping more than normal from the fight at the Tampa nightclub.

He arrived and inquired about a room for a day or two and a snook fishing trip. He signed in as Roberto Jorge and paid in cash. His trip was scheduled for nine in the morning. Breakfast would be available an hour earlier at the main lodge.

His room was a small cabin. It was pretty primitive, with large windows and a ceiling fan instead of air conditioning. Nick did not mind. His years in combat made him tolerant of lacking creature comforts and the breezes of the turquoise Caribbean were delightful.

Nick knew he had to be very subtle about asking too many questions about Anglo residents in this small village. His strategy was to ask workers among the village people, not the owner of the fishing lodge, store owners or the like. He would choose Latinos and ask in Spanish, using the ruse of wondering if there were any people like him who moved recently and might be good neighbors. He would state he was thinking about moving to the village or another similar one.

He went to the lodge for dinner but no opportunities to learn were presented. He had fish for dinner and a couple local Belikin Lighthouse lagers before walking back to his cabin for the night.

He texted Lola and gave his uninformative status report. Her report was much the same, about the run and how famously she and Finn were getting along.

"You realize what we said to each other when we parted?" she asked.

"I do. I never said that to anyone before. Ever. And I meant it," he replied.

"I did too, Nick."

She sent him a surprise photo which made his night just before they ended their call.

Nick was showered and ready in shorts, a tee shirt, boat moccasins, and a ball cap by eight to eat some breakfast before the cover snook fishing trip.

The breakfast was a buffet with eggs, sausage, bacon, tomatoes, refried beans, and bread called fry jacks. He sampled each and added Marie Sharp's hot sauce and a habanero salsa which was on each table beside the salt and pepper.

Instant coffee, a surprise, was on the table also. The server brought hot water and powdered creamer.

A coffee aficionado, the instant coffee was his only disappointment. He walked back to his cabin and washed up a bit and put on SPF as a protection against the blazing Belizean sun.

His boat and guide awaited. The boat was a seventeen-foot panga with a forty-horsepower Yamaha outboard, steered by the tiller handle on the engine.

The panga was a high-bowed, narrow-beam skiff. Its bottom was flat in the back.

It had been designed by the maker of the outboard sitting on its transom. The intended purpose was a utility boat for third-world nations. Sort of a Jeep of boats. He had always wanted to try one. They had become moderately popular in the US and several brands were made in Florida.

His guide was Marco, a man of hard-to-discern years. Nick took a stab at sixty-five or seventy. Regardless of his true years, Marco hopped aboard the panga and walked with grace and no effort along its centerline to the engine.

He had a cooler with some bottles of water and beer aboard. After catching and releasing five snook which would have been record quality in Florida (which Nick considered the number two snook grounds in the world, behind Belize), they drifted and drank a beer each.

Marco was pleased to have an unassuming American who spoke Spanish.

"It's a good life here, isn't it, Marco?" he asked.

"Yes, it is a very good life. There's not much money, but we get by very well without it. For now, the government is good. Next week? Who knows," he said with a shrug.

"I think I would like living here. I have nothing or nobody to hold me to Florida," Nick lied. At least about the "nobody" part, which seemed to have changed very quickly.

"Have other people from the US moved here? Latinos or Anglos?" he asked Marco.

"Only one. He keeps to himself. Tall like you. He is a funny color. I think he is sick."

"Oh? Where does he live?" Nick asked in a friendly but not overly curious tone.

"A big house. You passed it on the way here from the village. It is off the road and hidden in the trees," Marco said.

Certainly a house I need to check out after we get back, Nick thought.

As the tide changed, the fishing method adapted. Marco poled the panga into knee-deep water and anchored it. He stayed in the boat as Nick entered the water to fish. Marco watched his client use the light salt-water flyrod. He would snap it back and stop his cast at precisely the right angle to lay the line out and drop the fly in the very place he intended.

Marco, in his higher position standing in the boat, could spot snook cruising the salt flats easier than if he had been in the water. He seemed to Nick to be one with the beautiful fish with its lateral racing stripe as he turned and pointed a brown finger where to cast ahead of a snook looking to feed.

More often than not, the cast would yield a hookup. Nick would fight the strong fish, which hit the fly like a grenade going off, then release it.

While Marco grew up poor and eating all of whatever was grown or caught or killed, he appreciated the care his client took releasing the fish. It showed a stewardship for nature, something he did not always see among clients looking for large fish for bragging rights photos. This Latino American did not bother to have him take any pictures. To Marco, the pictures should remain in the heart, not some telephone device he had lived almost three-quarters of a century without.

The wind shifted. Marco told Nick they should head back. A front was coming in, and the water was already seeing some chop. They were several miles from the lodge and the guide throttled up on the Yamaha and the panga surged ahead. Nick was pleased with the performance of the simple rig. Before they got back, it was starting to rain.

The rain did not affect the guide. He had grown up in the tropics, as had his client.

Nick paid him a nice tip in US dollars and said, "I need to walk into town and pick up a few things. A little rain won't melt me, my friend." They nodded and Nick turned toward the village.

He reached the center of the village after a long walk. The house Marco had mentioned was largely hidden by the trees, but visible if one was looking for it. Nick had not seen it when he was walking to the lodge.

It had been raining here longer than where he and Marco had fished. Nick saw man-sized footprints in the soft dirt where the lane from the house met the gravel road to the village. They were headed toward the village and there were none going back toward the house. The prints were not the stride of a strong walker. They were more like a shuffle. Some dragged through the soft dirt.

It was difficult to determine how old they were since he did not know when the rain began here. Nick felt they were less than an hour old. The man was probably in town.

Nick walked on, still limping more than normal from the Tampa fight. He reached the village in a few minutes. His quarry was an American or European who was tall but had a sickly color and seemed to walk with a shuffle. On the surface, not such a difficult search in a small Belizean village.

He went straight to the grocery. In the old West, it would have been a general merchandise store. This one had food, light hardware, a postal counter, and what appeared to be a pharmacy counter.

The man he sought was at the latter, picking up a prescription. He paid in US dollars and turned toward Nick, nodding and walking past. He had never seen Nick, nor had Nick ever seen him in person. But from case photos, Nick knew he was Nate Boudin. The man-bun guy who got away from the task force raid just before Nick was shot by Boudin's latest client in Inverness. The Loch Ness Monster, Rory McCormick.

Marco had called it right. Boudin was very ill. His complexion was pallid, and his lips had a bluish tint. Nick's first thought was heart trouble.

He wanted to ask the clerk who delivered Boudin's prescription what the pills were for. However, the last thing he wanted was to draw attention to himself. To be in any way memorable. Or interested in this man in particular. He did not know yet what his dealings would be with the man who set up Madison's kidnapping in Tampa.

Nick would have considered waterboarding him. Now, having seen how fragile he was, he knew if he waterboarded him, Boudin would be the first person ever to succumb to the enhanced interrogation technique.

Nick bought a Cuban cigar for a quarter of what it would have been illegally in the States and asked for a pack of matches.

Stepping outside the store, he started to light it, then thought better. Where the hell was his OPSEC? Good operational security or awareness did not include going to a house and leaving a cigar smell for police to question.

Nick slipped the cigar into his pocket and walked after the man. After Boudin. How had he escaped? And how had he gotten here? He was clearly still involved in trafficking teenage girls through the wonder of cyberspace.

He walked up to within a hundred yards of Boudin and slowed to match the man's shuffling pace. Nick's own left leg thanked him for the easier gait.

Nick saw Boudin turn into the lane and disappear. There was sporadic traffic, so he could not be seen loitering by the entrance lane. He stepped off into the woods.

He was not happy about going into the bush. Belize has several varieties of coral snakes, moccasins, at least one variety of rattlesnake. Even worse, it had the dreaded fer-de-lance.

All are deadly. Especially the last. And Nick hated snakes. The Russell's vipers in Afghanistan were enough for him.

He decided chancing being seen beat getting bitten by a fer-de-lance or any other damn snake and moved back to the road immediately.

He quickly turned down the lane to the house where Boudin lived. He hoped the trafficker lived alone. It would greatly ease the questioning process.

Nick looked in a window and saw Boudin sitting at a table. He opened his bag from the pharmacy counter and set a small bottle on the table. He took a chain from around his neck and began to pray, holding the cross on it in his fingers.

He must really be sick, Nick thought as he watched.

Nick decided to use the direct approach. He walked over to the door and knocked.

Boudin came to the door within a minute and opened it without hesitation.

"Oh! I saw you in town. One of the few tourists without a rental car," he greeted Nick.

Up close, Nick realized this man was very sick.

"Yes. You were one of the few Americans or Europeans I have seen in town. I am at a fishing lodge. We have a few there.

"My name is Roberto Jorge. Bob is good enough. I have been thinking about moving here and wondered if you have a few minutes to spare. I would have caught up with you on the road, but it seems we both have a difficult time making headway very quickly."

"I saw you limping in the village. War wound?" Boudin asked, not bothering to introduce himself.

"Yes. Of a sort," Nick responded truthfully but misdirecting his answer.

"I am not feeling well, as you can see. So I will have to ask you to leave so I can prepare my meds," the man across the table told Nick.

"I see you are truly ill. I have come from Tampa Bay to find out something from you. I will find it out one way or another," Nick said.

"I am the former commander of the human trafficking task force which raided your warehouse and home. You are wanted on fifty kidnapping charges, human trafficking, and a bunch of other charges, including tax evasion.

"But I am not a cop anymore, Nate Boudin without your man-bun. I want to know where Madison Newton is. I know you were the alleged sixteen-year-old who engineered her kidnapping. Tell me where she is, or I will draw out your last days into a worse existence than you could ever visualize," Nick said.

"I see you are a Christian. Probably a Catholic. This is your one opportunity for redemption. Do it! You have nothing to lose."

Boudin was thinking. And it was apparent to Nick he was dying.

The man tried shakily to unscrew the cap on his new medicine. Nick took it and removed the cap and handed it back after reading the label.

It was nitroglycerine.

"I believe you should place a tablet under your tongue," Nick said.

"I know, damn you!" Boudin said as he put a tablet under his tongue and dropped the bottle on the table, the contents spilling.

"Where is Madison Newton?" Nick repeated. "Who has her? Do the right thing, Nate. Maybe, just maybe, God will forgive you at this last hour."

Boudin thought again, hesitating. Then he clearly came to a decision point.

"Mount Dora. The Jamaican has her," he said.

"Esson from the Mama Jama Club?" Nick asked for clarification, and the ill man nodded.

"Is he going to keep her?"

Boudin nodded, and Nick knew he was telling the truth.

All of a sudden, Boudin jerked. He grabbed his chest and his eyes widened. He jerked a couple more times and fell forward, his head hitting the table with a loud thud.

Nick reached over to his neck and checked his pulse with two fingers. There was none. He checked the wrist to be doubly sure.

Nate Boudin, trafficker of teenaged young women, was dead.

Nick stood up and went to the kitchen. He picked up a dishcloth.

Walking back, he wiped the nitroglycerine bottle and set it back down on its side as it had fallen. He left the pills scattered on the table and wiped his finger-prints off the cap. He had been careful not to touch anything. He had not touched the door handle. Boudin had held it wide for him to walk in.

Nick wiped the chair everywhere he might have touched it when he seated himself at the table. He even wiped Boudin's neck and wrist where he had checked for a pulse, though he knew anyone checking there for prints in an obvious heart attack death would be highly unlikely.

Nick had the knowledge he had come for and did not wish to be associated with having been there or maybe having prompted the fatal heart attack. He knew the man was near death almost immediately upon walking in. Now, he needed to get word to Lola about Madison's whereabouts and develop a strategy to rescue her.

He was able to lock the door from the inside, then close it once outside, again using the dishcloth. Nick stuffed the dishcloth in his shirt and walked to the end of the lane and peered both ways. Nobody was coming by foot or vehicle. He limped along the road to the lodge, now in driving rain. He arrived at his cottage soaked and changed into dry clothes. There was an umbrella in the corner, and he picked it up to walk to the main lodge for dinner. In the alcove inside the door, he called Lola. No joy.

10

The van was filling with heat and stifling fumes. Lola struggled with the seat belt shoulder belt combination which was holding her upside down. It finally came loose, and she fell, hitting the roof, now flat against the ground.

It dazed her for a second, but intuitively she needed to get out now to survive. She tried to open the passenger door to avoid climbing around the steering wheel. It was jammed shut from the roll.

The damned windows were intact and shut. She knew the electric window controls would not work and tried to kick the window out. No luck!

She drew her 9mm Glock Model 45 and fired several shots in a close pattern in the center of the pane. She kicked again, and the window gave. She kicked the jagged edges out and crawled through just as the flames enveloped the upside-down van. Pistol in hand, she crawled on all fours as fast as she could into the bushes and away from the heat of the van's flames.

When she had gotten ten feet away, the van

exploded. There was little shrapnel other than a few remaining shards of glass. She was not harmed and crawled further in case of another explosion.

Lola saw the big pickup and aimed her Glock at it from over a hundred yards. She could use a slight elevation—Tennessee elevation versus Kentucky windage—and hit the rear window and maybe kill the person who had tried to kill her. But the legality was ninety-ten against her. It ended up not mattering, because she fainted.

The site became busy within ten minutes. A fire pumper doused the remaining flames in the van. A trooper was photographing tire marks and estimating the number of rolls. He was able to get enough off the scorched license plate to run it.

County deputies were directing traffic. A second trooper was gathering and interviewing those first on scene, including the one who had called it in.

Lola crawled out of the bushes and began to crawl toward the FHP car.

She had gotten close before anyone saw her. The trooper investigating ran toward her. He stopped midway and looked at the bedraggled, bruised, and bloodied woman.

"Lola! Trooper Caldwell?" He resumed running and called for the ambulance to return. It had been summoned at the original accident call and left when no injured party was found.

He kneeled at her side. The fire had been too hot to look for a victim inside the van yet. Now he knew who the driver had to be.

"Were you alone? Or is there another victim inside?" he asked.

"Alone. Following a human trafficking suspect. His

bouncer was behind me. Did not know until he pulled up and I saw him. He dropped back and pitted me in a large dark pickup. I think a Ford F-350. Dark green or blue. He pulled over and made sure it was afire before driving off. It was as deliberate as hell, Hank!" she said to a trooper with whom she used to patrol.

"I have an ambulance returning. Lay still until they check you out. I'll get a firefighter to come over. One's a paramedic. Maybe both, I don't know."

He stood and yelled, "Paramedic with kit! We have a victim!" and one of the firefighters ran for the truck, retrieved a bag, and started their way.

The trooper put out a lookout for the truck with possible damage to the right bumper.

The paramedic did a preliminary check and said, "I think your injuries are all superficial, but you need to have an ER doc check you out. The closest is Lakeland Regional Health. I doubt they will keep you overnight.

"If you don't mind me asking, Lola, what the hell were you doing following a suspect in a PI agency van?"

"It's a long story, but I assure you it's all righteous. My boss is aware, and I am on a week's leave to help in the case. If you come to the hospital to take a full report, I will clue you in. This was attempted murder of a police officer. The driver and I knew each other, and he knew I was a trooper."

"I will get the particulars at the hospital. You ride there in the ambulance when it gets here. I will finish the investigation diagrams and initial write-up. It will be faster now I know what happened. Then, I will come to see you at the hospital. Anybody I can call?"

"Yes, the PI whose van is now a burned-out hulk with lots of surveillance equipment ruined. He's the former head of the I-4 corridor Trafficking Task Force.

He was shot in the line of duty and had to retire. His name is Nick Wolf." She gave him Nick's number.

As the ambulance left with Lola in the rear, the trooper called Nick. The call went directly to voice mail.

Nick was concerned he was unable to reach Lola. He ate and advised the owner he had an emergency back home and would have to curtail his visit.

It was too late to head to Belize City for a flight. He brought his small Mac laptop back with him to the lodge after dinner. Unlike his cabin, the lodge had Wi-Fi.

He logged into American and changed his return flight to the earliest available one in the morning, disregarding the extra fee.

Nick sent her a detailed text message delineating all he had learned but leaving out the part about Boudin dying in the middle of the interview. He would share that part in person.

He slept fitfully. The next morning he passed on breakfast and the lousy instant coffee. He had paid his bill the night before and began his walk to the village and the bus to Belize City.

As he arrived at the village's bus stop, he saw someone from the lodge having coffee at an open bar café. They had chatted about fishing during his dinner there the first night.

He walked over and found the man was returning to the airport in his rental car but needed some decent coffee for the several-hour trip. Nick offered to share the cost of gas for a ride back to the airport. The man told him to get his coffee to go and hop in. And, to forget the gas cost.

The trip was spent talking about fishing, though Nick tried several more times to call Lola. He was getting increasingly worried. He called the landline in his apartment office but did not get a response. Only his answering service.

He boarded the flight to Miami and barely made the very quick connection with the flight to Tampa several hours later. It had necessitated speed of movement he simply had not regained.

The first thing he did when he deplaned at Tampa was turn his phone on. He had a voice mail. It was not from Lola but a state trooper on I-4. His gut tightened as he heard the message about the accident and her being in the hospital.

He immediately rented a car at the airport and left for Lakeland Regional Hospital in a rental Chevrolet Malibu.

Though not severely injured from appearances, Lola had been tested for internal damages and concussion from her three rolls and almost immediate escape from the burning van. She was sent to a room for the night and observation.

Nick immediately went to her room. She had a bandage around her head, and he noted multiple bruises and small cuts and scrapes as he rushed through the door.

She looked up, and her first words were, "I'm sorry about your van."

"Screw the van! Lola, all I care about is you!"

Lola broke down, and all of the past hours' emotions flowed. He leaned over and kissed the tears.

"Do you have injuries I can't see? Or can I hug you? I have been so worried calling and texting you," he asked.

"What you see is what you get," she said.

He hugged her. "What I see is all I'll ever want."

She quickly told him her story. Her cell phone had gone the way of his cameras, shotgun, and everything else in the van. Total loss.

"When do you check out of here?" he asked.

"They said today, then I got up to go to the bathroom and fainted. Now they want to watch me until tomorrow and do some more tests just to be safe."

"When I get you tomorrow, I'm taking you to my place where Finn and I can look after you. But first I have to go to Mt. Dora and get Madison," he said.

"How did you know she was there? I was following Esson when I was intentionally rolled by the guy whose nose you broke."

"I found the 'sixteen-year-old' in Belize. He told me during a heart attack. He wanted to meet God with as clear a conscience as possible. He died before I left. But not by my hand. He was having the massive heart attack when I got there.

"I could not believe it. He was the guy who ran the trafficking along the I-4 corridor and got away before our big raid, the second half of which was when I was shot," Nick said.

"I have to go there and get her tonight. Because of the time it would take them to understand how I came to know her location and to get search warrants, I am going to keep law enforcement out of it."

"It's too dangerous to do it alone and unarmed!" she said.

"It's only mid-afternoon. I should be able to use my Florida concealed weapons license and some gun store's fast automated records check to buy what I need on the way there. I have to get going. I'll be back here in the morning to pick you up," Nick said.

"You damn well, better. I don't want you getting hurt. Watch out for the bouncer guy. He's likely to be there as Esson's bodyguard," Lola said.

Nick nodded, leaned over, and kissed her.

"If he is, he will be very sorry," Nick said, rushing out the door.

He called Pi along the way and had him do a search on properties owned in Mt. Dora by Esson. Five minutes later, Pi called back to tell Nick he had been successful.

"I have texted you the address, a local detailed map, and a Google Earth photo of the house. It's on the waterfront. There's a boathouse on the lake with what appears to be a second-story apartment. It has a one-vehicle parking space. It's not occupied in the photo."

"Thanks, buddy! Put it on my tab," Nick said and hung up.

Nick knew of a gun store in Tavares. It had been operating for many years. It always had interesting guns and he had driven up to look around several times in the past. He drove straight there. He knew he did not have time to conduct the mandatory function test fire of several hundred rounds for a semiautomatic, so he would look for a revolver.

He arrived in a bit over an hour and went to the used handgun counter. He asked to see one in particular. It was a round butt, three-inch barrel Smith & Wesson .357 Magnum. It was the medium K-sized frame. He tested the cylinder lockup and trigger pull. The grips and blue finish were worn, but the mechanics seemed good, and the bore was bright. It had been carried a lot but was well-maintained. They had a used holster with it. It was an inside the beltline one made of leather and well broken in. He added a box of Speer Gold Dot hollow points and a pack of two-speed strip reloaders, which held six cartridges each. His last selection before checking out was a mid-sized Kershaw tactical folding knife.

He checked out and loaded the gun and the spare ammo strips into the rental car.

It was already dusk. His next stop was the ever-convenient Walmart. Nick was still in his fishing clothes and needed something more operational.

A pair of dark-blue chinos, a matching tee shirt, a black dress shirt one size too large, and a black ball cap to replace his current tan one took care of his clothing needs. He added one pair of dark, heavy hiking socks and some long wire ties.

The next stop was a bank drive-through, where he exchanged a twenty-dollar bill for two rolls of quarters. He emptied the eighty quarters into one of the hiking socks and knotted the open end. He now had a perfectly legal sap.

He changed in a service station restroom and was now in all dark clothes. Nick had taken his high-lumen tactical flashlight to Belize and put it with the gun in the trunk. He was ready. Dusk quickly changed to night. It was time to reconnoiter.

He rode through the neighborhood and identified the house. There was no car in the driveway. The parking space for the boathouse was still empty. He did not see any small yard signs or window stickers with an alarm company name. Nick knew this did not prove there was no alarm but lessened the probability some-what in his mind. The bedrooms were on the second floor. Several window sashes were raised to pull in fresh air from Lake Dora.

It was good tradecraft to not idle by like he was looking at something but to casually drive by as if heading somewhere else. During his drive-by, he detected a way to climb to the second story without a ladder. As long as the windows were raised, even if Esson had an unseen alarm system, those windows were bypassed.

There was always his left leg to consider on any climb. And, if he had to exit the same way with a five foot six female, it could be a problem.

He doused his headlights and parked on the street.

He had already changed the lighting in the rental so the interior lights would not come on when he opened the doors.

Nick got out and walked to the side with the open windows. He heard a soft sobbing from the second window over from the lattice he planned to climb.

He looked both ways. No traffic. No neighbor's lights on. Using his good leg to bend and for strength, began to climb.

The first climb was onto an upside-down trash can he placed strategically. Then, onto a lattice with vines growing on it.

The good news was the cross pieced on the lattice were close together and Nick did not have to raise his bad leg high. The bad news was they were not very strong. They also were not very new. The third one broke.

Nick caught himself and hung there for a moment to see if the noise awakened anyone in the house. After a minute, he continued to climb. He could hear the crying. As a law enforcement officer looking for a victim, it would have justified entry without a warrant for life safety purposes. Nick did not give a damn. He just wanted to save the young girl.

He stretched from the top rung of his lattice ladder and slashed the window screen soundlessly. Closing the knife the way he had opened it—with one hand—he pocketed it and pushed upward on the window sash. It opened. It made a creak as the window opened more than to its normal fresh air height, but there was no stirring Nick could hear from within.

Nick grasped the windowsill with both hands and muscled up until he could get his head and torso in. Then he rolled inwards, still holding tightly to the sill to soften his landing.

This bedroom was empty.

So was the second bedroom.

Nick hit pay dirt on the third. It was larger and obviously the master. He saw a wig holder with a dreadlock wig on it. There was a blonde head in the bed, asleep but making sobbing noises.

He immediately took out his smartphone and began videoing the scene. He moved closely and focused on the bed.

He put his hand on the sheet covering the shoulder of the blonde and shook it lightly. There was no response.

Nick touched her neck, and her pulse was strong, though a bit erratic.

He lifted her to a sitting position and the sheet fell off her. Nick covered her unclothed body with the sheet.

He softly spoke to her.

"Madison. Wake up."

Her eyes fluttered open, and she tried to focus. He gave her a second and continued.

"My name is Nick. Your grandfather sent me to rescue you. Do you think you can walk?" She nodded, though he thought she was still sedated somewhat.

"Handcuffs," she said and shook the sheet down. Her hands were handcuffed in front and a thin rope was tied on the middle chain of the cuffs and disappeared down below her waist.

"Hold up your hands. I'll cut the restraint rope."

She did, and he cut the rope and left it where it was. Nick then quickly took off his dark long sleeve shirt and put it on her.

"Do you think you can walk?"

"I can try. I think the drugs the man from the club gave me are wearing off a little."

"Tell me your name. I need to make sure you are truly the person I came for."

"I am Madison, like you said."

He confirmed this by holding the photo on his cell phone up beside her face. Her eyes were somewhat open, but the lids were down more than if she was totally conscious.

Nick helped her up, but she was very unsteady on her feet.

He was going to have to carry her out. Using a fireman's carry to help his left leg while carrying her down the steps, he descended and placed her on a sofa. She had dozed off again.

He slapped her face very lightly. "Madison. Madison. You are safe. Wake up," he said softly to her.

She stirred and mumbled but never became completely conscious.

He searched the house with a quick, professional sweep. There did not seem to be a burglar alarm panel anywhere.

He decided to use the kitchen door. It was farther to his car on the street, but the route was all in the shadows. Nick picked her up again and carried her to the car.

The dark F-350 Lola had described was now parked in the driveway. He wanted to leave Madison in the car and go up and kill the man who had tried to harm his Lola.

Dedication to his mission held him back as he put Madison in the passenger seat and hooked her in. He straightened the shirt to give her as much decency as possible.

He started the Malibu and backed down the drive onto the lakefront road. In gear, he slowly drove out of town.

At a traffic light, he removed the emergency handcuff key he and every other cop carried in his wallet or somewhere else accessible on his person. He unlocked Madison. The light changed, and he drove on at a normal traffic speed.

Madison became increasingly alert over the next hour as Nick drove toward Tampa.

"Who...who are you again?" she asked hesitatingly.

"My name is Nick. I am a former sheriff's detective. Your grandfather hired me to rescue you. If I call him, do you want to speak with him right now?"

"Yes."

He called Judge Mabry's personal cell.

"This better be good!" came the surly answer.

"This is Nick Wolf. I have Madison in the car beside me. She is okay as near as I can tell but is coming out of sedation. How about I deliver her to you, and you have your physician there to check her out or he can take her to the hospital for a full check if he deems it necessary?"

"Yes. I will call him."

"I got her from the address. I will text you. Mt. Dora. Lake County."

"Okay. I want to talk with my granddaughter."

Nick handed the phone to Madison who spoke for a minute and then broke into tears. She handed the phone back to Nick.

"She's okay, Judge. Just overcome with emotion after being freed. It's perfectly normal. We will be at your house in forty-five minutes, according to my phone's navigation system. I'd better let you go to call the doc and the law."

"Thank you, Nick. This was really fast. God knows what you saved her from experiencing. I will also have a senior state investigator here to coordinate the arrests in Mt. Dora." The judge hung up with no further comments, and Nick focused on driving.

"Madison, who picked you up on the walk to school?" Nick asked.

"He was a giant. Big and ugly. Like a giant."

Nick tapped Photos on his phone screen. Recents appeared. Nick pulled up a photo of the broken nose man.

"Is this him?"

She nodded it was, and he put the phone away.

———————

As Nick was walking to the car with Madison, Esson's employee, Yerik Sokolov, had just arrived at the boathouse where he stayed when he was in Mt. Dora to guard the boss. He had seen a car parked on the street, but it was nearer to the residence next door, so he ignored it.

The sound of a nearby engine starting attracted Yerik's attention.

He quickly looked out of the window. Nick was carrying the girl over his shoulder to a car and putting her in it. He recognized the man from the club. The man with the woman he had killed on I-4.

He picked up his CZ 75 pistol, sticking the CZ 9mm in the belt at the center of his back.

Idiot! He ran down to his truck. No slashed tires. His truck started up without exploding. He would have disabled it or sabotaged it had he done the op.

The Power Stroke Diesel accelerated loudly as he took off after the sedan with the man who had hit him and the girl.

He called Esson.

"Boss, we got problem!"

"Wait one, I'm having dinner with friends." He excused himself and walked to a remote corner to speak to Yerik.

"Okay. What's the issue?"

"It is the man who hit me at the nightclub. The one with the woman I took care of. He just stole the girl from your house. I am after him in my truck," Yerik said to Esson.

"Yerik, you kill the man. And the girl! Do you understand me? Afterward, dump your truck and meet me at the alternate site. Make sure you are not followed."

"I will, I am waiting for the right time and place."

Esson returned to his dinner companions.

"I have an urgent work issue to which I must attend. Please continue without me," he said, handing two one-hundred-dollar bills to the server on the way out of the restaurant.

He drove to a storage facility on the edge of town. He

coded in at the gate and drove to his unit. He opened it and drove a Jeep Grand Cherokee out and replaced it with the Mercedes. Before he left the unit, he hung his current of two dreadlock wigs on a wig stand, baring a crew cut. He pulled on a golf shirt and jeans and left his Italian suit on the back seat of the Benz.

Esson, a different persona in looks and name, drove the Jeep thirty miles to a remote cabin located well off a state highway. He had an escape and financial plan. It was, sadly, time to put it in effect. He had learned earlier in the day his lieutenant, Nate, was dead of a heart attack in Belize. It was time to cut his losses and run. As long as the Russian killed the sonofabitch who had caused the downfall of a lucrative trafficking empire and the girl who could identify him.

Yerik was half a mile behind the Malibu on a dark and fairly deserted rural highway. He would roll the little sedan as he had the bitch in the van. *The woman of the man in the car ahead*, he thought. *She is dead. Soon this one who could testify against him will be also. The damn man who had sucker punched me. And a cripple! It was embarrassing. To have your nose broken by a skinny-ass cripple!*

Yerik found his spot on the two-lane state highway. It was a long straightaway and there was no traffic. He floored the accelerator, and the four hundred eighty-five foot pounds of torque kicked in, propelling the truck ahead.

Nick had seen the big truck gaining on him. This was no coincidence. He was hampered having the half-drugged victim in the car with him. He knew would be a final showdown with the big man. He had to kill him while protecting the girl from harm.

Nick was watching the truck. He knew what the

bouncer had in mind. The truck had almost twice the bulk of the rental car. But Nick was confident he was the better trained driver.

The truck came up on the left. The second the truck got even with his left rear tire to swerve right and PIT him, Nick stood on the brakes for a second and jerked the wheel to the left into the right outside rear tire on the dually. Nick floored the accelerator and pushed as hard as he could against the much larger vehicle. After a mere second, he hit the brakes again and let the sideways drifting vehicle get ahead of him. As the truck slewed over toward the right lane, Nick took the left shoulder and roared past.

However good a warfighter the Russian was, he did exactly the wrong thing to pull out of his sideways drift. He turned the wheel to the right not the left, causing the truck to go from a drift to a spin. It was simply too tall to do donuts on the highway and stay upright.

Yerik's truck rolled just as he had rolled Lola in the van. He ended up on the right shoulder, shaken but with the greasy side down.

Nick had stopped the Malibu at the truck's first roll. He pulled off the road and bailed out, .357 Magnum in hand. He could not afford to have this giant man in a giant truck keep coming for him. And, after Madison.

It had to end. End here. Nick walked toward the Ford pickup as the driver's door opened and the man, nameless to Nick, stumbled out and fell on his face.

Nick was within fifty yards. He narrowed it to thirty-five as the big man got to his feet and drew a pistol from behind his back.

Nick stood rock solid, using a modified Weaver stance. Though he knew he would generally use double action on the revolver in a defensive action, he eased the hammer back to full cock to give a shorter trigger press for more accuracy.

As the big man raised his own pistol, Nick pressed the trigger and send a 125-grain .357 Magnum hollow point into his chest just below the throat. He could see the impact.

He had been taught one is none, two is one. He smoothly pressed in double action and sent another round into the same place, making the wound even more massive. His aggressor died on his feet and crumpled into the grass without movie drama or fanfare.

Ever conscious of evidence in court, Nick took a photo showing his car and the truck with his large adversary laying on the grass, his pistol beside him. The latest generation smartphone camera accommodated for the darkness. The picture was usable. It would not take a graduate engineer to compare the vehicle sizes and come up with the distance between them. He walked over to the dead man and picked up the CZ with a pencil through the muzzle end of the barrel. Nick could not afford to have a person stopping unattended at the crash absconding with the valuable pistol. It was doubly valuable to Nick. It had the man's fingerprints on it and was his proof he shot in self-defense.

Nick holstered his revolver and called Judge Mabry as he walked back to the Malibu. He told him what he did to keep Madison safe. He knew "cover and evacuate" was the mantra of protection.

"Get back in the car. Leave your gun as is. Do not touch it again until you turn it over to law enforcement. Drive here. I will send the highway patrol to the scene and explain I ordered you to bring your protectee here and you will be interviewed here by a state investigator. Now, move!" the judge ordered.

Nick got back into the car. Interestingly, he had no damage from nudging the tire of the truck. The mid-size might be out of alignment. He would know when he drove it the rest of the way to the judge's house.

"Did you kill the monster?" Madison, now fully conscious, asked.

"I did. He won't bother you anymore, Madison."

"How about the man who owns the club? He was the really evil one. The one who scared me the most," she said.

"Your grandfather is sending police to find him now. The important thing is you are safe. They won't bother you anymore," he said, still realizing she was at risk until Esson was in handcuffs. She was the primary witness against him. The one who could put him away for a long time.

He watched as she assimilated what he had said and the past several days of captivity and stark fear. She stared ahead as he drove at a normal highway speed to the judge's fenced and gated home.

———

The judge's daughter was there. Despite her unlikeable personality, it warmed Nick's heart to see the reunion between the three.

The judge had a state investigator present as promised. He was a Florida Department of Law Enforcement agent, named Rob Gadsden. He took Nick's full statement about freeing the girl and the gunfight on the side of the road. Nick turned over his gun for forensic testing and the dead man's CZ for evidentiary fingerprints. Nick emailed him the videos and photos he had taken, and the state special agent reviewed them and added all to his report.

"Since these events occurred in different jurisdictions, I will likely need to provide all of this to them, too," he told the investigator.

"Probably not. I am going to claim jurisdiction and forward my report to the FHP, Mt. Dora, and Orange County, where the shooting took place," the investigator said with absolute confidence he could control the case.

At dawn, Nick was able to get back in the rental and head toward Lakeland and Lola. He was sore from the climb up Esson's house, tired and stressed. He needed breakfast and a nap. He stopped at a Cracker Barrel for the former and knew the latter would have to wait. Along the way he called his insurance agent and long-time friend, Ric, and told him about the wrecked van. He called an impatient Lola and told her he had an effective night and would fill her in on the drive back.

"Look, Nick. All I have is my light Kevlar vest, shoes, and gun. I am wearing a bare-ass hospital gown which would be a sight when I get out of the wheelchair and into the car. I need panties, shorts, a top, and a bra please."

"Roger wilco. See you after I go shopping."

This time, he stopped at a shopping center in Lakeland and this time, he shopped at an upscale anchor department store.

He had the clothes gift-wrapped and presented them to her in the room. While the nurse assisted her getting dressed, he went to security by pre-arrangement and claimed her FHP Glock, vest and badge wallet.

He rode down the elevator with an orderly pushing her in the mandatory wheelchair. She was adorned in a new sundress, matching purse and pumps instead of her running shoes. Lola attracted a great deal of positive attention all the way to the car.

"Where's the bra?" she asked.

"They were out of bras," he said.

"One of the largest department store chains in America and they were out of bras?" she asked incredulously.

"Seemed like they were," he said.

"You are an animal!"

"I've heard it said before. By you, as I remember."

"Just don't change."

"Okay."

"How are you doing after the shooting, honey?" Lola asked.

"Not my first rodeo. He almost killed you and was trying to kill me. I cannot think of a more righteous shooting."

"Me, either. How is Madison?"

"Nicer than her mother. She was very adult and appreciative."

"I interviewed her dad over in Largo the other day. He is far more human than the spoiled bitch he impregnated. She must have inherited her nice genes from him. You know? I need to call him and tell him she's okay. Do you think he might have seen the paper?"

"We were both mentioned. You hit hero status again. I think it will be great for our business," Lola said.

He looked at her when she said "our."

"Just trying it on. This will bring a big jump in the agency's workload, I bet. Maybe I can resign from the FHP and become your partner. Give it some thought," she said.

"I already have. A lot of thought. I believe we can pull it off pretty quickly. We'll have to check, but I think you can get your PI license immediately based on your LE experience. Can you carry over your state hospitalization?"

"I'm pretty sure I can," she said.

"Let's stop somewhere for lunch."

"You just want to see me jiggle into a restaurant."

"I do."

"Those words have a good ring to them. Keep practicing saying them," she suggested.

———

They went to Nick's apartment and office to check on Finn. Nick was neither surprised nor upset to see the yellow cat immediately gravitate to Lola.

"Well, how about you go through exactly what the PI firm does?" Lola asked. "All I know is from watching television. I suspect it's about as real on there as *CHIPS* was to what I do. No comparison!"

"You are dead right there. We do three things: investigations, the primary revenue source; security consulting; and executive protection. I also have a bail enforcement agent license, but only for a special purpose," Nick said.

"Almost all of the investigation work is from ten law and insurance firms. With you aboard, we can add more cases and more firms, I hope."

"You said bail enforcement? Like bounty hunter? I sure don't see you bounty hunting!"

"Actually, 'bounty hunting' is illegal in Florida. The state has a very precise licensing process. There is also no legal crossover between being a bail enforcement guy and a PI here. We both try to locate people, but the similarity ends there.

"Then, why did you get the license"

"After my group recovered around fifty trafficked teens, I was approached by a man named Guy Kellogg. He is known in a ten-county area, including Tampa Bay, as the 'Bail Bondsman to the Rich and Famous.' He has a network of bail bond offices near jails and court-houses all over. He also has his own office in a bank building in Sarasota where rich, important people who are arrested or whose relatives are, come to get them bonded out.

"He has a group of about five bond enforcement agents. I suspect they are very professional and effec-tive. However, he wanted someone who can concen-trate on finding skips who are special for one reason or another and have really big bonds. That was where he wanted me to come in. Find the person, then call in his other guys to arrest and transport them. My func-tion, done three times in the past three and a half years, has been more like PI stuff. But the law is so specifically written I have to be carried on his books and licensed."

"What do you get paid?" she asked.

"No salary. I am on call. I get twenty percent of the bond if I find the person and make the arrest. His guys who transport without all the footwork get five percent. They love it and appreciate how my participation allows them to spend time on their normal fifteen percent work and still get paid handsomely for nothing more than transporting the skip to the nearest police depart-ment for a receipt."

"Nick, how can five percent be considered 'hand-somely,'" she asked.

"When it's five percent of two hundred thousand dollars or ten thousand dollars."

"So, in the case you laid out, you earned twenty grand?"

"Yep."

"Sounds like I should help and get the license, too. It's a big payday even if it does not happen so often!" she said.

"I agree. Let me sell Guy on the idea of adding you as my partner and you should take the online course and apply for a license under his firm. After you get your primary license, the Florida Private Investigator one."

"How much of the consulting and bodyguard work is there?"

"I am asked to do more than I accept."

"A lot of people don't want to pay a security consultant what he or she is worth. On the executive protection, our contract wording weans out a lot of people from the start. Many are corporations that have out-of-town or out-of-country clients or buyers coming in. They want to be protected while entertaining them. Our contract says, 'The contract will be terminated instantly when illegal activity such as drugs or prostitution become involved, and the full fee will be forfeited.' I read it to an inquiring potential client upfront. Often they just hang up in my ear."

"Nick. I am no angel. I suspect you have found it out the past few nights. But I've spent my career upholding the law. I believe in the ethic which characterizes this agency and will be proud to include my name on it," Lola said.

She received just the sort of smile she hoped for from her new partner.

"How about I go through mail, and you research getting a PI license online? It has been four years for me, and the regulations may have changed," Nick suggested.

Nick brought her the Mac Pro laptop into the kitchen and set it up on the table with the Wi-Fi keyboard. He sat opposite Lola and began to go through the mail. Most of his bills were automatically paid by his company credit card. The good news was that the preponderance of the non-junk mail was checks from his insurance and law firm clients. He had a subpoena to appear in criminal court for his golf-playing allegedly wheelchair-bound suspect. The insurance company had referred the matter to the state for investigation and an arrest for insurance fraud had been made. The hearing was a week hence and the state already had his videos in evidence. He would review the case records in his files a day or two before his testimony to make sure he was still fresh on the times, locations, and other relevant facts.

"Nick?" Lola broke his concentration.

"Hmm?"

"What does the PI and consulting practice need to take off?" she asked.

"An agreeable partner, for one thing, but I think we have it covered now. Second, our own building. I have always envisioned a classy old house near here. Somewhere right on the line where residences and businesses are still currently intermingled. A building which would present a professional appearance for the firm but have a lot more room upstairs for a living area. Probably an alley in the rear and enough backyard to securely park three or four vehicles. Now, I had to keep the surveillance van in a rental garage a block down the street.

"The place would have dual residential and business

zoning, or the ability to get such zoning quickly and cheaply."

"Speaking of the van, I would think replacing it ASAP would be on the top of our to-do list," Lola said.

"You are right, especially given our primary business is insurance and law firms and the types of cases they generate.

"There is a method in my questioning madness," Lola said.

"Go on."

"A neighbor several doors down from my house is a retired engineer. He lives modestly but is very well off. His daughter just got divorced. He wants her to move into the neighborhood near him and asked if I would be interested in selling. He mentioned a price based on his doing sales comparisons on the neighborhood. If I were to take it, especially in a private, no-commission sale, I would net fifty thousand dollars. I guess my equity has risen a lot in the eight years I have had the house.

"We could use part of it for a replacement van and maybe forty thousand for a down payment on a lease purchase on the building we are talking about. I would think it would cover the lease portion for a year or so. If we are wildly successful, we can buy. If not, we are not in debt. Plus the majority of the lease would be a tax write-off," Lola said.

"Great thoughts! Where did this knowledge of real estate and taxes come from?" Nick asked.

"My dad was a tax lawyer. I grew up with this stuff. He wanted me to take over the business, though I always kinda yearned for a badge."

"Was he disappointed?"

"He never knew. He died and I helped my mother sell his practice. He had a lot of long-term clients with value. She needed the cash badly. It really bailed her out."

"Where is she now?"

"She is in our hometown. Princeton, West Virginia. She teaches school. Probably will for another twenty years before retiring."

"Would I like her, Lola?" Nick asked.

"No. You'd love her. One look and you'd see what I will look like in twenty years. I think you will like the prospect a lot!"

"Do you have photos?"

"Yes, but to see them, we need to go to Verizon and get another phone for me. Luckily, I let them talk me into insurance on it. The photos should all be safely on the cloud," Lola said.

"Let's get the phone tomorrow. Then, talk with your engineer neighbor. I have some good lawyers I work with daily. I know who could draw up a partnership agreement for minimal cost.

"We could also ride around the area and look at some places for an office residence. Then, try to find a van. I think we have the next seven days or so planned already," Nick said.

That night, with Lola sore and bruised all over and Nick stressed more than he wanted to admit about the snatch and the kill, they slept fitfully but happily, her raven hair spread out on his left shoulder, skin to skin. Finn happily curled up on top of the covers by Lola's feet. The way it was going to be for years to come.

They got a quick breakfast on the way to the Verizon store in the Jeep. The phone was replaced, and Lola paid extra for an upgrade. She had help loading the new phone from her cloud storage. Before they left for the next stop, she pulled up a photo of her mom. She was right. Nick knew she would look the same in twenty years, except for a few silver streaks in her dark hair. Mom was gorgeous. He, too, was right early on. Lola is a keeper for so many reasons.

They went by her house and made sure there was nothing in the refrigerator which could go bad. She put clothes, uniforms, and personal items in her GTI.

Her retired engineer neighbor's Ram pickup was in his drive, and they walked over at nine-thirty. He was pleased about the opportunity to buy her house and Lola asked if he was interested in buying it furnished. He was, and they promised a contract for the agreed upon amount before the end of the week.

State Farm had sent an adjuster to the junkyard where the burned-out hulk of the van had been towed. It did not take her long to declare it totaled. She could have done it just driving by seeing the burned-out hulk.

Ric said he could mail him a check for the value, or he could pick it up. Nick and Lola picked it up after dropping her car and the contents off at Central Avenue.

While in the apartment office, they again reviewed their combined finances. Nick had had several really good recent past years and a still-healthy savings account.

Lola lived conservatively and her house payments were low. Her personal car, like his Jeep, was paid off.

"I have saved a large part of my earnings since the military. The only two things I own now are the Jeep and a boat I keep over by Anna Maria Island."

"You have a boat?" she exclaimed more than questioned. "When were you going to share that with me?"

"Well, just then, I suppose. Do you like boating?" he asked.

"Of course I do, silly man."

"Did you pick up a bikini when you got some of your stuff just now?"

"No, darn it! Do you think I'll need one?" she smiled.

"I seriously doubt it," he grinned evilly.

"We should get a replacement van. It's a necessity with the cases I –or we—catch," he said.

"Where did you get the other one?" she interrupted.

"At an auction of county vehicles. It was clean because an inspector had it. He carried a ladder, but not much else, so it was not beat up inside and didn't have paint splatters and the type thing most work trucks have."

"Can we afford a new one?" she asked.

"Probably, but I would hesitate for two reasons. I have tried to operate on a pay-as-you-go basis, and it has held me in good stead. Also, a shiny new one might stand out too much. I think we'd do better to replace it in kind and keep a lower profile."

"Makes sense to me. Do they have these auctions often?"

"Cities and counties have them often. We should not have any problem finding one soon when you consider how many jurisdictions the Tampa Bay area has. I can call around to some of the former task force guys and see what they know about upcoming auctions in their area and how to get in."

Six phone calls to former task force officers later, he found out about an upcoming county vehicle auction and was promised to have his name waiting at the gate for entrance.

Nick composed a list of the equipment on the destroyed surveillance van. The cameras and monitors were from Amazon, so he pre-ordered them.

Finding a highly sought for Mossberg Shock Wave shotgun took longer but he located one and they picked it up immediately. He still had the regular length and shorty buckshot loads for it in his office. He would use the S&W .357 as the backup handgun as soon as he got it back from the state forensics lab.

They went to the auction several days later and drove a three-year newer van home. This time it was a Ford. Lola helped with the measurements, and they had a home supply store cut a piece of kitchen countertop like the one in the previous van. Everything was installed by the weekend, and they delivered the home sales agreement to Lola's neighbor and executed the sale immediately. He would take the signed agreement to the clerk's office and file for a new deed.

Lola and Nick put the rest of her belongings into the rear of the van and took them to his place. They stored items she did not immediately need in the garage where the van would stay.

Lola's vacation leave was up. She went to work in her FHP car and tendered her resignation. She had to work the full two weeks of the notice period. They continued to look for a better, larger combination living and working space during her off-hours.

Nick prepared a letter on the agency letterhead to his law firm and insurance clients advising he was adding an experienced partner and would thereby be able to handle more cases. He later wished he had held off a while since the letter generated ten new cases before Lola was available to work them.

Nick needed to exercise his injured leg, so he and Lola drove to the area where they wanted to find a new office home and parked. They spent an hour walking and looking at possible homes on the market.

They found what appeared to be a great choice several weeks later and called the realtor for an appointment.

They went to see it the following night. It had a living room which could be a front office, an adjacent dining room that could serve as a conference room with a wall the two of them could put up. There was a half bath downstairs for clients. A kitchen and utility room, and steps to a second floor with three bedrooms and a full bath completed the interior. There was no way to close off the stair entrance except using a movie theater velvet rope to stop people from going up. The rear had a yard of which half was concrete for parking but did not have a garage. An alley was behind the house.

They agreed to meet the realtor back there the next day so they could study it in daylight.

The following day they returned with notes and diagrams and a tape measure.

"It's not perfect. A garage would have been nice. But it's workable, I think. What do you think, Lola?" Nick asked.

"I like the backyard being fenced in with a privacy fence. How difficult would it be to add an electronic door opener to the gate off the alley?" she asked.

"Since it has concrete on the ground, I think a coaster wheel on the bottom of the gate and rod system could be installed pretty easily. A fence company would have to do it, but the expensive part is already here—the fence itself."

"Can we afford this place?" Lola asked.

"I suspect so. Since we both have the same bank, let's go talk to them tomorrow and see."

Lola fixed her first dinner for them. It was a Mediterranean chicken dish on rice with a mushroom, sautéed peppers, and onion sauce on the chicken breasts. It was delicious.

Nick already had her hooked with himself and Finn on European detective shows. They watched one and turned in early. Tomorrow would be the bank and Lola taking a late shift for the FHP. Nick would begin work on several outstanding insurance investigations.

Three months later found the partners handling a full load of cases from their insurance and law firm clients. The revenue quickly climbed past the breakeven for adding Lola and her giving up her FHP salary.

They worked most cases alone due to the caseload but had little night work since neither did domestic cases. It was a rare night Nick and Lola did not eat dinner together, either at home or at a local restaurant since both had long days and it was a treat.

Nick had an old friend who retired from a local PD to whom he referred all domestic cases, such as infidelity and divorce matters. Nick received a five percent referral fee from his friend on all of those. He considered it found money since he had never wanted nor accepted such cases from the start.

They were having dinner together at home tonight and discussing the agency's revenue flow.

"Nick, I was looking at cash flow. What do you think of doubling the amount we pay on the mortgage each month? We are already getting a tax benefit for a good portion of the house. We could pay it off before either of us reaches sixty. Maybe even fifty-five."

"I think it's a great idea. We are also getting to the point where we might need another surveillance van. Would you like a full size, or a smaller, compact van?"

"A compact would be fine. How about a magnetic sign board for 'Aaron & Caldwell Home Inspections' for this one?" she asked. "It might be a better cover for a female yet plausibly require a ladder to hide the camera dome," she said.

"I agree. But let's go with Aaron and Ashley, both of our middle names for the firm. Two A's would keep us in the front of any alphabetical listing. And give some anonymity. Good tradecraft!

Now, back to the smaller van. You would not have as much counter space to work your computer or eat lunch or whatever," he said.

"I know. I don't really use all the space anyway. Nick? Do they make a Shock Wave in something smaller than twelve gauge?" she asked.

"Mossberg does. They also make a twenty and a .410 bore. I think the .410 may be too small. By the time we need a shotgun, things have gotten pretty serious. A twenty is okay though. I am of the opinion our little one and three-quarter-inch shorty loads in the twelve are about equal to a standard length twenty. So, if you are shooting fast and want to hold the recoil down, those in a twelve will act about the same as a twenty gauge."

"Hmm. Makes sense. Since they are hard to find, I will be ambivalent as to which we buy then."

"I have a pretty hefty schedule tomorrow, honey. Do you want to look around for a smaller van between case-work? Or are you swamped too?"

"I can look around. I have a couple of traffic cases, as

you know. The insurance companies love having an ex-trooper working those and using my rolling measuring tape and drawing diagrams."

"I know they do. You can finish a couple of traffic cases while I am stumbling on one."

"Don't knock it, lover boy. You solving a traffic case is how we met."

"If you find a van that is a good deal and appeals to you, just get it, okay? No need to call and discuss it," Nick said.

———

A week later found them in the backyard of their new office home on Sunday, putting finishing touches on the rear interior of a two-year-old Ford Transit Connect compact van. They had already completed the camera installation and dome, put on and locked down the ladder, and installed the countertop. A metal tool cabinet that had a drawer long enough for the short shotgun was now being bolted in.

"Cold beer or iced tea?" Lola asked as they completed.

"I think iced tea. We have time left to slip over to Anna Maria and run the boat out to the Gulf if you want?"

"Have I ever made any sort of negative response to something with the word 'boat' in it?" she asked as they locked the small van and walked into the house.

The phone rang and was heading to the voice mail answer, "Aaron and Caldwell, please leave your number and a detailed message. Thank you," when Nick recognized the number and grabbed the phone.

"Hello, Guy. It's Nick. What can we do for you?"

"Nick, I have a hot one. Can you come down to my office in Sarasota as soon as possible today and meet with me?"

"Of course. Lola and I will be there in an hour," and hung up.

Already taking off her shorts and tee shirt, Lola asked, "What's the uniform of the day for this meeting? I don't know Kellogg, so I don't know what to expect."

"Business casual is fine," Nick said, stepping into the shower.

They switched places after a minute, and he pulled out dark chinos and a Cuban Guayabera shirt in black. Not only had he grown up in a long-term foster household where they were standard wear, they were common in Tampa Bay, and did a great job of concealing a handgun underneath.

As he slipped into sockless loafers, Lola had toweled off and chose a slightly more conservative mini-skirt than her normal, a button-up blouse and pumps. She slipped her Glock 19 into her purse. Nick had modified it for her as a replacement to the turned-in FHP Glock.

She ran her fingers through her raven hair and shook her head. Hair done.

"If you drive, I'll do my makeup in the car." He grabbed their two bug-out bags with clothes, toiletries, and extra equipment for two days each.

"Want to take the little van, now it's ready? I think we need a van in case we have to go on surveillance south of here and it would waste time coming back," she asked.

"Good thought! Let me grab the laptop and both of our SHTF kits," he said, referring to their "Shit Hits The Fan," emergency getaway bags with everything but the pistols they wore.

They were on the Sunshine Skyway ten minutes later. At the one-hour mark, they were parking and entering the bank building which housed Guy Kellogg's head office.

"Hi, Nick. This must be Lola, my newest bail enforcement agent," he greeted them.

Both shook hands and he motioned them to chairs in front of his desk. Sarasota Bay and Marina Jack's was the panorama behind him through the wide window.

"Here's what we have. My friend Brack, or Braxton, Williston made a fortune or two with ideally spaced distribution warehouses. He handled about every commodity.

"He lives over on Bird Key in a big house near the yacht club. Like in many such cases, his son, Brack Jr., is a worthless piece of shit. Flunked out of two universities. Has permanent white powder stains on his nose. You get the picture. Good looking kid at almost your ages, but beyond worthless.

"You may have read about the deal in one of our local marinas a month ago. Brack Jr. took his father's boat out to party with some similarly worthless friends. No permission was asked. Both drunk and high, like his crew, he came into the marina on plane in a forty-two-foot sports fish.

"Obviously, he could not stop in time. He crashed into several boats, sinking one. He threw it into full throttle reverse and hit a big sailboat and several boats docked for lunch by the marina's seafood restaurant. Thank God there was no fire. The police jerked his worthless ass off the boat and arrested him initially for DUI boating.

"The estimated damage is well over two million dollars. The state's attorney laid on as many charges as he could spell. Brack Sr. came to me for, and was issued, bail in the amount of half a million dollars. Junior had several arrests in the past and was a known bail jumper...a legitimate flight risk.

"The trial is set for next week. The little twit has already disappeared once. He had not officially missed his trial so there was no need in arresting him and causing me to lose money. With his father's concurrence, I sent two of my guys after him based on information his father gave. They brought him back in cuffs.

"I just happened to have an ankle monitor. It's the kind with a cellular signal to advise of location via GPS.

"Now, the worst has happened. The body of a dock hand was just found drowned about a half mile from the marina. He was working that day and disappeared. There was no immediate indication it was related to Junior's spree. Now, evidence shows it was. Manslaughter has been added to his charges. His dad said he freaked out.

"He had a friend come over. Junior got into his friend's car, and the friend cut the ankle monitor off with heavy wire cutters. Breaking the fiber optic cable set off an immediate alarm, and we knew from the GPS where he was. I sent two guys over immediately. But Junior was gone. The friend took Junior's Corvette and tossed the severed monitor with its GPS transponder into the bed of a passing pickup.

"We wasted time tracking its location, and my guys scared the hell out of some good old Florida boys.

"I want you to find Junior and bring him back. I have spoken with his lawyer and dad together. We cannot legally imprison him. We can petition to the judge to revoke his bail, return the money to me, I will take back my fifteen percent fee and give the rest back to Senior. Otherwise, I lose half a million dollars on the little twit.

"I want you to track him down ASAP and arrest him. I will get the warrant to you. Our petition is an emergency one and I expect to have it tomorrow. Given the warrant and Junior, take his worthless ass to the nearest police or sheriff's substation and turn him in for a receipt. He is simply incorrigible and does not deserve kid gloves or special treatment any longer."

"What's our fee?" Nick asked.

"You two do it alone, and you get my whole twenty percent, or one hundred grand. Bring in my boys to help and you get fifteen percent or seventy-five grand. They get five percent or twenty-five grand. Our usual deal."

"Has any work been done on the possible location or route of travel?"

"No. This happened several hours ago."

"Do you have the name and contact information of his friend? And, where he went before?"

"Yes. Everything I have been able to find out is in this folder. Take it and jump on this. I'd rather pay you the fee than lose a half million dollars, Nick."

"Is there something else we might learn from the father or mother? Or any siblings?" Lola asked.

"Possibly. The family information is in the folder."

"Has anyone spoken to the accessory friend?" Nick asked.

"We tried to reach him, but he is not answering. I sent some guys to his house. Neither he nor the Corvette were there," Kellogg said.

"Whose name is on the title of the Corvette?" Lola asked.

Kellogg looked at her oddly. "Why?"

"If Senior's name is on it and he did not give

permission for the friend to use it, he should report it stolen or unauthorized use. Then, we could have every cop in the state looking for it. With an 'accessory to the escape of a manslaughter suspect' addendum on the lookout."

"Damn, Nick. You did well associating with this one!" Kellogg said.

He made a quick phone call to Brack Sr. and found his name was on the title. He told him to dial 911 and what to tell the responding officers.

"We will go to his house now. I want to know the second his car and its driver are found. I also want to know information about his car. One of the ways we broke the big teen trafficking case was to use the GPS on the navigation system in a suspect's car. I hope we can use it to locate Junior," Nick said, adding, "Is information on the friend's car in the folder?"

"No. If Brack does not know about the car, he knows the parents."

"Any problem with us recruiting him to visit them with us?"

"I want to protect my half million dollars at this point. Try not to break the law in a fashion where you might be caught. Otherwise, bring the little piece of excrement back in cuffs."

"Please call Senior and let him know we are coming." Kellogg nodded and they left.

They left and crossed the bridge over to the Bird Key entrance and turned onto a drive near the yacht club.

"You must be the private detectives," the distinguished-looking man who greeted them at the drive said.

"We are. Lola Caldwell and Nick Wolf."

"You guys look like you are out of central casting."

"Thanks. We have varying looks. Tomorrow, you might not recognize us."

"Guy said you two are more likely to get my errant son back safely than anyone," Williston said.

"We will try, Mr. Williston. But we need your help," Lola said.

"Come on in, and let's talk."

The interior of the house had art on the walls, which looked like it should be in the Ringling Museum of Art a few miles north on the waterfront.

"This is my wife, Gloria, and our daughter, Erika. These are the two detectives Guy Kellogg sent to find Brack and bring him back safely."

Neither private investigator corrected Williston. Their job was to arrest him safely and turn him over to the police to be held until trial, which was a bit different.

"Exactly how long has your son been gone, Mr. Williston?" Nick asked.

Brack Williston looked at his Patek Phillipe watch and said, "Two hours and thirty-seven minutes."

"We just received the file from Guy and have not had a chance to review it in detail. Please tell us about the friend who helped him get away and whose car he has," Lola asked.

"His friend's family also lives here on Bird Key. They are virtually neighbors. His name is Brad Cole. His parents are Bill and Amy Cole."

"What kind of car does he drive? The one he switched with Brack."

"A restored 1964 Porsche. It's dark green," Williston said.

"Good and bad," Lola said. "Good because it's odd enough to be spotted easily. Bad because we had hoped it would be new enough to have GPS we could track. How about Brack's Corvette?" she asked.

"It was my old toy he inherited. A '68 Mako Corvette with an engine and transmission upgrade."

"But still no GPS, right?" Nick asked.

"Right."

"I have to ask you this for our protection. Did Brack have access to any guns?" Nick asked.

"We have a small gun safe. He knows the combination. I will have to go check it," Williston said.

"Thanks."

"Mrs. Williston, do the Coles have any other homes? Since Brack and Brad are both MIA, maybe they are meeting at one."

"Yes. They have a cabin on a canal leading into Charlotte Harbor in Charlotte County. The Burnt Store Marina area."

"Have the police been here to take a report on the Corvette yet?" Lola asked.

"No, not yet. It's been almost half an hour since Guy told Brack to call them."

"When they get here, stress it is not a theft. Just your son loaned it to Brad but did not have your permission to do so. May as well keep family relations good. We may need the Coles," Lola suggested after rethinking using Brad's parents.

"Thanks."

"Have you been to this cabin?" Nick asked.

"Oh, yes," Gloria said, "many times."

"Can you get an address for us to put in our navigation system?" Nick asked.

"I'll call his mom and get it:

"I noticed you drove up in a little van with a ladder on the top," Erika said.

"It's our number two surveillance van. Want to see it while your mother is on the phone and your dad is checking his guns?" Lola asked. Lola had sensed the girl wanted to say something and was looking for a private moment away from her parents. She had been unable to signal her feelings to Nick.

While Nick waited for the directions and gun information, Lola and Erika walked out, and Lola opened the rear of the van.

"You seem like you want to tell me something, Erika."

"Well, kinda. Yeah," the youngest Williston spoke hesitatingly.

"Spit it out. Nick and I are probably your best bet at getting your brother back quickly and safely."

"Err, Brack, took some money and some cocaine with him. He also took some whiskey or something from the wet bar. He's an addict. He is real different when he's under the influence of anything. I just wanted to warn you," she said with a tear rolling down her cheek, almost immediately joined by one on the other side.

"Thanks for letting me know. You should know Nick was an Army Ranger in combat and a detective sergeant. I was a state trooper who patrolled alone, often at night. We try to be ready for anything, but advance notice is always appreciated, Erika."

"I love my brother. You won't hurt him, will you?" Erika sobbed.

"Our intention is to arrest him and turn him over to the police in the safest way possible. It's not to harm him. If we react violently, it won't be because we started it," Lola said softly and hugged the teen.

Nick came to the door and motioned her in.

"Brad's mother thinks he is headed to the cabin. The cabin is actually a four-bedroom house with a boat lift out back. She said he left an hour ago in the Corvette. He took his .22 rifle with him, but she said that was pretty normal," Nick said.

"Mr. Wolf, a 1911 .45 made by Springfield is missing. And a box of twenty hollow points, I am afraid to say. I have no idea what was in his mind to take a pistol with him in flight like some criminal," the senior Williston said, clearly distraught by his finding.

"We appreciate your help, folks. We'd better get on the road. I'd like to get Brad before he teams up with your son. Pairs tend to have dumber ideas than individuals in my experience. Thanks again. We will keep you apprised through Guy Kellogg," Nick said, and they left, both faces reflecting the new seriousness of the situation.

"Guy, this is Nick. We are heading down to Port Charlotte. The friend who broke him out seems to be heading to a family cabin down there according to his mother. We have learned that Junior took cocaine and liquor. Both are armed. Junior with his father's .45 automatic, friend Brad with a .22 rifle."

"Okay. I might head a couple guys down that way in case you need them. Be safe. Brack Williston, Jr. is not worth dying over. But, if you get a chance to hook him up, do so. If you need to bust his jaw getting him into the back seat, go for it. Keep me advised," and Kellogg hung up.

They drove four miles above the speed limit except where they could go faster in a group of vehicles. There was no time for a traffic stop.

They got to the Burnt Store area and cruised past the house. The Porsche and Corvette were both there. The house seemed buttoned up.

There was a man mowing his lawn next door.

"Hi! My name is Nick. We are looking for Brad. His car is here but the place seems locked up. Have you seen him?"

"Brad? Yeah! He and some other young guy were here and left in the boat about thirty minutes ago. I know because I had just come out to mow the lawn. Looked like they had camping gear. And a rifle. I heard the other guy say Marco Island."

"Marco? Isn't it eighty or ninety miles from here?" Nick asked.

"About. I doubt they will make it tonight. Maybe if they push hard. But not this time of day. I don't think that boy knows anything about driving a boat at night."

"I have not seen it for a while. What kind of boat do the Coles have?"

"A Grady White with a two-fifty on it. I think it's twenty-four or five feet. Nice boat!"

"I'll say, it is! Any good places to stop between here and there in a motel?" Nick asked.

"Sanibel. Maybe Naples. But those places are plenty expensive. I'd say they would pull over and anchor and sleep in the boat. Mosquitos would eat them up though," the older man surmised.

"You're probably right. What's the closest place they would get fuel?"

"The marina here." The man pointed over and they could see it in the distance.

"Thanks for your help. We'll catch up with them. Somewhere!" Lola said with a disarming smile she had worked to recover from her trooper days.

They drove over to the marina and went to the fuel dock. A dock hand came out.

"Can I help you?" he asked.

"We hope so. We were supposed to go on a boat excursion with a friend. He got our message about meeting him here confused and left without us.

"Have you gassed up a twenty-four-foot Grady White in the last thirty minutes or so?" Nick asked.

"Sure did. Pumped two hundred dollars in. But his credit card covered it okay."

"Did he say where he was going?" Lola asked, smiling at the young man.

"Yep. He said they were going down to the Ten Thousand Islands to hang out a couple days. You can get lost in there forever if you don't know what you are doing."

"Boy. Different plans. Can you check the credit card and see if it was our man Cole?"

The dock hand did.

"Brad Cole on the charge slip he signed all right!"

"I don't know what got in Brad's head. Did he say where he was going to stay tonight? Maybe we can catch him there."

"I think sleep in the boat. It was big enough even though it does not have a cabin."

"We should rent a boat and try to catch him. Where should we rent one?"

The young man pointed, not unlike the grass mower did.

"Thanks!" Lola said, and they headed to the boat rental, where they secured a twenty-foot center console with a one-fifty outboard for two days. The tank was full and they transferred their two go bags and the case with the short-barreled shotgun and locked the van. Using the chart which came with the boat, they headed out the Intracoastal Waterway southbound, dressed in their street clothes.

Nick looked up at the sky. It was dark gray, going to black.

"This is not a day I would be heading us out in our boat," he said. Lola had patrolled Florida's highways in the worst weather the Sunshine State could throw at her. She nodded serious agreement to her partner.

"We don't have caps, even," she said.

"If there is any good news, I included both plastic ponchos and bivvy sacks in our emergency bags."

"I saw a little pouch labeled 'bivvy sac.' What on earth is a bivvy sack?"

"It's a kind of a cross between an emergency sleeping bag and a one-person tent. But the tent does not have any supports to hold it up. You just crawl into this insulated, weatherproof bag, snug down the open end, and survive."

"Won't it be hot?" she asked.

"Normally in Florida, yes. But feel how the temp is dropping as this storm rolls in? It may feel good. We may both fit in one sack. We'll see."

She smiled at the prospect and dug out a poncho from each small day pack. She handed one to him. It was already sprinkling. When it hit, it would hit hard with driving rain.

"What we make off arresting Brack will be well worth a miserable wet night," Nick promised as the rain came down harder.

They were heading south in the Intracoastal Waterway. The sky was almost black.

"I have to believe Brack and Brad will pull over. Regardless, we will as soon as I find a wide spot where we can anchor safely for the night," Nick said.

He found a workable spot just after they entered Pine Island Sound.

"Honey, will you man the wheel and try to hold us steady right here while I deploy the anchor?" She stepped behind the wheel and bumped the throttle from reverse to neutral to forward as required to hold the boat more or less in one spot.

The location was in the lee of a small cove in the Sound, where they were somewhat protected from the worst of the wind. Nick was pleased to see the rental had a good ground tackle or anchor chain and line. He had noted the depth finder before stepping forward. The depth was six feet. For a storm, he wanted to play out six times that in scope which was the length of the anchor line. He put out an estimated forty feet and asked Lola to bump the throttle in reverse. He could feel the anchor did in with his hands and quickly did his figure eight wrap on the front cleat to hold it at forty feet or line, or rode, length. The tide swung the boat around. It was now bow toward the nearest shore. If it changed, they still had enough clearance so the boat would not hit the shore with its stern and motor.

The center console boat was self-bailing, so rain would not be an issue. Nick assured the scuppers which drained it were clear of anything in them which would block them.

"The tee top will not give us any protection. Let's move a bivvy sack up to the open bow area. I'll open it if you put our pistols in Ziploc bags we can keep nearby and dry. Undress under your poncho, and we can put semi-dry clothes inside the console for tomorrow. We'll just sleep in our underwear."

Lola put the two plastic bags with the Glocks near where they would sleep. The boat was already rocking and the rain coming down hard. Thunder and lightning were nearing.

Nick held the bivvy bag while Lola, poncho still on, put her bare feet and legs in. He changed his hold to the poncho as she slid her panty-clad body all the way in.

"Does it feel like there will be enough room for me?" he asked.

"I think so. We'll have to be real close all night. Like always," she said, her voice almost obliterated by the wind, rain, and thunder.

"I'll be with you in a minute."

He slipped off his loafers and trousers and tossed them into the dry compartment in the steering console then removed two more items from his getaway bag.

Nick erected the all-around white light pole clipped on the inside of the boat. He needed an anchor light to warn off any unlikely boaters in the area. However, he was hesitant to use the boat's starting battery to power it and chance a dead battery in the morning.

He snapped a white Cyalume light stick to light it and held it up against the top of the light pole. Nick then secured it tightly with several wraps of a small bungee cord.

He went back to the bivvy and slipped out from the poncho and his Guayabera shirt and slipped into the sack beside a very soft and beautiful woman.

She snuggled up to him.

"This could be a lot worse, you know," she said, chest to chest and her face inches from his.

"I know. We'd better get some rest," he said.

"Not quite yet..." she responded.

The storm got more fierce as the night passed. They imagined the two fugitives were absolutely miserable unless they left the Grady White boat and pitched a tent on the shore. Even so, the tent would be stressed by the high winds.

———

Each bag held a bottle of water and a couple of protein bars. Lola and Nick would not be deprived of breakfast but nonetheless tried not to think of eggs, bacon, and pancakes.

The boat held and the Cyalume stick maintained its bright watch.

At dawn, they packed up and started the engine to continue south on Pine Island Sound.

Each had clean tee shirts in their bags. Nick decided to wear his over his somewhat damp tartan boxers in the boat. Lola donned her black bra, which with the matching panties, looked like a bikini. Especially under a tee shirt.

Nick sped up to just above planing speed while Lola kept a close watch on the shoreline and any docks they passed for the slightly larger Grady White boat and their fugitives. At the speed they were going, it would take over an hour to reach Sanibel Island.

Almost immediately, they spotted the Grady White with two male occupants pulling away from the coastline.

A muscular guy in plaid shorts and a pretty woman in a tee shirt over her bathing suit did not arouse any alarm on the part of the two young men.

Lola waved and smiled as Nick began to overtake them.

Beside them at about thirty miles per hour, Lola raised the Mossberg twelve gauge and Nick motioned them to stop.

As expected, they did the stupid thing on the deserted waterway just after dawn.

Brad pushed the throttle of the larger engine all the way forward and the boat leaped ahead of them.

Lola aimed a shot across their bow like a Coast Guard cutter might, but Nick shook his head no.

The Grady White's speed was approaching fifty, a good five to ten miles per hour faster than their rental boat could go.

They watched as the boat pulled ahead of them and Brack took Brad's place at the helm.

Brad removed the .22 bolt-action rifle from a case and worked the bolt. He aimed at the pursuing boat and fired. Nick swerved the boat and dropped his speed.

First, Lola shot a video of him aiming the rifle at them and caught the small puff of smoke as he fired from the speeding boat and missed.

Second, Lola ducked out of the way and took some two and three-quarter-inch rifled slug rounds out of the shotgun case and replaced the buckshot with the seventy-two caliber lead slugs.

She went up to the bow and Nick slowed for her to aim steadily. She fired a slug at the big Yamaha outboard, but Brack swerved, and it sailed past harmlessly.

The noise of the shot caused Brack to jump, and he let go of the wheel. The boat hit a telephone pole-sized channel marker at fifty miles per hour. Both Brack and Brad were thrown overboard. Since Brack did not have his kill switch attached to his person, the wrecked boat continued on, beaching itself at high-speed half a mile ahead.

Brad swam with powerful strokes toward the nearer shore some hundred yards away.

Brack was floating face down. Nick pulled the boat up within thirty feet.

"Lola, take the wheel and stay down current from us!" he said as he jumped in and swam toward his fugitive.

Brack began coughing and shaking his head as he came to.

Nick decided unconscious would be easier to deal with and clipped him with a knife-edge hand on the back of the neck.

He cupped his right hand under Brack's jaw and began to swim him back toward the rental boat. Lola idled it in and cut the engine at Nick's request.

"I am going to wait for the prop to stop spinning and we can try to muscle him aboard over the swim platform," Nick said.

It was difficult to get the unconscious man's torso up on the swim deck in deep water, but Nick got him far enough up in it for Lola to reach under his arms and drag him aboard.

Once Brack was out of the way, Nick put his right foot on the ladder, and with a pull on either side, thrust himself up onto the boat, dragging his left leg.

"I almost died when you went overboard! You swam fine though!" Lola exclaimed.

"Yeah, it's the walking part that gets me," he said.

"Let's put one of those silly yoke life vests in the console stowage onto him for safety, then handcuff him from behind.

"Then I guess we need to get presentable," Nick said.

She stepped around the console and pulled her blouse and skirt over the black lingerie and tossed him his shirt and slacks. She put her Glock in her purse, and he holstered his once he got his pants up and belt fastened.

"What do we do about Brad and his wrecked boat?" Lola asked.

"We should call 9-1-1 and tell the Lee County Sheriff's Office. He fired at us and is an accessory to a fugitive escape, so they should be pretty interested in speaking with him. And, of course, we can hand Brack over to them. I will call Guy Kellogg first and see the status of our arrest warrant," Nick said.

Kellogg said he had the warrant in hand. It had been issued late last night by a judge whose friend had lost a boat during Brack Jr.'s marina demolition.

"How about texting me a copy to keep on the phone and sending a fax or email copy to the Lee County Sheriff. I will tell them it's coming, and I will meet them at Pine Island Marina to hand over Williston. Start cutting the big check please."

"In lieu of losing half a million dollars, I am tickled to write your check, my friend. Was it an easy capture?"

"No, it was just a quick one. We had a boat chase after sleeping in a bad storm in an open boat. The friend who sprung him shot at us. Lola fired at their motor with a shotgun slug, but he turned the boat and it missed. Brack was driving and hit a channel marker. Both were thrown clear, and the boat went about half a mile before beaching.

"The friend swam ashore, leaving Brack floating face down. I jumped in and we pulled him into our rental boat. He came to with no injuries, but I tapped him behind the neck so we could put a life vest on him and cuff him. He's an obnoxious big mouth.

"He's waking up now and cursing like a drunk sailor. Brad Cole is still running in the woods on the west shore of Pine Island Sound. If Lee County can get to the Grady White they wrecked quickly, they can recover a .22 recently fired and Senior's .45 auto."

"Okay, Nick. I will call them myself and tell them to have a car meet you at Pine Island Marina. Feel free to place the little shit under arrest for skipping bail. It's going to be the least of his worries. Good job to both of you. Oh! You can swim? I thought..."

"I can swim. Just not run or climb mountains. Swimming was a final part of my physical therapy."

"Good. Gotta go and call Lee County. Later!"

––––––

"Brack. Be thankful. If Nick had not pulled you out of the water, you'd be dead now. So, shut the hell up or I will help you go sleepy-bye again. Got it?"

Braxton Williston, Jr. found he was more terrified by this woman who was taller than he was than by the guy driving the boat.

"Where's my friend?" he demanded.

"He's still running for his life. He did not seem to care much about yours. He swam ashore, leaving you floating face down. Now shut your mouth. You caused us a miserable night and I am looking for any reason I can to bitch slap you like the little girl you are," Lola said. He shut up with that, but she slapped the hell out of him anyway.

Two sheriff's cars were waiting for them at the marina.

One immediately began taking a preliminary report. "The bondsman gave the story to our lieutenant and sent us the warrant. Have you arrested him for skipping?"

"I have."

"Has he been Mirandized?"

"No. Our warrant was for skipping bail. There was no reason to question him. We knew he skipped. Sarasota PD has a manslaughter warrant in addition to the reckless endangerment and other for tearing up a marina with a yacht while drunk and high on coke. I think they will probably want to pick him up today."

"How about the other guy who shot at you? Our marine unit is at the boat. They found the rifle with a spent shell that had not been ejected yet. And a .45. No sign of him."

"The runner is named Brad Cole. Sarasota address. He swam to land after being thrown out of the boat about a half mile north of where the boat beached. Same side of the Sound. There's not a lot along there, so he's probably hiding in the woods, thirsty, hungry, and scratching a million mosquito bites. The Springfield 1911 was taken without permission from his father. It was not used against us."

"Good! We should be able to get him. Will you testify he shot at you?" the deputy asked.

"We both will. Plus, we have a smartphone video of him shooting at us. My partner, an ex-Florida trooper, fired back with a shotgun slug, but they swerved, and it went clear. Our prisoner, Williston, was driving so the other guy could shoot. They crashed into the channel marker when the driver took his evasive maneuver. The runner left our prisoner floating face down in the water. I had to go in and swim him to the boat."

"I noticed you limping. Do you need an EMT to look at your leg?"

"No thanks. Bullet wounds which earned me a disability retirement from wearing a uniform just like yours."

"Pretty ballsy jumping in to save him with a disability," the deputy commented.

"He was a fugitive. I had to do my best to get him. He deserves all the years of Florida Graybar Hotel hospitality he has earned."

The deputy nodded his agreement.

"If your partner can give me her version, we can speed this up. We'll arrange to leave your rental boat here and give y'all a ride to the office. I will have the report entered onto the computer and print a copy for you to have and one to sign for us. We'll give you a receipt for Mr. Williston and a ride back to the marina so you can return your boat and go about your lives."

"Thanks for your professionalism, deputy. I've always heard you guys have a top-notch operation down here."

He interviewed Lola, whose report mirrored Nick's. The interviewing deputy gave them a ride to the office. They signed their reports and got the receipt to trade for a very large check in Sarasota.

Upon return to the Pine Island Marina, they got in the rental boat and drove it toward the original marina.

"This would be a great trip with real swimsuits and a cooler full of lunch and snacks," Lola remarked.

"If we play the weather right, we could bring our boat down here. Maybe stay at Cabbage Key for the night and have a hamburger in paradise."

"Like Jimmy?" Lola asked.

"The very same, who allegedly penned the song there."

"You have a date! With the check we are going to pick up in Sarasota, we could put out extra water and food for Finn and do the trip really soon!" she said.

At the boat rental at Burnt Store, the dock hand replaced their gas and put it on the credit card. Nick took the receipt for the rental and gas and included it in their case file for tax deduction purposes.

Their clothes were damp but fairly presentable. They spread the ponchos and bivvy sack out in the rear of the van. It should protect them from mildew until spread out in the sun at home.

They headed back home, stopping at Sarasota to pick up their check and at the bank to deposit it at the drive-through window. Showers and a nap with a very happy yellow cat snuggled between them followed.

"This has been quite a two-day period for us, hasn't it?" Nick asked Lola before she slipped into dreamland. She nodded sleepily and kissed two fingers. She reached across Finn and touched her fingers on Nick's lips, closing her eyes.

"Quite a lady we have here, huh, Finnie?" Finn made a noise Nick took to be "yes."

Nick stroked the back of the cat's head until both went to sleep.

A flurry of cases came in the following day. With the addition of Lola, the number of accident investigations for both insurance and law firm clients soared.

Their original plan was for Lola to be the primary accident investigator, but the numbers required Nick to take many of them. While not the most exciting PI work, they paid the same and were often faster from assignment to money in the bank.

Both wanted to pay off the home office and vehicles as quickly as reasonable and operate debt-free, something which was tough for small businesses. At the way they were going, it appeared achievable within a relatively few years. They continued to pay down the mortgage first and foremost.

The boat trip from Anna Maria Island down to Pine Island Sound was put off but not forgotten.

The Lee County deputies located Brad Cole and arrested him on numerous charges including aggravated assault with a firearm. His case is pending in Florida's Twentieth Circuit. Nick and Lola knew they both would be subpoenaed to testify for the prosecution.

Brack Williston's case was held and he is awaiting sentence. The senior Williston, though thoroughly disgusted with his errant son, hired the best Florida defense attorney around. Guy Kellogg told Nick what should be the thirty-year sentence recommended by the state's attorney may end up to be ten years in prison.

Nick shrugged at the proposition of the reduced sentence when he got off the phone and told Lola.

"Ten years hard time would be a long time for the spoiled pretty boy. Every day in prison would be the worst day of his life. I'm not worried about duration unless it's something stupid like two years. But this isn't California. It's just not going to happen here. Besides, we earned the largest single fee in the agency's history, so we have no complaints no matter what the judge says!"

"I agree, Nick. Plus, we put the major part of the fee against the mortgage and it jumped us years ahead in paying it down. Not bad for two days, wet and mosquito-ridden or not."

Nick had repeatedly expressed his concern to Lola about her carrying the larger Glock off-body. He was always in favor of carrying a firearm on oneself instead.

She relented and he bought her a Sig 365 like his. The one she chose had the longer barrel and grip. Nick installed a Wilson Combat grip module for better ergonomics. A DeSantis inside the waistline holster and several magazines completed the purchase.

Lola found the ergonomics were so good she could actually shoot the smaller firearm better than the one with which she had so much familiarity.

Nick had carried the military version of the AR, or Armalite Rifle, in combat. It was the latest iteration of the M4. Despite its many fine attributes, he chose a Ruger Mini-14 to add as their rifle.

The same caliber, it was wood and steel and not a black rifle. He liked the traditional feel. Nick was a fan of the .223/5.56 NATO cartridge because in a home environment, the tiny high-speed .22 bullet tended to break up on interior walls. Walls which even a 9mm or buckshot load would penetrate and endanger neighbors. They carried it when a case risk evaluation suggested the possibility of gunplay. Otherwise, it was kept hidden, but with easy access near their living room office. Nick had gotten the .357 back from state investigator Rob Gadsden and kept it clipped underneath his desk. The only thing on their wish list now was infrared night vision to use for surveillance.

The agency was assigned and completed several more bond skip cases by Guy Kellogg over the next several months. The time expended was similar to an accident investigation billing, but the money tended to be better. Just nowhere near the twenty percent fee applied to five hundred thousand bail as in the Williston case.

————

Six inmates from Tampa Bay were loaded into a county jail van for transportation to Florida State Prison, generally known as Raiford Prison. Raiford houses one of Florida's three death row cell blocks and the state's execution chamber.

Two of the passengers on the van were heading for death row. They may or may not receive a lethal injection after years of appeals and whatever were the politics *du jour*, either in-state or nationally. The other two were just felons facing varying amounts of prison time.

The prison is located on State Road 16 near in Bradford County near its line with Union County. The two correctional deputies settled in for the hundred-and-seventy-six-mile trip. Both were professionals. The trip was one they made frequently and without interruption. They took I-275 north to I-75 north and onto the Ocala exits. They picked up 301 north along the old speed trap section to Waldo, then Starke where they planned to turn onto State 16 to Raiford.

Unfortunately, it did not work the way they planned.

The van was slowed by a cement mixer on a fairly deserted stretch of US 301 North just south of Waldo.

The mixer slowed for the jail van to pass. As the van got beside the large vehicle, the mixer's driver jerked his steering wheel to the left. The hit knocked the van off the road into mud beyond the shoulder. Only the deputy's expert driving kept it from rolling.

Two Suburbans pulled up beside it and four masked

men with heavy and highly illegal automatic weapons bailed out.

The guards were smart enough to not resist against overwhelming firepower.

They were disarmed and tied with plastic handicuffs which rendered their hidden handcuff keys useless.

The prisoners, still cuffed, had bags put over their heads. They were loaded into the two black-windowed Suburbans. Two were specifically chosen to ride in the first. The other four were crammed into the second and the two SUVs powered off. The cement mixer, its actions unseen by any passerby, continued onward, showing no damage. He had earned his two thousand dollars and was thinking about parking it in his lot and driving his pickup to a lunch of chicken fried steak and some green beans.

The Suburbans headed south. The second one pulled over and unloaded its four new passengers. The driver and his confederate injected the prisoners with a powerful sedative and dragged their limp bodies into the woods.

They would be out for an hour. The two thugs uncuffed them and left them, heads still bagged, in the woods. They departed to catch up with the other Suburban, which had the two death row prisoners.

The four felons who were dropped off awoke over the next fifty to sixty-five minutes. They were not totally sure what had happened.

They knew one thing. They were free in the middle of nowhere. They needed civilian clothes instead of jail uniforms. They needed money, guns, and transportation.

They saw a truck coming in the distance. One prisoner pulled off his jail pants and shirts and ran out on the highway in his underwear, flagging the truck down in feigned panic.

"I need help! I done been carjacked!"

The truck pulled over and the man in underwear ran up to the driver's side and pulled him out.

A second prisoner grabbed a large rock and killed the pickup driver. The first man donned the dead driver's clothes. He searched the truck and found a .32 Harrington & Richardson revolver in the glove box. It was old and weak but loaded.

The prisoner who had flagged down the truck got behind the wheel, gun tucked in the waist of his new pants. The murderer jumped in beside him as did a third prisoner.

"We got to rob a store and get us some beer and clothes!" the rock-wielding killer said. "You have to hop in the back," he said to the fourth prisoner.

The fourth man shrugged and said, "Nah. You guys go on. I'd stand out like a sore thumb back there in this uniform and get y'all caught. Get outta here. I'll be fine."

The driver spun the wheels of the old pickup as he took off toward the north and looking for the nearest 7-Eleven or similar. Money from the till, beer, and tourist tee shirts would go a long way to getting them over the Georgia line. And a dead clerk would not identify them.

The man alone on the side of the road was no less lethal than the fools who had just driven off. He was, however, much smarter. He had seen several houses and mobile homes only a few miles south. They would be a logical source for clothing, money, and a vehicle. He was not particularly worried about a gun. He had no intentions of trying to shoot it out with country boy deputies who grew up shooting tin cans and hunting.

He began his walk south, staying in the woods since he was still wearing orange jail scrubs with orange socks and shoes.

It took him forty-five minutes to get to what he thought was the best house. It had men's clothes drying on a clothesline. They looked to be about his size. The pickup pulled in behind the small house was maybe five years old, he guessed.

It would be virtually unnoticeable, yet new enough to be dependable.

He went in. The woman was young. Not as young as he liked, but he had his way with her before choking her to death.

He found a suitcase and filled it with her husband's pants, shirts, and underwear. The outfit he chose to put on fit well, so he assumed the rest would also fit.

There was a pistol in the drawer. It was a loaded Smith & Wesson M&P in forty caliber. He took it.

The man wiped down everything he thought he might have touched. Truck keys, some cash, and a debit card were in her purse. He smiled as he read the card's PIN written on the back in black Sharpie. He also took her cigarettes and a Bic lighter.

He then had a thought and slapped himself in the face in anger. He left his DNA in her.

He picked her up and carried her out the back door and far into the woods behind her house. He put her under a fallen log and covered her with brush.

A medical examiner could collect his DNA unless the body was totally destroyed. He went back to the house and opened the tool shed. Taking the five-gallon can of gas and a can of motor oil into the woods, he doused her until both were empty.

He flicked the lighter on and set her afire. He ran

back to the truck and left, heading south before the smoke and flames got someone's attention and sent fire and police there. He just hoped she would be immolated sufficiently to destroy the evidence he had been too excited to think about until too late.

———————

Lola and Nick were in the office. A new insurance company had visited to talk about investigative services and had left with the agency's signed contract in his portfolio.

Nick was finishing a glass of iced tea and getting ready to file the new contract. Lola was putting the final touches on an accident diagram for another client.

A car pulled up in the front and Nick saw it through the window.

"Lola, get out of sight and armed. The little hairs on the back of my neck just rose. I have a bad feeling about the guy walking up our sidewalk."

She got up and went to the former dining room, now conference room. The semiautomatic Ruger Mini-14 rifle was there. Nick heard her pull and release the operating handle, chambering a cartridge.

The man walked in through the unlocked door. He was tall and tan-skinned with a crew cut. He was almost handsome in an exotic way, but the handsomeness was ruined by his angry expression.

It hit Nick. The man was Jorell Esson without his dreadlocks wig!

Esson reached behind his back as Lola stepped out, the Ruger Mini-14 rifle shouldered. A gun appeared in his hand, and she pressed off a shot.

The little fifty-five-grain high-speed bullet hit him in the chest and tumbled. He aimed toward Nick and fired.

Nick had already rolled away with the .357 Magnum in his hand. He aimed with one hand and fired three times.

The Mozambique or failure drill. Two to the center of mass and one to the head. A pink spray came out the back of Esson's head as the bullet went out the door and somewhere beyond his stolen car.

There was no need to check a pulse on Jorell Esson. He was clearly as dead as dead could be.

Nick let out a long-held breath and looked at his beloved partner.

"You okay, honey?"

She lowered the short rifle and nodded.

"Esson was our only open cold case," he said.

She looked at him and spoke softly.

"Case closed."

ACKNOWLEDGMENTS

Appreciation to Denise Kearns for her contributions as initial manuscript editor, daughter Heather Tilman Blanton for the title, as well as to Dr. Aaron Stecker—former SWAT Medic Holley Wade—for the consultative advice, and Sheriff Bob White (retired) for help with the use of FirstNet communications by the task force.

A LOOK AT BOOK TWO:
ELUSIVE HEIRESS

When a simple missing heiress case lands in the laps of private investigators Nick and Lola, little do they know it's just the tip of the iceberg.

As the duo digs deeper, they find themselves entangled in the treacherous world of Honduran crime and the ruthless Bosnian mob. And the heiress? She has a knack for vanishing without a trace, leaving our intrepid investigators chasing shadows.

In this explosive sequel to *Stolen Lives*, the stakes are raised to new heights. A million-dollar bond violator becomes their target, leading them on a thrilling international manhunt. Yet, they soon discover they're not the only ones on the hunt, as drug cartels unleash their own deadly assassins.

With bullets flying and survival at stake, Nick and Lola must navigate a web of danger and deceit. As their investigations unfold, they're drawn into the sinister underworld of human trafficking, fighting to bring down the merciless kingpins behind the abduction of teenage girls.

Get ready for a relentless rollercoaster ride through the darkest corners of crime, where bravery, determination, and a touch of audacity are their only weapons. Will Nick and Lola overcome the odds and unravel the mysteries that threaten to consume them? Find out in *Elusive Heiress*, a gripping tale that will leave you breathless and craving more.

AVAILABLE OCTOBER 2023

ABOUT THE AUTHOR

G. Wayne Tilman is a full-time author. He is retired from the Federal Bureau of Investigation, and prior to the FBI, he was a Marine, bank security director, deputy sheriff, investigator, and security contractor.

Wayne holds baccalaureate and master's degrees from the University of Richmond and has been an adjunct faculty member there and several other universities. He holds the internationally recognized Certified Protection Professional board certification, generally accepted as the highest in the security profession. He also earned a US Coast Guard 50 Ton Inspected Vessel Master Captain's license.

Wayne writes espionage thrillers, mysteries, and westerns. His impetus to write in those genres comes from both personal experience and heritage—having a direct ancestor who was one of the first sheriffs in America, another forebearer who singlehandedly captured the real Desperado of song fame, and a mother who served as a counter intelligence agent.